Extracted

Anasius Trilogy

Book 1

Rich Castro

Reformation
Lightning

Reformation Lightning

www.ReformationLightning.com

First published by Reformation Lightning in 2021

Cover design by Chris Iliff

Printed and bound in Great Britain by Clays Ltd, Elcograf S.p.A.

Reformation Lightning
10ofThose
Tomlinson Road
Leyland, PR25 2DY

ISBN 978-1-8381883-4-4

3 5 7 10 8 6 4 2

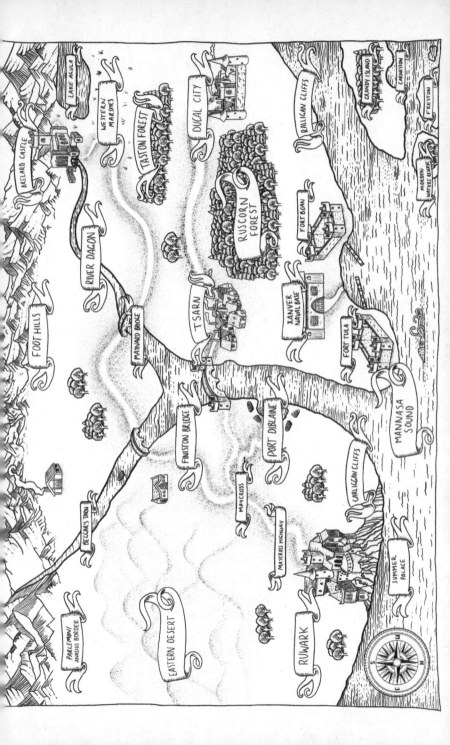

A Dangerous Game

"Unless something changes in the next few seconds, I'm going to get caught," Jason thought.

The combination of fear and sweat were making his skin clammy. Almost imperceptibly, he pulled his black cloak lower over his face and pressed himself further into the dip in the ground. Three Notalians were enjoying the lingering warmth of the dying sun as they moved slowly towards him, deep in conversation.

Until now, their voices had not carried well across the forest floor. Jason was breathing as quietly as possible and he had turned his right ear towards them to try and hear better. The ants were beginning to bother him, but he gritted his teeth fiercely and lay statuesque.

The tall cruel-looking man with a completely shaved head had a rich black-velvet cape, striking red breeches, a sheathed straight sword strapped to his waist and a bright gold medallion on his forehead – clearly he was one of the royal princes. The second man was slightly shorter, much broader and his close-cropped hair was such a light blond it was almost white. He had dark, penetrating eyes, and he was clad in a mail-shirt and carrying a sword. He had the forbidding Notalian military insignia tattooed onto his forehead and a dagger strapped to his calf with a wide leather band. He was General Qong of the Notalian Liberation Army and Commander of Notalian Tactical Operations, a ruthless and formidable leader about whom Jason had heard a good deal, none of it pleasant. The third man looked vaguely familiar, but Jason could not place him. He was younger, perhaps only a few years older than Jason, with a dull-grey long-coat covering his mail, a gleaming peaked helmet clamped over his shoulder-length black hair, and an evilly curving sickle at his side. It was obvious that the three men were discussing tactics.

The royal prince had a harsh Notalian accent which was particularly difficult to understand. As Jason strained to hear the conversation ahead of him, he felt it was almost inevitable that he would be discovered. If that happened, the dungeons of Crask along with their infamous torture chambers were a virtual certainty. Ordinarily, his cloak would have been perfect camouflage against the usual dark browns and blacks of the forest floor, but against the carpet of orange flowers on which he lay, his body shape would be unmistakeable, even in the evening's lengthening shadows.

He pressed his body hard against the earth, hoping desperately that the men would change course. He knew that any movement would draw attention to himself, but the ants were crawling up his arms towards his face. Every muscle was taut as he strove to resist the urge to shake them off and scratch himself.

As the three men moved slowly along, their words became increasingly plain. Jason knew that knowledge of their plans would be invaluable to the Anasiun defence, so he lay like a rock, listening intently and praying for darkness. The ring around his ear glowed brighter beneath his cloak.

General Qong was speaking: "...unexpected. Tranton can be taken easily – there is no garrison there, and from there the route to Tsarn is swift."

The younger man replied, "But the plan will never succeed unless we can get through Tsarn. And how are we going to manage the ferry?"

"An undisguised Notalian in Tsarn would stand out like a sore thumb," agreed Qong. "As for the ferry, we're working on it."

"Working on it?" The tall man was angry. "You've had three months! If you don't have a plan yet, you don't deserve to command my army!"

Qong responded with a quiet, deliberate and dangerous voice that was impossible to challenge.

"Our plans are final and flawless, Your Royal Highness, but they are not for all to hear." He was staring directly at the tall man as he spoke, with eyebrows raised. The tall man looked at him carefully and then nodded almost imperceptibly.

The youngest man bristled. "As a fully-fledged member of the NTO, I should know all our plans." His voice was rising.

Qong was immovable. "All in good time, Qinoda, all in good time." He changed tack. "Now, we need a plan for bringing large numbers of troops through Ducal City and up into this forest. And we need detailed plans of these woods so we can find a quiet path through and reach Tranton from the west, unnoticed."

The prince grinned and said, "From there, a rush through Xanver and onto Tranton will be straightforward enough."

Qong continued, "The ferry is a tough problem. Security is tight on both banks of the river. Full shipping passes are needed before they even allow you into the terminals. Now, Qinoda, can your friend get them?"

The younger man replied, "I've not yet asked him. So far, he's simply been our eyes and ears. He won't be too happy with us for asking for more."

"He'll be paid well."

"He'll need to be – he's risking his life as it is."

Jason saw that the men had begun to move off to the right. But he didn't allow himself to breathe relief yet – they were still within spitting distance. He stayed glued to the ground and furiously ignored the ants, even as they explored his neck.

"How many men are allocated for this mission?" asked the prince.

General Qong didn't hesitate, "The Anasiuns are a weak people, with few warriors amongst them. We can overwhelm them with less than 20,000 troops."

"So in three weeks, all Anasius will be ours, and they will never see it coming!" grinned Qinoda. "I'm looking forward to the battle."

General Qong frowned. "As the prophet Zoantha said:

'Desire not the war, but the win.' We all know you are mighty in battle, Qinoda, but the key is to be mighty of mind as well as of body. Both are needed for success." He turned to the prince. "Your Royal Highness, might I have an audience with the king tonight?"

"I know you ask only because it is necessary. I will arrange it. Most options have been considered."

The Notalians turned and began to walk away from Jason.

"...garrisons...the Uplands...Ducal..."

Jason heard them laughing in the distance, their voices fading into the growing darkness. Then, finally, he could neither see nor hear them. He clawed recklessly at the ants.

At a different time, in a different place, on one fateful afternoon, Jason had his history homework propped in front of him. A coke sat opened on his desk, and he was meant to be revising the Second World War. "We take our stand for freedom..." he scribbled as he tried to remember the words of Churchill. But he was distracted. He kept dreaming of Anasius. He knew that war was coming, a war for which most Anasiuns were woefully unprepared. A war that would be ruthless, vicious and catastrophic, and he could think of no way to avert it. And then, even as he started typing a message to Zak, there was a familiar jolt of electricity from his phone and, for a split-second, he disappeared. His bedroom vanished and he was standing back in Anasius once more. He had been extracted.

It was only much later that Jason realised he had heard the sirens passing his bedroom window.

The king was worried. He had heard reports from right across Anasius – reports that many were ignoring the Scrolls, the ancient words that had kept the kingdom safe for centuries. There were whispers that Notalia was building its army and planning to invade. Anasius and Notalia had an alliance, to be sure, and an ancient one at that, but he could not be certain it would be heeded, especially when the Anasiun miners were not only bringing gold, but had now found seams of platinum deep in the Arelard mountains. He knew that Anasius was an attractive land, and he knew his military forces were thinly spread. How could he prevent invasion? He took his Scroll and flipped it open. He read again the legend of the snake and it gave him an idea.

1

An English Education

A year earlier, Trey was reminiscing about his first two months in England. Two weeks before Easter, his family had packed up all their belongings in North Carolina and his dad had flown off to England to start a new assignment. He and his mum had stayed in a motel for another four weeks whilst his mum finished up her job. As an only child, living in a motel when your dad's in a different country and your mum's working all hours is the epitome of boring. So Trey spent most of his time hanging out with friends, playing Xbox or Ultimate Frisbee.

A month later, he and his mum packed what little remained, left the motel and flew to London. His dad had found a great house in a quiet neighbourhood in the suburbs, with good transport links to the city and an "outstanding" local school for Trey to attend. Trey and his mum were excited to see everything, and his dad was enthusiastic to show them around the house. There were three good-sized bedrooms, which meant they had a spare room for when friends came to stay, and it had a nice garden. It was not big – their house in Charlotte had been much larger – but according to his dad, houses near London were all very expensive.

Shortly after they arrived, Trey started school in England. Back home, he had worn jeans and a T-shirt to school, but here in England his school had a special uniform, like you'd see in an expensive private school in America. So he and his mum had spent the previous day at a "school uniform" store where he'd had to try on and then buy shirts, ties, sports kit, blazer, socks and a whole host of other seemingly unnecessary paraphernalia. Everything he tried on was emblazoned with the school logo. He felt ridiculous wearing it, and he wondered how any kid could get used to it. Apparently, though, no-one else seemed to have a problem with it, so Trey's mum duly bought the lot.

When the first day of school dawned, Trey was awake early, with knots in his stomach and his brain running in overdrive. Did he have everything he needed for school? What if they had the wrong uniform, and kids laughed at him? Would anyone like him, or would he be shunned as the new kid? What happened at lunch? What if he got lost? Would he make any friends? What if he didn't understand any of the lessons? What if he was stupid? He got up in a hurry, trying to distract himself from his own thoughts.

He showered, dealt briefly with his short brown hair and got dressed. His stomach was still jumping about nervously, but he tried to ignore it. Sheepishly, he went down the stairs to breakfast in his uniform. His mum was standing there with a camera, her smiling face framed by her wavy blonde hair, and her blue eyes twinkled at him.

"I need a photo, Trey," she teased. Trey was already embarrassed by his clothing, and the last thing he wanted was a picture that his friends back home might see. He tried to hide his nerves – he didn't want his mum to think he was scared.

"No, mum. I look like a private school kid – I don't want my friends to think I've changed."

"Trey – this is a new beginning for us and for you. I want a picture to mark the day. Just smile for me and then you can have your breakfast. I made sausage and egg as a treat," she said persuasively.

Trey breathed heavily. "Okay, mum," he said. He managed an awkward smile and heard the repeated click of the lens as his mum tried to get the best shot. He was impatient, because whilst he might be nervous to start a new school, he was also starving. As soon as she was done, Trey raced to the kitchen and left his mum in the hallway proudly inspecting the pictures of her tall, well-tanned, fourteen-year-old son.

An hour later, he and his mum arrived at the school office. A short kid called Mark had been assigned to show him around and help him to get integrated.

"Hi, Trey," he said a bit awkwardly.

"Hey," Trey returned.

"We have to go to our tutor room first, so I'll take you there now. Do you have a locker?"

"A locker?" Trey questioned.

"Yes, to keep you PE kit and stuff in?"

"Errr, no."

"Okay, you'll have to carry it all, then," Mark said without explaining any more. Then he led Trey down a long corridor, up a few stairs, round to the right, along another corridor and then down a shorter corridor on the left. The school felt like a perfect maze, and by the time they arrived at Mr Lomar's classroom, Trey knew he could never find his way there without directions. The door stood open and the sound of excited voices was wafting out of the room.

Their tutor, Mr Lomar, was a short, pale-faced and ginger-haired man, balding slightly and wearing a cheap suit. He was sitting at his desk, asking people various questions and greeting students as they came in. He looked up as Mark entered, followed by Trey.

"Hello Mark," he said. Then, "And you must be Trey."

"Yes, sir," Trey replied.

The classroom had got noticeably quieter, and lots of faces were turning towards them. Trey felt himself beginning to go red. Why couldn't he just hide in a corner somewhere?

"Let me introduce you," Mr Lomar said to Trey.

Mark had sat down next to another boy who turned out to be called Raf.

"Good morning everyone, and welcome back to Raynesborough County. Before anything else, I'd like to introduce you to Trey Osborn. He and his parents moved here from North Carolina in the Easter holidays, so he's new to the school. Please make him feel welcome."

The room of twenty-eight students didn't look

particularly enthusiastic, but maybe that was just because it was the first day back at school after the holidays. The knots in Trey's stomach were back with a vengeance.

"Trey, I know you'll settle in quickly, and if you have any questions or problems, you come and ask me, okay?" Mr Lomar said. Then, without waiting for a reply, he picked up his glasses, put them on his long, pointy nose, and continued, "Now, everyone, get your planners out, because we have a few things to get into the calendar straight away." He reached across his desk and picked up a small book. "Here's a planner for you, Trey. Why don't you sit here next to Jacob?" He pointed to a seat about half-way back.

"Oh, sir," Jacob protested. "That's for Calvin."

"No, Jacob. It's for Trey. Calvin's late, so he can sit somewhere else. Take your bag off the chair and let Trey sit down." Mr Lomar turned to Trey, "Jacob will show you where we write our calendar items."

Jacob muttered a swear word under his breath, and opened his own planner. He didn't even look at Trey, but he whispered harshly to him, "You stole Calvin's seat – you're going to be sorry."

Trey was sorry already. His heart was pounding, he was sweating, and his face was on fire. He looked at Jacob's planner and then opened his own planner to the same page. School was not starting well.

The first week was a complete blur. Trey was the new guy nobody knew, and he was alienated pretty much from the moment he arrived. Mark was not enthusiastic about helping him settle in, and after the first day of taking Trey to each of his lessons and meeting him for lunch, he basically left Trey to his own devices. Mark was trying hard to get in with the popular group, and the popular group would not be seen dead trying to help out some needy American kid who seemed to have no clue about anything. They knew Mark was helping Trey because he had to, but even so Mark felt he had a far better chance of acceptance if he ditched Trey. The popular group seemed to consist of kids who swore more than anyone else, enjoyed boasting about risky exploits, and liked intimidating and laughing at others. And they were all rich. Since Trey didn't fit into any of these categories, he was a dead loss as far as Mark was concerned.

That first week, Trey got lost around school two or three times a day, and was then laughed at for being late to lessons. He shared a desk only when someone had no option but to sit next to him because there were no other chairs in the room and he found himself wandering the corridors at break and lunch, trying to look busy and feeling utterly alone. In the second week, he found the library and decided it was a good place for sanctuary. You weren't allowed to talk in the library, but you could sit and read or do your homework without being bothered by anyone. None of the popular group went in the library – it was for nerds and geeks – so he was safe from Calvin, Jacob, Joe and the rest. He noticed at breaktime that Max, a quiet boy in his tutor group, was also in the library fairly often. At lunch, though, Trey was mostly alone – Max usually hung out with his own friends over lunch.

For lessons, sometimes Trey would be ready for the lesson to begin, only for someone to barge past him, accidentally knock his books off his desk, shove him or blank him entirely. His voice set him apart, too, and lots of kids mimicked his accent (usually really badly) every time he spoke. In fact, they would mimic his accent both when he was around and also when they thought he wasn't, and then they would laugh so that he didn't know whether they were laughing at him or laughing at someone's poor attempt at an American accent. People would look at him and then look away, as if there was something wrong with him. He would sit at a desk and everyone would choose to sit somewhere else, or worse, someone would ask him to move so that they could sit next to their friend. Most of this happened out of sight and out of earshot of teachers, who were far too busy to notice anyway.

Slowly, Trey was moving from being a happy, contented young man, to a quiet and withdrawn student who avoided eye contact and had a lump in his throat at some point most days. His parents were busy with their jobs, sometimes out of the country with work, and Trey did not want to bother them. They had their own problems. But he hated school and he didn't want to think about it a second longer than he was forced to. When he got home from school one Wednesday, though, he couldn't hold it in anymore, even though his mum was there. He rushed to his room and the tears flowed. His mum knocked on his door.

"Trey, Trey – whatever is wrong?" she asked frantically.

She came into the room to find Trey curled under his

duvet sobbing. She sat on the bed and tried to hug him through the duvet. But Trey didn't respond. His heaving sobs meant he couldn't speak anyway, and he didn't know what to say.

"What on earth has happened? Did you get in a fight? What is it?" she pleaded.

Trey managed to choke out, "I hate school. I hate England."

"Oh Trey, I know being somewhere completely new is hard – we thought it would be. But this is more than that, isn't it? Something happened at school."

He uncurled a little bit as his mum continued to hug him. But how could he tell her the nightmare of the last few weeks? He couldn't stop crying. He missed his friends. His missed the sunshine of summer in Charlotte. He missed his school where he knew everyone, got good grades and was okay at sprinting. Why did everyone hate him in England?

"I just don't fit in, mum," Trey said.

"But Trey, you had loads of friends at Parkdean. You're good at making friends. What happened today?"

Trey uncurled a bit more and leant on her shoulder, still crying, and she put her arm around him.

"I speak differently, I don't cuss all the time, I'm the only new kid and I don't know anything. I'm weird."

His mum seemed suddenly angry.

"You're not weird, Trey. You're a decent, strong, committed kid with lots to offer, whatever they say at school. And not cussing all the time is a good thing, not a bad thing. You're new – sure, but you'll figure it out. You always do – you're tough, Trey. Who called you weird?"

How could his mum call him "tough" when he was bawling on her shoulder like a toddler?

"I did," Trey said.

His mum rolled her eyes.

"But they all think I'm weird. Why can't we go home?"

"I don't believe they all think you're weird. And we can't go home because your dad has been posted over here for the next three years. We've got to figure this out. I've not seen you like this since grandpa died three years ago. So what's happened? Something's happened, I know it has. What was it?"

"No, mum. I..." he choked up again. How could he tell her about today? How could he describe the acute humiliation he suffered at the hands of Calvin and Joe after PE? She would want to get involved, and how could that make anything better? He decided not to be specific. Stay general, he told himself – that was safest. "It's not just today. The kids ignore me, or shove me, or push my books on the floor, or steal my stuff. They mock my accent all the time. They..." Again, he was struggling to talk. His mum was still sounding angry.

"Who, Trey? Who does this?" she demanded.

"Everyone."

"Everyone?" She sounded unconvinced. "Give me some names, Trey."

"There are loads of them, mum. Do you want the names of everyone in my tutor group?"

"Trey, there must be some kids who don't treat you like

that?" she asked incredulously.

"I dunno."

"Trey, no-one should be treated like this. Even if kids don't really get on with you, they should at least respect you and be polite. It sounds like they're not even doing that. Maybe we need to find you a new tutor group or something..."

"Mum," Trey protested, "that's not going to help. If you do that, everyone will know why I moved tutor groups and everything will just get worse. I need to handle it myself."

"How long has this been going on for, Trey? Is it just today?"

"No, it started on day one and it's just got worse."

"In that case, we need to do something, okay? I won't do anything without talking to you about it, and your father and I need to talk about it. But we definitely need to do something – this can't go on. Your father and I will defend you to the hilt. And we'll pray for things to improve, and for an idea about what to do going forward. Okay?"

"Okay, mum."

In reality, Trey couldn't really imagine things getting much worse. Maybe his parents would think of something, but he had no idea what. He began to calm down a bit, and he stopped crying. How was he going to face anyone tomorrow? He needed to be off sick – a headache, or a horrible cough, or something.

"Trey," his mum's voice interrupted his thoughts. "Trey, I still think something specific happened today, and I'd like to know what it is when you're ready to tell me. And I want to know names, Trey, not just a vague, 'everyone'. It's not good for those kids to get away with treating someone badly – they need to face up to what they have done, and learn from it. They need to understand how much it can affect someone. So I will need details and names. I know you don't want to do that right now, but please think hard about it. We need to start fixing this mess, and we can't do that without details."

"Yes, mum," Trey said. But he didn't know whether he could. Cricket had happened after lunch, and when training was over, Trey had gone for a shower. Then someone had thrown his towel over the shower door and it got soaked. He finished showering and came out wrapped in his sodden towel. When he got back to the bench by his locker, someone had hidden all his clothes except his boxers which they had thrown in the toilet. Everyone was laughing, and no-one would tell him where his clothes were. Then he'd got angry and shouted at Joe, "Where've you put them?"

Then Joe had got in his face and said, "Is the new kid accusing me of something?"

At almost the same moment, Calvin grabbed at Trey's wet towel, pulled it off, and ran off with it, accompanied by gales of laughter from the other boys. Trey was naked, angry and humiliated. He ran to the toilet and locked himself in. He felt the tears pricking his eyes, but he swallowed fiercely. He would not give in to those boys. One of them was banging on the door.

"Do you want your towel, Trey?" Calvin whined with a fake American accent.

More laughter.

"Hurry up, boys – don't make me come in there," Mr Longmore commanded from out in the corridor.

The tormenting came to a sudden end and the boys rushed from the changing rooms and headed back to class. No-one messed with Mr Longmore.

Trey scooped his boxers from the toilet, rinsed them out in the sink and tried to dry them under the hand dryer. He was terrified someone was going to come in and find him naked, so he worked fast. A few minutes later, after skulking around the changing rooms wearing his not-very-dry boxers, he finally found his clothes. Someone had stuffed them into an open locker at the other end of the room. He got changed in relief and then went to his tutor room, keeping his head low. There was a smattering of laughter as he traipsed in, but then Mr Lomar put a stop to that and started talking about sports day. Mercifully, Trey was forgotten.

And now his mum wanted him to tell her all about it. How could he possibly do that? He didn't want to re-live it, and he certainly didn't want his mum to hear how humiliated he had been. His cheeks were beginning to burn again even just thinking about it, and the familiar lump was rising in his throat. He didn't even know who had hid his clothes – it could have been anyone. It was probably Joe and Calvin, he thought – they were the most likely. He swallowed hard, but his shoulders heaved, and the tears flowed once again.

Trey slept only fitfully, and the next morning he still had a churning stomach and a racing brain. He was trying to forget what happened in the changing rooms, and everything else, but he was failing. He stayed in bed hoping desperately for a sick day. He could smell pancakes – his mum was cooking the perfect breakfast on a day when Trey needed to be off sick. Perhaps if he had a bad cough, he could still eat? He tested his cough out a few times in his room.

He put on his dressing gown and went downstairs, coughing at strategic intervals. His mum was sitting at the counter, looking worried.

"Morning, Trey. Are you feeling a bit better than last night?"

"I've got a cough, mum," he said, and coughed loudly to prove it.

"You might feel a bit better after breakfast," she suggested. "And I still need to know what happened at school yesterday."

"Nothing really. I guess I made a big deal of something that wasn't that big."

He was hoping to convince his mum that he'd just had a bad day yesterday, but today was going to be fine. Except that he had a bad cough, so he shouldn't go to school because someone else might catch it. He coughed again.

"I'm not sure that's true, Trey. You were extremely upset about something, so why not let me decide whether or not it was a big deal. I need to know what happened."

She handed him some pancakes as she was talking, and Trey drizzled maple syrup over them. They smelled delicious, but his stomach was churning horribly. He wasn't sure he was going to be able to eat them. He coughed hard again.

"It's just some boys being mean again, mum. It happens all the time, and not just to me."

But his mum was not going to let go of this one. She was like a dog with a bone when she wanted to know something. Trey knew he'd have to tell her eventually. He tried eating a bit of pancake.

"At the very least, this ongoing nastiness towards you needs to stop. But I need to know what happened yesterday, too. What did they do, Trey? Did they hit you?"

"No, mum," Trey managed to say, playing with the pancakes on his plate but not managing to eat them. "They just hid my clothes after cricket."

"What? When? Where were you? What time was this? What do you mean, 'they hid your clothes'? Who hid your clothes? Was it Phil or Max or Joe?"

His mum's questioning was relentless, and Trey had no choice. He told her the story, but he was careful to miss out names. As he explained what had happened, his mum's expression grew increasingly horrified and angry.

"I am coming with you to school, and we're going to see Mr Mason," she announced.

Mr Mason was the headteacher of Raynesborough County School, and he was pretty scary. Trey had a coughing fit.

"No, mum – it's not going to help. They were just being kids. And anyway, I'm not feeling too good. I think maybe I need some recovery time today." He coughed again. And he couldn't eat – his stomach certainly wasn't feeling good.

"Trey, I wouldn't blame you for not wanting to be in

24

school today. However, running away never solved anything. We're gonna get this thing sorted out. I am not having my son treated like that, and I can't imagine Mr Mason would think anything different."

"But mum..." Trey began.

"No, Trey. There are times for being quiet and times for speaking out. This is a time for speaking out. Let's go."

Trey groaned. Now he had no choice. He coughed again, suggestively, but his mum was not going to give in. They were heading into the lion's den.

After their meeting with Mr Mason, school continued much the same, although Trey was very nervous about what might happen now he had talked about being bullied. He could not imagine anything getting better now adults were involved, but he supposed they couldn't get too much worse, so that was a vague encouragement. Nothing changed that day, which in a weird way was quite comforting. He did notice that Max was pulled out of physics by the deputy headteacher. Max! Max hadn't done anything. Why weren't they talking to Calvin or Jacob or Joe? Trey couldn't understand it. Also, Trey suspected that Mr Mason had talked to Mr Lomar, because Mr Lomar seemed to be looking his way pretty often in registration and tutor time that afternoon. The rest of the day went by pretty much as usual, with maybe less shoving and barging than usual. Friday was a normal day, too, although Mark was late for English because he had also been talking to the deputy headteacher about something.

Trey breathed a sigh of relief when the bell rang and

school finished for the week. And only one week was left before the half-term holiday when he didn't have to go near school. He couldn't wait.

His mum greeted him as he came through the door.

"Hi Trey – how was today?" She was still worried, and her brow was furrowed. She had not slept well for the last two nights after the shock of what Trey had been experiencing at school.

"Okay," he said.

"I need more than that, Trey. Were people nasty to you today? Has anything changed?"

"I don't know, Mum. Today was fine. Not much happened I guess. I was in the library at lunch, so no-one talked to me and that was fine by me. And lessons were all right."

He didn't mention that Calvin had kicked his chair or that Jacob had stolen his pencil case for most of his physics lesson. Those things were mild compared to what he'd had in the past. Generally, people had left him alone.

"Has anyone spoken to you about what happened this week or said what they're doing about it?" she persisted.

"No, mum. Max was taken out of physics to see the deputy head, but I don't know why that would be relevant. Max hasn't done anything. Mr Lomar definitely knows something because he seemed to have his eye on me for the whole of tutor time. That might be why no-one did anything then."

"Okay," his mum sounded uncertain. "But if nothing happens on Monday I'm going to see Mr Mason again."

"Mum..." Trey began to complain.

"No, Trey – he is in charge of a school where at least one student is being bullied. He needs to do something about it."

"What can he do, mum?"

"I'm not sure," she said. "At least those boys should get into a lot of trouble, get the parents in, suspension...I don't know. But something major needs to happen. You experienced physical and emotional abuse. They can't be allowed to just get away with it."

"But mum, it's my word against theirs, and they'll never admit anything."

"Maybe they will and maybe they won't," she said confusingly. "But something needs to be done."

"Mum," said Trey, wanting to change the subject, "when does dad get back?"

"Tomorrow night. Then he and I will talk about it."

"Okay. So what are we doing tomorrow?" Trey tried again, and this time he was successful.

She smiled at him. "I have to go into town to do some shopping, and I wondered, do you wanna come with me?"

Trey groaned inwardly. Shopping with his mum was not top of his list of exciting Saturdays. But what else was there to do – he didn't really want to play Xbox by himself all day.

"Okay. Can we go to Five Guys?" He expected a negative response, but at least it was somewhere that vaguely reminded him of home. "And can I Skype Caleb when we get back?" Caleb had been his best friend at school, but it was still early morning in North Carolina so he couldn't call him until later.

"Sure, honey."

"Five Guys, or Skyping Caleb?" Trey wasn't sure what she was saying yes to.

"Both."

"Thanks mum."

The following day, once the shopping was done, Trey was sitting in Five Guys drinking Dr Pepper, wondering about his friends in Charlotte and trying not to think about school. Suddenly, as he stared out of the window, Phil, Joe and Calvin walked past. Trey groaned inwardly and tried to hide behind his bag of fries, but he was too late. Calvin had seen him and he nudged his two friends and pointed. There was Trey, sitting opposite his mum, drinking soda, in town on a Saturday afternoon. They all looked in his direction, and he could see them laughing. Phil pretended to take his clothes off, and mouthed cuss words at him and the three boys cracked up. They knew that he was with his mum, and Trey knew he would hear about this again on Monday. He could imagine the laughter.

He sighed. "Mum," he said, "can we go now? I want to Skype Caleb."

Five Guys had lost its appeal and Trey just wanted to get home.

"Sure, honey."

They left and headed back to the car park.

Trey took out his phone and started sending Caleb a message. There was a jolt of electricity. Trey was extracted.

2

Training

Trey had no idea what happened. It was as if he had been plunged into a very vivid dream, but he knew he wasn't dreaming. One moment he was walking away from town, the next moment he was sitting in a room laid out rather like a lecture theatre, half-filled with, perhaps, 100 people, none of whom he knew. His phone had vanished. He was almost at the top of the tiered seating, and off to one side. Everyone was watching the stage ahead and below, on which a white-haired man stood, tall, ramrod-straight and striking in appearance. The man was dressed in black trousers which covered his feet and reached to the floor, a pure white un-collared shirt, and a black cloak that reached down to his knees. The cloak was fastened almost together at the front, by way of a scarlet band of cloth that encircled the man's chest and was tied off on his right side, with two tassels hanging freely from the knot.

Evidently, he had just arrived at the podium. Trey's mind was reeling.

"Ladies and gentlemen," the man began. "We meet in the

name of Xcion the Sovereign. My name is Marnak. Please open your Scrolls and we're going to read the prophecy of Halkon."

Everyone removed what looked like a credit card from their lapel, and then unfolded it into a black rectangle about the size of an A4 piece of paper. As they unfolded it, it glowed brightly, and Trey realised these rectangles were, in fact, foldable screens. Most tapped their screens a few times and then settled back as the man at the podium began to read.

"This is the prophecy of Halkon the son of Malandra. Harken to the words of Xcion:

'Foreign peoples trample on the weak and project
    glory onto the merciless;
They reject the truth and follow the gods of gold
    and sceptre;
They embrace lies as if their life depended on it.
They refuse sanctuary to the poor; they demand
    money from the penniless;
They torture the innocent.
They live as lemmings, each yearning for approval
    as they run towards the cliffs;
The blind rejoice in seeing;
The senseless cavort in their cleverness;
The dead carouse through life;
And there is no hope for them.
Why, Anasius, why do you applaud them?
Why do you seek after all that is not good,

Turning from my prophets to the promises of a
    powerless delusion?
Your poor cry out, your weak fall and rise no more
    whilst you clutch at your momentary trinkets.
You have gone the way of Zagon,
And your destruction awaits.
Sing the songs of Xcion again.
Dance before me and delight in me.
Turn from your rebellion,
Your chasing after the wind.
Reject the lure of darkness.
Stop embracing fleeting pleasures that can never
    quench your thirst,
And turn back to me. I sourced you,
I founded you,
I brought you into this pleasurable land,
But you ran from me as a toddler runs from a
    parent.
Your pride knows no bounds,
But I will bring you low if you will not stoop.
I will turn Anasius over to the nations around her,
And you will be dispersed,
Until you turn and acknowledge me again.
I am Xcion the inexorable,
Xcion the unparalleled,
Xcion the Sovereign."'

The man at the podium stopped reading and looked up at
his audience. Some of the people around him began to fold

up their sheets, but he stopped them. Trey felt like he must be in some kind of religious service. His eyes were darting here and there, his mind racing, trying to work out what had happened to him. Was he hallucinating? Was any of this real? What had happened to him?

"Please keep the Scroll open as we work through it this afternoon," Marnak said. "These words, written down by Halkon in the year 14, almost 300 years ago, are as relevant today as they were then."

Trey's mind was jumping – had he fallen into some kind of parallel world? The year 14 was 2000 years ago, not 300. Marnak was still speaking.

"Back then, Anasius had just signed the PAN treaty a year before, a treaty with Notalia and with Parlemoni, agreeing to boundaries, individual sovereignty, defence against mutual enemies, free trade across our borders, and so on. Legally, that treaty still holds. But, as we all know, we live in very different times now.

"The Notalians are growing their army, strengthening their defences, increasing their wealth, and developing their political power in any way they see fit. Their military intelligence is no longer shared with us. They tax goods traded between us. These words of Xcion the Sovereign through Halkon." The man waved his own screen as he spoke. "These words fit the Notalians almost perfectly. They promote the wealthy, give more to those who have much, take from those who have little, trample on the weak, and as for what they do in Crask..."

The man continued to talk, but Trey couldn't focus.

He was trying to understand what was going on, trying to understand what had happened to him, trying to make sense of everything. How was this possible? Had he been in an accident? Was he dead, perhaps? He shook his head to try and clear it, but that just made his headache worse.

This meeting reminded him vaguely of his home church back in North Carolina. The man was giving something a bit like a sermon. They were reading from an ancient text. It felt religious. But what was being discussed was beyond his understanding entirely. He tuned in again.

"But, friends, we are doing the same things. This text is not just about the terrible things the Notalians are doing. We're doing them too! We don't torture people, maybe, but we do pursue wealth above everything else. We do educate only the rich. We do look down on those who have less. We do not provide for the needy. We have more than enough resources for every citizen of Anasius to be housed, well-fed and educated. Yet a quarter of our citizens live below the poverty line.

"And then we come to temple and pretend we're upright and worthy and decent and moral people. Friends, let's remember the words of Xcion the Sovereign: 'I will bring you low if you will not stoop.' We have no hope unless we trust in and depend upon Xcion. We must forget our momentary trinkets and reflect our gratitude to Xcion..."

Trey became aware that a woman had come quietly down the stairs of the aisle to his left. He looked across. She was beckoning him to come with her. A few of the people in the auditorium had also noticed and were looking his way.

He got up obediently, ignored the staring eyes, and followed her up and out.

As soon as they were through the doors, she began to speak.

"Hello, I am Heldta. Welcome to Anasius."

"Errr...hello," he said uncertainly. "How did I get here? Am I dead? What's happened to me?"

"Okay, okay. You're not dead, no. And there'll be time for more explanation later. But for now, you were summoned here because we need your help. I've been asked to bring you directly to the Overlord Academy to begin your training, although you'll need some less conspicuous clothes before that." She looked him up and down. "What are you wearing?" she asked, wonderingly.

"Errr." Trey shrugged. "Jeans and T-shirt. What's wrong with that?"

"Well...nothing, I guess, if you really want to be noticed. But I'll find you something else to wear in a moment. Anyway, Xci2 will meet you at the Overlord Academy and you may ask him your questions. Come, we have little time."

She led him outside, and to his surprise he found that the large building was nestled in a clearing in the middle of a forest, a forest that contained some truly enormous trees, like the giant redwoods he had seen in California on holiday the previous summer. She marched him through the woods until they stopped before one of them. It had a thick vine running up one side of it, and he noticed that the vine had some parts at the end that looked almost like they had been tied together.

Heldta pointed to the vine, started to put the loops over her arms and legs, and told Trey to do the same. He copied her rather uncertainly. Then she touched a small branch at the bottom of the tree, and the vine loops tightened. He felt trapped, but before he could do anything about it, the vine was pulling them both up the tree. The journey was short but very fast, up the bare trunk and then through some branches and leaves. Within seconds they must have been eighty metres up, before they stopped rising and landed on a platform. The vines went slack and dropped back down the tree. Heldta and Trey were standing on what appeared to be a wooden bridge, so high above the forest floor that Trey had not noticed it at all from the ground. In front of them was an irregularly shaped high-roofed treehouse with an arched door and large windows. How it was secured so high up, Trey could not tell. But he had no time to think about that now. He was ushered quickly through the doorway. He had been in Anasius less than thirty minutes, and his Overlord Academy training was about to begin.

3

Worlds Apart

Marcia and Kia, both from Trey's class, were discussing ideas for the forthcoming school talent contest. Kia's singing lessons were going well, and Marcia was already known around school for her own soprano voice. Perhaps this year they had a chance at the title, Marcia thought. She was certain that if they practised hard, they could impress the judges. As they reached Kia's house at the bottom of the hill, Kia suggested they meet up later for a run-through. Marcia agreed, and Kia turned into her driveway. Marcia left the gate and started up the long hill to her own home, pulling her phone from her pocket as she went.

She wandered home slowly, browsing through her considerable playlist. She loved music and kept getting distracted by great songs which sadly would not work as a duet. She flipped over to her messages and as she did she felt a jolt, like a surge of electricity, emanating from her phone. Her phone clattered to the pavement. Her body flickered and glitched like a TV with bad signal and her body disappeared for a nanosecond and then appeared again.

The moment was so quick, it was like nothing happened, but from Marcia's perspective, that nanosecond lasted for weeks.

In one brief painless moment, that jolt, that electrical surge, encompassed her whole being. At the time, she got the distinct impression that someone needed her urgently. Later she realised that "needed" was the wrong word – she was not needed so much as summoned. Unequivocally and irresistibly summoned. The spark,   as she came to describe it, was over in a moment, but its effect was inescapable and spectacular. She found herself in a completely unknown world.

Utterly disorientated, she shook her head and blinked. She seemed to be in a little clearing in a wood, or perhaps it was a great forest – she had no way of knowing. This was no ordinary forest, either. The trees were huge, towering dozens of metres overhead, and forming a ring around her as if forbidding her to leave the clearing. Except for the little triangular space where she stood, the floor of the clearing was covered in thousands of tiny neon-orange plants that glistened and danced as the rain dropped on them.

She was poorly clothed for such weather and already beginning to shiver. Her long dark brown hair was sending a stream of water down her back and the smell of wet earth was rising to meet her. The huge contrast between the spring sunshine at the top of the hill back home, and this forbidding alien land made her feel queasy.

She noticed that some of the trees had thick braids of dull green ivy climbing up them. In fact, those with the ivy had large dark shapes perched high in their branches, but she did not notice them at that moment because it never crossed her mind to look upwards into the torrential rain. Her first thought was to run in amongst the trees to find some shelter, but she had hardly begun to move when she froze.

Ahead of her stood a small crowd of people. There were perhaps forty or fifty of them in all, gathered together under the nearest trees. Most of them were wearing dark brown breeches, buttonless and seamless shirts which finished at the elbow, thick black leather boots, and long cloaks made of a dark coloured material, thrown over the shoulders and hooked together at the front with a wide silver hook, coming from the left and fitting neatly into a perfectly circular silver hole on the right. Many had the hood of their cloaks up against the rain, covering their heads and concealing their faces. A few, the leaders perhaps, were bare-headed except for a gold ring that entirely encircled their right ear. Some wore something like a credit card, clipped to the top lapel of their cloak. Others carried what looked like a piece of black paper in their left hand. Almost all were armed, although she didn't notice that to begin with.

She saw them before they saw her, and she managed to stifle the cry that jumped to her throat.

How did she get into this mess? Could she run to the opposite side of the clearing? She wasn't a great athlete and she knew that as soon as she was spotted, trying to outrun them would be impossible. She was confident she only had a few seconds before she was discovered. They were taking it in turns to speak in voices so quiet that she couldn't make out what they were saying. They appeared to be worried about something – deeply worried. It was as if they were trying to plan but unsure how; unsure of what opposed them, perhaps. Then, even as she watched, one of the men glanced in her direction and gave a start and a low cry. The others followed his gaze, and the low voices died away. Hands reached inside cloaks for weaponry. Some of the gold rings glowed more brightly. Within a minute, Marcia had become the centre of attention. All eyes were on her, and few of them looked friendly.

Marcia's brain was in overdrive. Her shivering had really taken a hold now, and whilst it was partly due to the wet and cold, it was also a result of terror.

What are they going to do to me? What sort of weapons do they have? What have I done to deserve this? she thought.

Her heart was trying to crash through her ribcage. Panic was rising. Will they torture me? How will I cope with the pain? Or am I dead already and this is the afterlife?

The questions tumbled through her head at lightning speed. Did I get killed by a car or something? What happened to me?

She tried in vain to push the panic down and think logically. She shook her head again, and the water from her hair sprayed around her.

The crowd advanced towards her. Their weapons were out now – swords, knives, bows and arrows all at the ready, and she knew that running away was a hopeless enterprise. If they weren't going to kill her straight away, then they might want to question her, she thought. And she would be unable to answer their questions even if she wanted to. She had no idea where she was or how she had got there. How could she convince them she was no threat? Or perhaps they didn't care. Maybe they just took pleasure in torture and death. One or two warriors were moving swiftly ahead of the crowd. They were only seconds away. Shaking to the core, she decided that she would not be seen as a coward. She tried to speak, but managed only a ragged croaky sound. She stopped, clenched her jaw, stood up straight and waited for death.

4

The Summons

Zak, a central figure in the friendship group in Mr Lomar's tutor group, was one of the most experienced in extraction. On and off, he had been part of the Modern Era in Anasius for at least a year. He knew the Anasiun approach to life – peaceable, progressive and moral. He loved that their advanced technology ran in harmony with nature – such a different approach from life back in England.

Getting extracted for the first time was an accident. Clicking that random pop-up on his laptop was a mistake. He didn't mean to click it. He was reading about the famed Bermuda Triangle for his English homework when a pop-up appeared that seemed to be asking for warriors looking for adventure. A cheesy ad for a travel company, he thought. And he meant to close it, but his mouse slipped at the last moment. To Zak, it looked like nothing happened but when he eventually clicked away from the ad a small piece of code duplicated from his laptop to his phone and his Xbox and then sat dormant behind the scenes, activated only when he was needed. When required, the code provided a small pulse of electricity that summoned him to Anasius.

The first time it happened, he was cycling to meet Joe and Zika at the leisure centre, and he had stopped for a drink. He chugged his water bottle and then checked his phone for messages before cycling off again. As he tapped his phone, he felt a sudden pulse up his arm. His surroundings disappeared and he found himself outside, standing on a stone hump-backed bridge overlooking a wide river that rushed quickly beneath his feet. Ahead of him was a slowly rising undulating terrain that led to snow-capped mountain peaks on the horizon, although it was hard to see in the half-light. He fancied it was just after dawn, but he wasn't sure why he thought this.

A great forest stood off to his right and then some low country that stretched as far as he could see. And he was trying to understand what had happened – perhaps he was dreaming somehow, or perhaps he had been knocked off his bike. But he had no time to contemplate that now. He heard a tapping noise behind him and turned slowly around. The source of the noise was a stout wooden staff with which its owner had rapped on the flagstones. She was a middle-aged, green-eyed woman with greying hair pulled into a tight bun on her head. She was dressed in breeches, a tight bodice and a black cape that was fastened at the front with a bright silver hook. She had a gold ring encircling her right ear, and it was shining brightly. The woman stared at him.

"Oh..." Zak gasped involuntarily. "Who are you?"

"Shh – keep your voice down." The command was quiet but authoritative. "The more important question is, who are you, and where did you come from?" Her voice was barely above a whisper. "I'm sure you've come to help because you've only just appeared, but your clothes are all wrong."

Zak considered his jeans and yellow T-shirt.

"What's wrong with them?" he asked indignantly.

"Shhh – too loud. If you have come to help, and, if that is the case, I'm not even sure how or what you can do, but if that is the case then choosing something so conspicuous is not a great way to start. And I wish you'd stop staring as if I was the one who'd just appeared out of nowhere on Maynard Bridge. I know you've been summoned by Xci1, but you don't look like a warrior to me. Still, looks can be deceiving, I suppose. Where's your Scroll?"

"Scroll? What scroll? And who's 'sigh-one'?" he asked, copying her pronunciation, but having no idea how he might spell the word. His mind was in a whirl and he couldn't make sense of what she was saying, whoever she was. "I'm not a warrior," he explained, "and I'm not sure how I got here. Perhaps there's just been some kind of mistake..." Zak was beginning to ramble.

"I see we have a lot to do," she interrupted. "Come with me, quickly, and speak no more. And Xci1 does not make mistakes."

To Zak it was clear that her voice, though quiet, was not to be disobeyed. He followed her meekly, wondering what strange adventure lay ahead.

They left the bridge and moved swiftly away from the rising sun. He noticed she was wearing thick, shin-length boots which meant that she was comfortable as she strode rapidly through the tall, dewy grass. But Zak's experience was very different. His trainers were soon drenched and his jeans got increasingly wet and clung to his legs – totally the wrong clothes for hiking. The woman kept quietly urging them to go faster, and as the journey stretched on and on, Zak began to sweat and his T-shirt clung to his back making him even more uncomfortable. There seemed little hope of a drink. After what felt like hours, when all Zak wanted to do was have a rest, and his head ached from lack of water and from the glare of the sun, the terrain changed from wide open grassland to scrubland leading up to a forest. There were little groups of trees here and there and large dense bushes dotted about. They were getting much closer to the woods, too – clearly their destination lay that way. Aside from the swish of their feet as they moved through the long grass, the only sound came from the maddening trickle of the brook to their right. Everything else was eerily quiet – too quiet, Zak thought. There were increasingly many places a person might be hiding if they wished to remain unseen, and this, coupled with the woman's repeatedly furtive glances this way and that, made Zak nervous. The way the woman travelled suggested that they might encounter dangerous enemies at any moment – her rapid pace, her insistence on silence, her staring into possible hiding places. But they saw no-one until just before the forest. And even then, Zak didn't see them until it was too late.

All at once, without any warning whatever, the woman hissed to Zak to keeping moving down the path, and she slid off to their left in a silent, zig-zagging manoeuvre cross-country. A small silver sword had appeared in her right hand, and she was waving it about, as if cutting some invisible enemy. Then there was a bright but soundless flash of electricity from the tip of her sword that shot off into a clump of bushes. There was a sound like a whimper from the bushes, and then a whizzing noise and a second later, blood bloomed from the woman's left shoulder. She cried out, but she didn't stop moving forward. She reached the bushes within moments and then Zak, further down the path, heard the sound of a struggle, an agonised squeal, a deep cry and then a low groan. After the silence of the past hour-and-a-half, the noises were shockingly loud, but they were over within seconds. The woman emerged from the bushes, her sword dangling from her left hand, and her right hand clutching the wound on her left shoulder. She was breathing heavily, and she looked weak and pale, but she urged Zak onwards.

"Almost there," she panted. "Quick. Keep moving."

"But you're hurt," he said. "You need help. What on earth happened back there? What..."

"Shhh." She cut him off. "Don't talk. Just move."

In a few minutes they reached the edge of the forest. Most of the trees were extremely large, perhaps three metres in diameter at their base, and at least forty metres tall, Zak guessed – like the giant redwood trees he had once seen in a documentary on the Sierra Nevada. They grew at regular intervals, with other much smaller trees growing between them. The forest floor was strewn with clumps of grass, bracken, nettles and holly bushes, and it smelt fresh and clean. Perhaps finally they were going to stop for a rest.

The woman moved swiftly to the opposite side of one of the huge trees just inside the forest, and she pushed the tip of her sword into a little knot in the wood of the tree. At first, nothing happened. But then two tiny parallel lines appeared from the knot and travelled down the tree to the ground. The lines became cracks and then the wood of the tree between them seemed to fall backwards into the tree itself. The gash got larger still until it was about one metre wide, and then a gleaming metal door rose into view, filling the gap entirely. The woman replaced the sword in her cloak and tapped three times on the door. It slid smoothly upwards, like a giant mouse-trap door, and she motioned Zak forwards.

"You look like you've never seen a subway in your life," she murmured as she saw how big Zak's eyes had become. "Come on – we have a train to catch."

She stepped through the opening, and Zak followed. As soon as he was inside, the metal door slid silently closed behind him, a soft warm light came on above his head, and the box in which they now stood sank down into the ground.

From the outside, the metal door slid shut, the crack in the tree came together again, and the tree looked perfectly ordinary, apart from its great size. The whole process took less than thirty seconds. It was a mechanism that had remained a secret for nearly two centuries. But this time, someone was watching. Someone carefully camouflaged ten metres inside the forest, with a pair of binoculars glued to his eyes. He made careful note of the tree and then slunk away with a grin on his face. The overthrow of Anasius grew one step closer.

Zak was relieved to have stopped the relentless march through the grass, and was hopeful of a drink. But the lift, for that's what it seemed to be, dropped into the ground like a stone into a canyon and Zak's stomach was left somewhere high above his head.

The woman smiled at him weakly. "Bit quick for you, is it?" She was panting, bleeding and struggling to stay standing. She continued, "They don't make warriors as they used to, that's all I can say."

Before he could say anything in response, the lift slowed rapidly and came to rest. This was the fastest elevator he had ever experienced, for sure, and now he guessed they were a long way underground.

"At last," the woman murmured. "The train's ready for us."

As she spoke, the door slid silently upwards and the woman stumbled through it with Zak at her side. They did not stand on a station platform, as Zak had fleetingly expected, but rather in a beautifully furnished carriage. At least, he assumed it was a carriage, though it looked more like a room in a posh hotel. Zak was wet through, breathing hard, slightly dizzy with the suddenness of the last part of the journey, and desperately thirsty, but he forgot most of these things because of the wonder of his surroundings.

The air was fresh and pleasantly warm. At regular intervals, there were plush armchairs covered in a material that looked like deep-blue velvet but that seemed smoother somehow, and all the more inviting for it. There were no windows, and the walls boasted ornately-framed portraits hung at intervals – portraits of royalty or aristocracy, he supposed, given their fine, if unfamiliar, clothing. The light was soft and warm and came from sleek round-bottomed uplighters attached to the walls. The floor was stone – marble, maybe – and there were rugs here and there to soften the effect. He noticed that there was a bar at the far end stocked with all kinds of food and drink, most of which he didn't recognise. It reminded him of his deep thirst.

He noticed that the train had begun to move, but the acceleration was so gentle and the movement of the train so smooth, that he soon forgot he was travelling at all. A man wearing a dark green shirt and black breeches was approaching them rapidly, looking deeply concerned.

"Gloria – what happened?" he asked loudly and urgently. She had crumpled into a nearby chair, and she looked back at him and whispered something.

The man shouted, "Dr Krinton! Dr Krinton! Some help please."

A bright-eyed grey-haired man rose from a chair half-way down the carriage, reached for a bag by his feet, and rushed over to the woman.

"Gloria – how did this happen?" he asked as he walked towards her.

But there was no response from the woman. She had passed out.

"Get her flat and we can tend to this wound. Did she say anything?" the doctor asked as he got to work.

They both glanced at Zak expectantly.

"Errr..." he began awkwardly. "I...I don't really know. She had a fight with someone in some bushes."

"Who?"

Dr Krinton responded, "Professor – look at the boy. He is dazed, wild-eyed and exhausted. Get him to Xci1 while I attend to Gloria."

The younger man offered his hand to Zak. "Professor Chan at your service," he said. "You are most welcome. I am sorry for the secrecy of your travels and your difficult journey here. There are spies throughout Anasius these days and you can't be too careful, as you have discovered. Let me get you a drink."

He paused by a chest-high countertop and picked up a pear-shaped bottle. He removed the lid and offered it to Zak. Zak nodded his gratitude and, despite his thirst, carefully put the bottle to his lips, uncertain what it was he was about to drink. But it was delicious – fresh, citrusy and thirst-quenching. He drained it in seconds. The professor smiled and offered him a second bottle.

"We have a new Scroll for you, some clothes for you to change into, and you may choose your weapons, but first you need to see Xci1. He is waiting for you in the next carriage."

As he spoke, he led Zak to the arched doorway at the end of the room.

"Your Majesty, Outer Warrior One!" he announced, and ushered Zak through, bowing and then retreating back into the first carriage. Apparently, not only was Zak "Outer Warrior One", he was also being presented to royalty.

A tall, black-haired man was approaching him with a big smile on his face. "Please forgive me," he began, "I expect you are very confused. I am Xci1, Prince of Anasius and first heir to the throne."

He was dressed in clothes very similar to those of the other three people he had seen, and he had the single gold ring encircling his right ear, just as the others had. He wore brown ankle-high boots with gold laces, carried no weapons, held something black, thin and rigid in his left hand, about the size of a piece of A4 paper, and had a thin but ornately carved band of gold encircling his head.

"In these dark days, it has become necessary for us to summon certain people for help. We need young people, people not related to Anasius, people with no axe to grind, people whom we can trust and train. In essence, we need people from a different world. Aside from me, only two others in Anasius know your origins, and those two will never betray you. We summoned you because we need your help."

Zak needed to sit down. He was reeling from everything that happened in the last few hours. His extraction; Gloria; the lengthy hike through the grasslands; the deadly fight in the bushes; the lift in the tree; the train; and now, this information. He was just a teenager from Raynesborough County School. He was no warrior. He was a keen cyclist and footballer. He was good at maths and physics and useless at history and languages. He had a loyal group of mates. And he was not a warrior.

"Your Majesty," he began hesitantly. "I'm not sure who

you think I am. My name's Zak. I'm just a school kid – I'm not Outer Warrior One, whoever that is. I'm not a warrior at all. I think there's been a mistake."

Xci1 motioned Zak over to a chair, and replied simply, "No mistake, Zak."

He paused as Zak sat down.

"But you're right – you're not Outer Warrior One. Not yet. But you will be, when we've trained you. And you will have a vital part to play in the defence of Anasius in a year's time. There's a lot to do before that."

"But...Your Majesty," Zak protested, "I have my own life in my own country. I don't know where I am or how I got here, and I need to get back. I'm supposed to be going to the leisure centre with my friends..."

Xci1 interrupted him. "You'll go back and forth a few times before war comes to us, Zak. And we'll summon you when you're needed, so don't worry about that. As for returning to your own country, that can happen only when you reach the outer marker – you'll know it when you see it. But you can't return until then and you can't make it happen by yourself."

"But they'll wonder where I've gone. I mean, they must already be wondering where I've got to. If I stay much longer, the police will be called and there'll be a heck of a storm to deal with. And how will I explain where I've been?"

"Zak – you have been extracted via a piece of code we lodged in your phone. Our worlds do not run parallel. No time passes in your world whilst you're here, although time does pass in our world whilst you're in your own. If a person were watching you very carefully when you were extracted and returned, all they would see would be a little glitch, rather like a tiny bit of interference. And they would dismiss it as a trick of the mind. But very few people watch carefully, so I don't think there is anything to worry about."

Xci1 was very sure of himself, Zak thought, but he had no reason to disbelieve him. And anyway, Xci1 had said there wasn't anything Zak could do about it whether or not what he'd been told was true. He settled back into his chair, grateful for the rest, and certain of one thing only: nothing would surprise him from now on. Which just goes to show how little he knew about his future.

5

Combat Training

It was more than a year earlier when Jason had begun his training. Xci3 was an older grey-haired man, dressed smartly in the usual Academy professors' attire of black trousers, buttonless shirt, red sash across his chest and the ubiquitous gold ring encircling his right ear. He began the first combat training class in his usual way, with a large white screen behind him and a mannequin standing a metre from his right side. The mannequin was dressed all in black and carried a broadsword in its right hand.

"The first rule of combat is disarmament. If an enemy is armed and you are not, then you must do everything you can to level the playing field. In a combat situation, what happens if you are not carrying your weapon and an armed assailant approaches you? Unless you disarm him, almost certainly you will fall, never to rise again. Disarmament capability is a keystone of effective defence."

As he spoke, he moved closer to the mannequin.

"I want you to imagine that Jerry here is really an enemy

soldier approaching me from my right and in front of me. Watch carefully what happens, because I would like one of you to describe my technique to your fellow students. I am also recording this so we can review it later."

As he finished speaking, with a movement so lightning fast that it was over in an instant, the sword from the mannequin was lying on the floor, and Xci3 was turning away from the dummy. It was so fast, and so jarringly unexpected, it left Jason almost breathless.

"So what happened?" Xci3 asked as he finished straightening up. It seemed impossible that anyone could tell how Xci3 had done it.

Still, one trainee replied confidently, "You used your right foot to kick the blade free."

Xci3 studied him carefully. Then he smiled. "Let's take another look."

The lights dimmed and the screen behind him came to life. On screen appeared Xci3 and the dummy from a minute or two earlier. Then the movie began to roll and the scene they had witnessed was re-enacted again.

"Is he correct?" Xci3 asked.

Jason had no idea. It was too fast. No-one said anything.

"Let's try at half-speed," Xci3 suggested. He punched a few buttons and the screen came to life again. This time, at half-speed, whilst Xci3 was moving very fast, you could see that his right leg had moved upwards and outwards and his body had made a quarter turn to the left. Maybe the trainee was right?

"Now quarter-speed," Xci3 said and pressed a few more

buttons. This time everyone could see that Xci3 had lifted his right knee, kicked his foot out and struck the top of the sword-hilt with the inside of his right foot, continued the movement around to the left and planted his right foot over a quarter turn from its starting point.

Xci3 mused out loud, "This is the first occasion when one of my students could tell exactly what happened first time around. Perhaps I'm getting slow as I get older."

Jason almost laughed, but then he realised that Xci3 wasn't joking. Whilst he had moved unbelievably quickly, Xci3 actually thought he might have been slower than he used to be? How was that even possible?

Xci3 returned to his lecturing. "In the next few weeks, I will be teaching you disarmament techniques like the one I used here on Jerry. You will train and practice harder than you have ever done before. Your muscles will ache, your heart will tell you to rest, your brain will tell you that it is an impossible task. About a third of you will drop out before the end. But if you have stayed the course and completed your training, then by the end of two months you will be able to do far more than disarm Jerry in the way I just did."

Jason wasn't sure he believed him. Surely there was no way he would be able to move as fast as Xci3. But whilst he began to doubt whether he should be at the Overlord Academy at all, he reckoned he was going to learn some interesting things. Xci3 was clearly an expert in his field. Jason wondered about the other students. He glanced around the room. There were eight of them including himself. Five other guys and two women, all older than

Jason. They did not look like a band of hardened warriors. Most looked either scared or worried. They wore the same clothes that he had been given on arrival at the Academy: standard issue dark brown breeches, seamless shirt, and strong black above-the-ankle boots. One of the girls, Riley, half-smiled across at him, and he got a brief nod from Carson, a short, stocky lad who was only a couple of years older than him. The others were fully focused on Xci3.

Xci3 went on. "In weaponless hand-to-hand combat, killing someone takes time. Irrespective of the combat technique, one of the fastest ways to kill a person is by strangulation, and that is not particularly fast. Breaking someone's neck is often successful, but death is never instantaneous, and some have survived and recovered from such an injury. You might hear of gold-band qualified southern warriors who can kill with a lightning-fast punch to the back of the neck, but such is the stuff of legends, not life in the real world. Such a blow could incapacitate someone, knock them out, even put them in a coma, but it would take some time for them to die, and again, they might recover. This is why warriors carry weapons.

I know that most of you are keen to learn combat techniques, both hand-to-hand combat and the effective handling of weapons. All that is to come. But remember, the people of Anasius are a people committed to the true and the good and the right, as described in the Scroll – the people of Xcion the Sovereign, who stands true in all things, over all worlds, and beyond time itself. We train in armed combat not because we undervalue human life, but rather because we value it highly. We value our own people, reflected in our lengthy and detailed course in self-defence. And we value the lives of our combatants, finding ways to incapacitate without killing whenever we can.

There is no place in Anasius for humiliation or torture. We all know that in the dungeons of Crask the Notalians specialise in inflicting maximum pain without killing people. It is an ongoing evil that makes me sick to the stomach; an evil that tears at the heart of the Scroll, assailing the value Xcion the Sovereign has placed on all people, and inviting His righteous punishment. But Crask is in Notalia. Here in Anasius, there is no place for such atrocities. We continue to campaign for the rights of those incarcerated and to argue for justice. Despite the Notalian rhetoric, national security is never an excuse for maltreatment of prisoners. As you will know, the three people of Anasius whom they have in the dungeons of Crask are private citizens. None of them have connections with our nation's military or civil leadership at all. But they are probably being tortured even as we speak."

Jason was now leaning forwards in his seat, eyes fixed on Xci3 who paused for breath before continuing.

"But be that as it may, if war comes, and it probably will, we are training to be warriors. Warriors defend the weak and the poor and the defenceless. Warriors stand firm for their country. Warriors do not give up and they do not give in. And in times of war, warriors are called upon to kill their enemy invaders, enemy assailants and enemy fighters. Their death is necessary to secure our ongoing freedom. Warriors stand in the gap. They shout loud and clear, 'If you want to take my country, my land, my people, then you need to go through me.' And they hold fast to the end..."

For a moment Xci3's voice tailed off. Then he seemed to regain his composure, took a drink from a glass that was in front of him, and continued speaking.

"As I explained at the start, we begin with disarmament. In all likelihood, an opponent will be armed with something. Your first job in hand-to-hand combat is to level the playing field as much as you can. Disarm your opponent. That is your primary task. I will show you a total of five techniques, each of which you are required to practice until you can complete them without fail at least nine-out-of-ten times, irrespective of the weapon used. We will assume for the moment that your opponent is holding a straight knife a bit like this one."

He selected a knife from the weapons arrayed on a table to his side and held it up. The blade was about nine inches long, and the handle about six inches. It looked extremely sharp.

And with that, Xci3 began to explain the first technique for disarmament.

Jason was engrossed.

6

A Lunchtime Conversation

On Monday at Raynesborough County School, something happened after lunch. When Trey reached his tutor room, Mr Mason's secretary was there and took Calvin, Joe and Phil out of the classroom. They did not return that day. And when Trey got home from school, his mum was waiting for him. She had just finished a phone conversation with Mr Mason, and she was wondering how things were going at school.

"Hello, Trey," she hugged him as he came down the hallway. "How was today?"

"Okay."

"I need more than that, Trey. Was anyone nasty to you today? Did people mimic you? Did they shove you or kick your chair or get physical?"

"Nothing major, mum. And then three boys got taken out of tutor time and didn't come back. No-one seemed to know what was going on, and I didn't really know, either."

"I've just been talking to Mr Mason."

"Right, okay," Trey responded uncertainly.

"Mr Mason told me that last week he had spoken to two

of the most reliable and committed students. Both are part of your tutor group. He had asked them what was happening around the school, in particular how they thought you were getting on, because he was worried you were not looking very happy. After some prompting, they said that people mimicked your accent, knocked books out of your hand, and so on. They also said a bit about what happened in the changing rooms last Wednesday, although they weren't there for all of it. They left when someone grabbed your towel. In fact, they left to go and tell Mr Longmore that the boys were messing about in the changing rooms, and that's why he came and shouted at the door. After some persuasion, they also named names."

They named names? Trey was worried again, and he felt the familiar churning in his stomach. This might all come back on his head. He knew the two boys were Max and Mark, but he didn't know them very well.

His mum was speaking again. "Mr Mason told me that he has just suspended three boys, and that one of them – the one who took your towel – would not be returning to Raynesborough County School. I got the impression that he's been in trouble for lots of different things over the past year."

Trey wasn't sure what to think. Everyone would know they had been suspended because of him – wouldn't he be branded a snitch? Would any of the bullying really stop, or was this just a smooth bit of road before the potholes began again? As he thought about it, he realised that Calvin, Phil and Jacob were the main problem, with Joe just tagging along. He knew that Calvin, Joe and Phil had been sent home, and he suspected that Calvin was the one who wouldn't be returning. Perhaps Jacob would be annoyed at him because his friends had been suspended? Like Joe, though, Jacob only did things when his friends were around him, so maybe he'd be okay when they weren't there. He didn't know.

"I guess that means the next couple of days might be a bit better," Trey said uncertainly. And anyway, he thought, they certainly couldn't get worse, and he couldn't be shunned anymore than he was already.

His mum said, "Well, Mr Mason wants me to call him tomorrow and let him know how the day went for you. And he wants to chat with me again on Friday to see how things go once the other two boys have returned. In the meantime, he wanted you to know that the school will do everything it can to sort this out. He has talked to Mr Lomar, who is trying to keep an eye out, and he's asked Mark and Max to keep him informed, too. It all sounded quite good to me, Trey, although I remain alarmed that any student would think such behaviour is okay. Personally, I don't think any of those three boys should be allowed back to school."

"Mum, they're not the only ones who are nasty to me. And the school can't expel everyone who is nasty to someone else. If they did that there'd be pretty much no-one left. Maybe school will be a bit better with them gone for a bit; or the other kids might turn against me because they think I snitched. But I didn't, mum. I didn't say anything. Even to you."

"I know you didn't. And Mr Mason knows you didn't, too.

But whatever happens, I want you to talk to me about it. I want to know who did what, what was good, what was bad, how you felt. All of it. The thing is, Trey, we need to make this work. I can't homeschool you again – you need subject-specific teachers to get you through your exams. I also want you to have some decent friends and enjoy school. That might seem like a pipe-dream at the moment, but we're praying you will get there."

"Okay, mum."

The following day, Calvin, Phil and Joe were not in school, and it wasn't long before Trey's tutor group knew the reason. Half-way through morning registration, Mr Mason arrived. This was a very unusual event, and the room fell silent in seconds.

Mr Mason began, "I'm sure rumours are now flying, because they always do, so I thought I ought to come and explain what has happened. Three boys from this class have been caught bullying others and subjecting someone to emotional and physical abuse. As a result, I have discussed the matter with the local police but they have agreed not to intervene in light of what I proposed to do about it."

As soon as Mr Mason said the word, "police", there was an audible intake of breath from some in the room. If Mr Mason didn't have everyone's undivided attention before, he certainly did now.

"There is no place in this school for that kind of behaviour, so Joe and Phil have been suspended until Thursday, and Calvin has also been suspended pending expulsion. He will not be returning to Raynesborough County School. When

Joe and Phil return, they will be on a school contract, in agreement with their parents. This means that if they are ever involved in similar behaviour again, their place at this school will be forfeited.

"For all of you sitting here, some of you have also been involved in bullying. And most of the rest of you have been well aware of what has been going on but you have lacked any moral courage to do something about it. As I have said on previous occasions, there is no such thing as an innocent bystander when bad things happen – either you actively try to stop things, or you are responsible for allowing them to continue. I have not yet managed to discuss these events with Trey..."

Trey dropped his head and stared at the floor. His face was on fire. He was horrified to be named publicly like this.

Mr Mason continued, "...but I am convinced that he has experienced the very worst of what any group of young people can offer: mimicking, isolation, rejection and humiliation. In essence, through no choice of his own, he has come here from another country and, instead of welcoming him and seeking to learn from him, you have subjected him to verbal, emotional and physical abuse – that is why I sought advice from the police. Trey must now have the worst possible idea of what it means to be a British teenager, and undoing that conviction is going to take considerable time and effort. But undoing it must be done, nevertheless.

"I am in no position to instruct people about who to be friends with – that is not my job. But teaching all our students the importance of kindness, moral courage, responsibility, discipline and integrity lies at the heart of what Raynesborough County stands for. If you do not share those values, then you should not be at this school. Common decency demands that we interact politely and respectfully with one another, and our school code of practice demands that intimidation, disrespect, humiliation and abuse have no place here, or, in my view, anywhere else in the world. Now as I said, I have not had a chance to discuss the truth of this with Trey, but I remain convinced that I am right. And I am expecting that every one of you is taking on board what I am saying and that I will hear no more of this in the future. My ideal is to come to registration in order to sing your praises, not to express my disgust, but I have been forced to do the latter. I do not wish to have to intervene any further, but I will do so if necessary. Does everybody understand me?"

No-one said anything. Trey's heart pounded. His eyes were fixed on the floor. He was unable to speak even if he had wanted to.

"Does everyone understand me?" Mr Mason demanded more loudly.

"Yes sir." The response rippled around the room.

"Good. Now you need to get straight to class without being late, so I won't hold you up anymore. Thank you for your time, Mr Lomar." And with that, Mr Mason left.

In silence, the other students gathered their belongings and traipsed out of their tutor room. It seemed that no-one knew what to say. Trey tagged along, carefully lagging behind the others, wondering what on earth his day was going to be like after that. He did not have to wait long to find out.

It turned out that he wasn't the only one lagging behind. Zak was trailing as well. Trey was worried. It was almost as if Zak wanted to talk to him, but that would be weird, because he'd mostly kept himself to himself up until now. There were less than four days remaining until half-term – couldn't he just be left alone until then? He knew Calvin was not returning to Raynesborough County, so that was good news. But he had been named out loud in front of his whole class, so he was probably forever the outcast now, and Joe and Phil were returning in two days, which was even more worrying. And now Zak was trying to get him alone.

Trey tried to figure out how to avoid Zak, but they were both going to RE, so that was difficult. Maybe he needed to speed up a bit to get closer to the class – there ought to be some safety in numbers, especially with the girls around. But he didn't get a chance.

"Hey, Trey," Zak said to him in a low voice. "Can I talk to you for a minute?"

"It's a free country last I checked," Trey responded coolly. He didn't know what Zak was going to hassle him about, but he could bet it was something to do with the boys getting suspended.

"Trey," Zak said urgently, "it's about Anasius."

Trey's heart missed a beat. He swallowed. Had he heard correctly? What did Zak know about Anasius?

"About who?" he asked, thinking he must have misheard.

"Not 'who', you idiot. Anasius. I was extracted on Saturday on my way to go swimming with Zika and Joe."

Trey's heart was racing. Zak was friends with Joe – that could only mean trouble. But Zak had been to Anasius as well. What did he want? They had almost reached the classroom now, so there was no time to ask any questions. Zak was speaking again, now in an even lower voice.

"Meet me at lunch – I need to talk to you. Okay?"

Trey didn't know what to think. Being alone with a friend of Joe seemed like a horrible idea. Who knows what Zak might want to say or do to him. On the other hand, if Zak had been extracted then there was something major he and Zak shared – something they could actually talk about.

"Okay, Trey?" Zak's urgent voice interrupted his thoughts as they reached the classroom door.

"Er, yeah, sure," Trey managed to say.

Then they went into RE.

Trey could not concentrate that morning. His heart seemed to have a mind of its own, and he was surprised no-one else could hear it beating so hard. His brain was full of recent events with Calvin, Joe and Phil, Zak's insistent request, and Anasius. RE, biology and French seemed pretty meaningless in comparison and he simply had no time for them at all.

At lunch, Trey went and sat at a corner table by himself as usual, aware of the stares and whispers of various students as he walked across the dining hall. He got his lunch out and tried to ignore everyone as he ate his sandwiches. Then

Zak came to find him and joined him at the table. This was the first time Trey had eaten lunch with anyone at school – it was turning out to be a very strange day. Zak started speaking as soon as he arrived with his lunch tray.

"Trey, are we okay? I mean...I haven't really spoken to you much since you got here. I...I guess I've just carried on with my own life and...like...are you okay?"

"I'm fine," Trey said, not really answering Zak's question, and finding Zak's sudden interest in him a bit weird.

"The thing is, I was extracted to Anasius on Saturday. I was there for nearly a month, although I guess it was a millisecond of our time, and towards the end of that month I had a long chat with Gloria, who told me you had been extracted as well. You know Gloria, right?"

"Yes," Trey said. He softened a bit and said, "Gloria was in the health clinic at first, but I met her a few times at the Academy later on." This was so weird – he was having a civilized conversation with someone at school.

"She helped me come to terms with everything that happened in Anasius. It had taken me a good two weeks to come to terms with being extracted and then to submit to getting trained at the Overlord Academy. I was proud and stubborn and, after the initial wonder of going to a whole new world, I just wanted to come home. I spent almost all of those first two weeks living in the building next to the auditorium, eating when I wanted, sleeping when I wanted, roaming the woods as I pleased. I had been told I was welcome to visit and listen to the lectures, but I only went twice because I thought they were boring. After my initial whirlwind day in Anasius, when Gloria was injured and when I met Xci1, I became someone no-one wanted to know. I shouted at Heldta who was supplying me with food almost all the time, and trying to help me acclimatise. I shouted at Gloria, even though she was the one who had saved me from being shot at, only to be shot herself. She was supposed to be in recovery from that arrow wound, but I shouted at her nevertheless. And overall, I generally pouted and sulked. Then, on day eleven, I wandered away from the Academy and managed to get myself hopelessly lost. I discovered that I was useless at navigation, useless at providing for myself, and useless at sorting myself out. I roamed for hours, refusing to call out for help. But after spending most of the day without food or drink, and with no idea where I was or how to get help – the whole place seemed totally deserted – eventually, I broke. I sat at the foot of a tree and blubbed like a little kid who's lost his mum at the shops. I had no idea what to do.

"It turned out that they had fitted a loco-audio tracker into my clothing. This meant that not only did Xci2 at Overlord Academy know where I was, he also knew that I was crying like a baby. It took them less than twenty minutes to get to me. And when they did, and I discovered that they had heard me bawling, I was so embarrassed and annoyed that it still took me three days before I finally agreed to being trained.

"At this point, Gloria interrupted me and told me that this is when I began to be useful. I didn't really understand what she meant. So I asked her about other people's experience of extraction. And what she said completely blew me away. She said that you were extracted on the same day as me, and that while it had taken me two weeks to acclimatise and submit to training, it had taken you thirty minutes."

Trey grinned, suddenly enjoying Zak's story. He said, "Being somewhere else where people were nice to me and wanted to train me and prepare me for something – that was a breath of fresh air. I have no friends here at Raynesborough."

"That's not true anymore, Trey," Zak countered, grinning back. "Our church youth group are meeting up for a BBQ in half-term. Maybe you'd like to come?"

Trey's grin faded. "You don't have to pretend, Zak. I know I don't fit in, and I don't want a pity party. I just want a quiet life without people hassling me. I…"

Zak interrupted. "I'm not pretending. I want you to come."

"I'm not sure about that," Trey said. "No-one else is going to want me there."

"The girls will. And I'll handle the boys. Tim's our youth leader, and he'll be there – he's a great guy, and he'll make sure you're included. We're having a fire and games and there'll be tons of food. Think about it at least, will you?"

Trey nodded, "Okay. Sure. I'll think about it." Then he remembered Joe. He was Zak's friend and was bound to be there. He couldn't possibly go if Joe was going to be there.

But Zak was moving on, "I'm telling you my story of Anasius because I realised that I've not been very nice to you since you came here. I've either ignored you or ignored it when other kids mock your accent or shove you around or whatever. I was there in the changing room last Wednesday, Trey, and I laughed along with everyone else. I did nothing to help. I just made it worse. I'm sorry, Trey." Zak seemed unsure what to say next.

"It's okay," Trey said. "Nobody helped. But I didn't snitch – I really didn't."

"I know," Zak said. "Mr Mason's good at his job, and he knew who to talk to and what to say. That whole thing should never have happened. Calvin's not coming back, and good riddance – he used to bully me, too."

Wow, Trey thought, today was indeed packed full of surprises.

"I reckon Joe's learned his lesson now – it'll be okay with him now."

"I'll believe that when I see it," Trey said.

"Fair enough," Zak conceded. "Let's go and play football."

Trey knew he meant soccer, but he let it pass.

7

Half-Term

Zak was still feeling really bad about his failure to stand up for Trey, and for joining in with the bullying. He hated himself for being weak and just letting stuff happen. And he hated that Trey had had such a horrible experience at school. So now he was determined to make Trey's life much better. Following that first lunchtime meeting, Zak made sure Trey ate lunch with him and his friends from then on. He knew this would be fine for Marcia and Kia (in fact, Kia had told him she felt bad about Trey, too), and Max, Jason and Zika were pretty easy-going, so they wouldn't be a problem. He worried a bit about Joe, though. Joe was currently suspended because of what happened with Trey, and he probably assumed Trey had snitched. Joe was also quite hot-headed, and whilst he was a fun friend to have around, he was an act-first-think-later type of person. Zak resolved to talk to Joe as soon as he could and try and sort things out.

Trey didn't say very much over lunch, but Zak hoped he was happy simply being included, and listening to their inane conversation about Mr Davidson's latest fashion disasters, errors in the latest Marvel movie or why you couldn't actually make cheese on the moon. Slowly, he thought, Trey was becoming a part of this little friendship group.

When Joe returned from his suspension on Thursday, though, he avoided talking to Trey directly and mostly seemed to ignore him. As a result, lunch was a bit more tense than the previous couple of days, although Marcia and Kia did a sterling job of keeping the conversation going. All in all, Zak thought, it wasn't terrible. He knew that Joe did not have all the facts, and he kicked himself for not managing to talk to Joe before his return. He would tell Joe the truth as soon as he had a chance, but somehow in those last two days, there wasn't the opportunity.

On the Sunday at the start of half-term Zak's family were rushing to get to church on time. This was not unusual – his mum was not a morning person, so they were usually waiting for her. They arrived with about a minute to spare and managed to find seats towards the back. As the service started, he spotted Trey and, he assumed, Trey's parents. He decided that after the service he would introduce Trey to Tim, his youth leader. But for now, the service was under way, and the usual hymns, prayers and sermon unfolded. Pastor John closed the service with a prayer and, moments later, Zak met with Trey and they went to find Tim.

"Trey, this is Tim, our youth leader," Zak explained a few minutes later.

"Hi," Trey said and extended his hand.

"Hello Trey," Tim responded, shaking his hand warmly. "It's great to meet you – I have seen you here a few times before, but I've not had the chance to say hello. Zak tells me you're one of his friends at school, and he's hoping you'll come to our BBQ on Friday night. D'you think you might make it?"

"Errr, probably," Trey said uncertainly. "What time is it?"

"It's at 7 pm at the Partridge's house. Zak can show you where that is, easy enough."

"Oh, okay. I might be able to come. How many are going?"

"I'm not sure. It's half-term, so some folks are away. But we should still get 10 or 12, I would think. And it'd be great to have you."

"Thanks," Trey responded. "Do I need to bring anything?"

"No – just yourself. Oh, and old clothes. We're having a fire and stuff, and you might get a bit grubby."

"Okay, thanks," Trey said again.

"Hopefully I can get to know you a bit then, Trey. Sorry I can't hang around now – I have visitors for lunch and I'm not very well prepared. I'll see you Friday."

"See ya," said Zak as Tim left.

"Bye," Trey said.

Zak laughed, "Well, Trey – you didn't seem to need much convincing!"

"It's hard to say no to him," Trey admitted. "Anyway, it's not like I've got anything else to do."

"Great. I'm looking forward to it, for sure," Zak said. He hesitated, wondering whether or not to invite Trey to his gathering of friends tomorrow. Eventually he said, "What are you doing over half-term?"

"Not a lot. A bit of work, I guess. Dunno."

"Work?" Zak raised his eyebrows. "Sounds like a boring idea." Then he decided to ask. "Well, if you're around tomorrow, I'm having a few friends over and you'd be welcome to come."

"Errr, yeah, maybe..."

Zak pressed him a bit, with a grin on his face. "Oh, come on. Imagine I'm Tim and I just asked you."

"Okay, okay," Trey smiled. "Let me know when." Zak noticed Trey's parents beckoning him from the doorway, and pointed them out.

"You better go Trey," Zak said. "I'll message you."

Half-term was a welcome break from the problems of school. Zak hadn't made any specific plans for Monday's gathering. Joe and Jason were both away, but the rest of the group were coming. They'd probably end up playing on the Nintendo Switch, he thought, although Marcia and Kia wouldn't be up for that. Maybe they could wander to the park or something. And pizza was definitely in order – his mum had bought loads ready to throw in the oven when they got hungry.

Zika arrived first on his bike, as always, and he and Zak played FIFA while they waited for the others. Then both Marcia and Kia arrived, and proceeded to talk about school-work as if it mattered. Zak and Zika tried to bring the conversation around to the summer holidays or sport or something interesting, but it was an uphill struggle.

Max arrived ten minutes later carrying two bottles of coke, followed almost immediately by Trey, who came uncertainly to the door, bearing a tub of chocolate brownies.

"Hey," Zak said to Max and Trey, "Come on in. Brownies and coke is exactly what we need to distract the girls from discussing Latin."

Max grinned. The girls were always going on about work. He and Trey followed Zak back to the lounge with the refreshments.

"Coke and brownies," Zak announced, and much to his relief, the conversation changed to discussing food – a far more enjoyable subject. Marcia commented that the brownies were the best she'd ever tasted, and they agreed that the crisp top and chewy insides were completely delicious.

"Thank your mum, Trey," Kia said with a smile.

"Yeah," Max said. "I agree – these are great."

Trey went a bit red and then said, shyly, "I made them this morning. Mum's recipe, though!"

"Really?" Zika said incredulously. "I've never been any good at cooking. My mum always says that I use the smoke alarm as an oven timer."

This caused laughter all round.

"I'm useless too," Marcia said. "Although I'm a pretty good at burnt toast. How did you come to be great at cooking, Trey?"

"I'm not. Not really. But when mum went back to work, she stopped making brownies. I really like them, so I decided to learn to make them myself. I can't really cook anything else," Trey said.

"No need to," Max responded. "Anyone could live off these brownies no problem!" He took the last one from the tub. "And any time you feel the need to make brownies, I'm happy to come and help you eat them!" He crammed it into his mouth in one go.

"You're disgusting," Kia said.

"You remember when we played Chubby Bunnies and Zika managed to fit eleven marshmallows in his mouth?" asked Zak. "That was disgusting. It was all drooling out the sides, and..."

"Ugh, stop," Kia interrupted. "Why are boys so gross?"

"They're made that way," Marcia explained. "Something to do with their brains, I think. I read about it somewhere."

"Yeah, yeah," Zika said. "Come on – what shall we do now?"

The friends cast about for a bit, and then Zak brought out some playing cards. He riffled the cards expertly, dealt them out, and they played Cheat for over an hour. Zika lost because he was terrible at pulling a poker face. The others had varying success depending on the round, and Zak virtually always won because he was an expert at cards. Zika was suspicious that Zak manipulated the cards somehow to give himself a good deal, but he could never see it happening so he wasn't sure. He asked to shuffle and deal one round, but his shuffling was so messy and his dealing so inaccurate that the others told him to let Zak do it again.

They ate pizza, went to the park and hung out around the kiddy swings and generally whiled away a few hours before they dispersed home.

"See you Friday," Zak called to Trey as Trey left.

"Sure," Trey said, "and thanks!"

The rest of half-term was increasingly boring and uneventful. By Friday evening Trey found himself looking forward to the prospect of a night out. He ate supper with his parents and then cycled over to Zak's. They had planned to meet at Zak's house and then go to the BBQ together from there. He got to Zak's house in under five minutes, and Zak was waiting for him at the gate. Together they hurtled off down the street, weaving expertly in and out of the traffic and jumping onto the pavement when the traffic was slowing them down. It took less than ten minutes to cross town and head up the lane to the Partridge's house. "House" was a bit of a poor name for the mansion that came into view as they crested the hill and glanced to their right, seeing the smoke rising from the BBQ.

The house and garden were down off the road, so as they turned into the top of the long drive, Tim and one or two kids were easily recognisable in the garden. Zak and Trey arrived at the gate a few moments later, pushed their bikes against the hedge and sauntered through into the garden. Tim spotted them.

"Hi," he said with a smile. "I'm glad you're here. There's a shed-load to eat, and only five of you here so far."

Zak and Trey saw Marcia and a girl who turned out to be called Ellie, bouncing on a large trampoline. Ellie went to a different school from them but she seemed nice enough. There were two small kids, who apparently belonged to the

Partridge family, playing on a bouncer and a tricycle up near the house. Tim was barbecuing some chicken wings and thick burgers, and chatting to Jason about his half-term. Zak and Trey joined them.

"What did you do this week, Zak," Tim asked. "Off cycling again?"

"A bit," he admitted. "We spent Tuesday at the beach – it was really hot and my dad had the day off. Apart from that, though, not much. I went into town yesterday, but didn't do anything interesting. You went to Snowdonia, didn't you Jason?"

Jason told them about his four days in Wales. Initially it sounded great, staying in a bunkhouse, climbing mountains during the day, getting away from everything. But then Jason told them that they'd had to carry all their gear and cook all their food and had walked for hours through incessant rain. That, coupled with little phone reception and Internet, meant that suddenly it sounded far less fantastic. Trey was almost glad he'd had a week of boredom.

"What about you, Trey," Tim asked.

"Didn't do anything, really," Trey replied. "Both my parents are at home this weekend, though, so we're hoping to head to London for the day. We don't really know what to do, but I've not been before, so hopefully we'll have some inspiration."

"You should visit the London Eye, Houses of Parliament and the Tower of London, at least," Zak said. "I've been to London loads of times, but those things are really worth doing. They're pretty easy to get to on the tube, too." Trey wasn't sure what the tube was, but they sounded like good ideas to him.

Zak was wondering whether he should offer to go with them, but was worried that would be a bit weird. He didn't know Trey's parents, but on the other hand he hadn't been to London for quite a while and always enjoyed visiting. His mind began to race ahead, planning out a route and what to do and, most importantly, where to eat. His face was thoughtful and he was frowning a bit as Trey said, "I'll try to remember those – mum was asking me what I wanted to do in London, but I had no idea. The thing is, we've only been in the UK for two months, so we don't really have a clue!"

There was a pause. Then Tim said, "Penny for your thoughts, Zak. What's on your mind?"

Zak went a bit red. "Well, errr..." This was a bit embarrassing, but going with Trey could be a fun day out, and he didn't have anything else to do. "The thing is, Trey, I was wondering...would it be weird if I came with you? I mean...I know where everything is, and what's worth seeing. I'd pay for myself and everything, of course, but..."

"That's a great idea," Tim responded, knowing a little bit about Trey's school troubles from what Zak had told him, and how much Trey needed to be developing friendships. "What d'you think, Trey?"

Trey was hesitant, "Well, it sounds good, but I don't know what my parents will think. Dad's been away for a bit and now that he's back, they might just want us to have a family day. I'll see what they say."

Zak was still a bit embarrassed but also hoping it would

work out. His weekend was going to be pretty dull if not. Trey texted his mum, and the conversation at the BBQ moved on.

About ten minutes later another three guys arrived. Two of them Trey did not know. But the third was Joe. Trey was instantly wary, but as it turned out, Joe seemed to be a different person that evening. Trey did not know it, but Zak had finally managed to talk things through with him the day before, and, while Joe still didn't quite understand how bad things had been for Trey, he at least accepted that Trey was not a snitch. He had decided to give Trey a bit of a break.

So now Friday evening had arrived, Joe was polite, pleasant and even chatty, although he did show off his parkour skills a bit too much. In fact, Trey admitted to himself later, Joe was pretty decent, all things considered. Maybe he didn't have to worry so much about Joe, although what Joe would be like when he was with his other school mates was yet to be seen.

After the food, the little kids were taken inside, and the youth group had the garden to themselves. They spent a bit of time on the trampoline, although Joe was far better than any of them and could do all kinds of flips. Then they had an awesome all-in game of giant Jenga, which Marcia lost spectacularly when the pile toppled with a crash and nearly knocked her over.

Then Tim said it was time to light the bonfire. Mr Partridge had collected huge piles of hedge trimmings and other garden waste ready to put on the bonfire once it was properly going. Tim had fetched a small can of petrol from his car, which he then passed to Zak. Zak poured most of it over the woodpile, and then poured a little trail out towards the seating area. He got rid of the can, and then Joe flicked a match at the trail. Nothing happened. He tried again, and this time the spark set the trail ablaze. The flame raced to the bonfire almost in the blink of an eye and then the bonfire went up with a bang loud enough to shake the ground and bring Mr Partridge running into the garden. The girls looked a bit startled, but the boys were creasing with laughter, including Tim, their youth leader. Mr Partridge realised quickly enough what had happened and that all was well. With a brief, "Be careful, guys," he returned to watching the cricket in the lounge. Soon after, they threw the great piles of hedge-cuttings onto the flames and it wasn't long before the bonfire was huge. Then the boys began an idiotic game of trying to jump over it.

"You're going to burn yourselves," Marcia said.

"We'll be fine," Joe said as he ran across the grass and took a flying leap over the pile.

Marcia gasped, but Joe landed safe and sound quite some distance from the far side of the bonfire. Zak followed him, then the others.

"Boys never were that clever," Ellie remarked to Marcia. "My mum says that boys don't grow up, they just grow bigger."

Marcia grinned, despite her worry. "She's right about that," she agreed.

The boys tired of it eventually and then as the bonfire began to die down a bit, Tim got out some marshmallows and skewers. They spent some time melting and eating the marshmallows, in the midst of which Trey got a text from his mum.

"Sure Trey – of course Zak can come. Be good to have a tour guide. Can he meet us at 8 am at the station?"

Trey grinned and passed the message on to Zak.

"8 am? Bang goes my lie-in," Zak groaned jokingly, but really he was pleased. He loved to visit London, and he thought it'd be good for Trey for them to get to know each other a bit more. Plus, now he had something to do the next day and he might even be able to persuade them to go to his favourite restaurant for lunch.

The fire was sinking now, and the group drew closer in, watching the flames, staring at the glowing embers and enjoying the heat from it as darkness began to fall. Tim started telling them a story about when his friend Mark from college asked him to do a bungee jump with him to raise money for charity.

"I hate heights," he explained, "but I didn't want Mark to think I was scared, so for some reason, I agreed to it. We set up an online funding page and got lots of sponsorship for some kids at a cancer unit in town. When the day came and we arrived at the crane ready for the bungee jump, loads of college mates had turned up to cheer us on, all laughing and joking. My stomach was turning somersaults and I thought I might throw up. I decided it would be better to go first and get it over with, so they took me up this huge crane and stood me on this tiny platform with just a bit of elastic tied to my legs. I could hardly stand up, I was so scared."

Joe laughed, and some of the others were smiling broadly as the fire crackled.

Tim continued, "My friends were cheering and yelling up at me. Didn't they realise I was about to die?"

Tim said it so dramatically that everyone was grinning now.

"Eventually, gritting my teeth and wishing I was anywhere but there, I tried to focus on all the money we were raising. I thought about the kids at the cancer unit who really needed the help. And then, for some inexplicable reason, I stepped off the platform. Apparently, I screamed the whole way down, but I had my eyes shut and my jaw clenched, so I don't know how true that is. When I finally stopped bouncing and they got me down, I sat on the grass and took some time to recover. It was then that I realised all my mates were laughing at me, and Mark was right there beside me. I looked at him. 'Your turn now,' I grinned, relieved it was finally over. Do you know what he said then?"

The friends shook their heads.

"He said, 'You must be joking! You'll never get me up there doing that. I am terrified of heights. I just wanted to see if you'd do it!'"

Now everyone in the circle was laughing. Tim was smiling too.

"Unbelievable," he said. "Unbelievable!"

After Tim's story, other stories followed, and it was getting late when Tim broke up the party and urged people to head for home.

When Zak got home, he discussed the London trip with

his mum, and she thought it was a great idea. In fact, she was really pleased that Zak had decided to try and befriend the new American boy in his class – Zak had told her a little bit about Trey's difficulties. She insisted on collecting together snacks and lots of drinks for everyone, which filled Zak's backpack. She also made him get Trey's parents' mobile numbers so she could have a conversation with them and check it was all okay. She did make a fuss, Zak thought, but he guessed that most mothers did, too. And he didn't really mind – instead of playing Xbox by himself all day, he was going to a place he loved, and he was excited to show off his knowledge to Trey and his parents.

Trey's family got up early and got to the station just after 8 am. Zak was already there, carrying his heavy backpack and checking a tube map. Zak explained about London travel, the tube zones and what sort of tickets they needed. They bought the tickets and took the train into Waterloo. From there, Zak led them on a walk out to the Thames, where Trey saw his first glimpse of Big Ben and the Houses of Parliament as they waited in line for a ride on the London Eye.

"I've been on this twice before," Zak said, "but it's still fun. You can go at night, too, and see all the lights – must be awesome at Christmas." He pointed out various landmarks as they ascended. The panoramic views across London were amazing. Trey was fascinated by how old many of the buildings were – all built long before the USA was even founded. Here was ancient history in real life, he thought.

After the London Eye, Zak suggested a tour boat down

the river, since the queue was quite short. On-board, he dug into his backpack and brought out more drinks and snacks for everyone.

"I can't make your brownies," he apologised to Trey's mum, "but London always makes me hungry and thirsty, so my mum made sure I came equipped!"

"Equipped for all of us, I see," Trey's mum laughed. "Please thank your mum! I'm very grateful to you as well. We're having a great day already! Thank you for coming."

Trey's parents listened to the tour-guide explain everything they passed by. Zak had heard it before, but Trey tuned in every now and then, particularly when they passed the Globe theatre, the Tower of London and Tower Bridge. They continued all the way down to Greenwich where they got out and walked up the hill to the observatory.

As Trey's parents read signs and explored, Zak decided that Trey's parents were all right. He wondered whether they'd appreciate his lunch plans as he led them back down the hill to the river. Zak confided in Trey as they walked, "I planned today around my favourite restaurant," he said. "Do you fancy Nando's for lunch?"

Trey grinned. "Sounds awesome," he said.

The queue was long but it was worth the wait. After lunch, they took the Docklands Light Railway to the Tower of London, where they spent the rest of the afternoon. Trey's parents chatted with a couple of the Beefeaters, in their striking red and navy uniforms and top hats, and then told the boys they would meet back at the entrance in a couple of hours' time, so Trey and Zak went off together to explore the tower.

They read about its history, from William the Conqueror onwards. They climbed hundreds of stairs as they moved through the White Tower and explored its exhibits. They stood by a giant sculpture of a dragon made entirely out of weapons, and had a discussion about weaponry in Anasius. Then Zak took Trey across to the Jewel House. Security was very tight.

There was a new video-exhibit of Queen Elizabeth II's coronation, most of which the boys watched, but it was the walk past the crown jewels themselves that was breathtaking. Suits of armour, swords, maces, spoons, bowls, pitchers, crowns, all gold or silver and sparkling with gemstones. Trey had never seen such grandeur, and the weaponry rekindled their discussion of warfare in Anasius. Finally, they made their way back to the entrance and reunited with Trey's parents. They took the tube back to Waterloo and made their way home.

Trey returned home happy and relaxed. The BBQ the day before had been like a new beginning where he finally made a few friends, and today with Zak had been great. The worst two months of his life were over. The second half of term was going to be way better. Or so he thought.

8

Arelard Castle

Kia stood up from her desk chair and simultaneously clicked "Sleep" on her laptop. As she clicked the button, there was a jolt of electricity and she was extracted for the first time. Completely disorientated, she stared around, wide-eyed. Her bedroom had disappeared. Now she was standing in a huge room with a white-panelled ceiling, an oak floor and large oil paintings hanging from the walls. Towards one end were three wide steps leading up to a stage on which stood a gleaming musical instrument, a little like a grand piano. At the near end of the room, recessed into the wall, was a huge fireplace, and on the enormous grate, three large logs were burning steadily. The narrow windows were hung with plush red curtains, and most of the light in the room came from five great chandeliers which hung at intervals from the ceiling.

Standing near the fireplace was a heavy-set woman with a high forehead, brown hair tied back into a long straight plait, a circle of gold around her right ear, an ankle-length skirt and a buttonless blouse. She wore a black cape over the blouse, a black credit-card clipped to the top lapel, and shin-length black boots, laced perfectly.

"Hello, my dear," she said. "You must be Kia. I know this must be a shock to you, but time is of the essence, and we really can't wait any longer."

"What?" Kia stammered. "What's happened to me?" Her voice seemed to come out in a daze. "Am I dreaming? Did I fall?"

"No – you are not dreaming, and you did not fall. You're in Arelard Castle," the woman explained. "And I'm Betsy. Please do sit down." She motioned to a few low-backed chairs and a sofa that rested a dozen feet from the fire.

Kia sat down gratefully on the sofa. "Am I dead? Did I have an accident?"

"No," Betsy smiled. "You are very much alive. You have just been extracted into Anasius, and extracted for a specific purpose which we'll come to presently. Would you like a drink?" She turned to a small, high table against the wall and picked up a metal shaker and stemmed glass.

"Err, yes, please," Kia responded, suddenly realising she actually was thirsty. "Extracted? I don't know what that means. And where is Anasius? I don't think I have heard of such a place, and my geography's pretty good."

Betsy responded, "Anasius, Notalia, Parlemon and all the other countries here are part of a world that runs alongside your own. You have been brought from your world into ours." She poured something green from the shaker into the glass, and gave it to Kia.

"Thank you," Kia said, eyeing the green liquid doubtfully. Finding her senses a little, she asked, "You mean this is a parallel universe?"

"Yes, sort of. Except that for a parallel universe, there would be no cross-over between the two; no means by which a person could move from one to the other. But in this world, very occasionally at the specific command of Xcion the Sovereign, and only in times of great peril, a few from your world have been summoned here."

"But why? I mean...why me? I'm just a school kid. Whatever 'peril' you are in, I don't see how I can help. There must be millions of more suitable people. Can't you just send me back?"

"Xcion the Sovereign has summoned you here, because in these dark days, we need young, fresh and uncorrupted help. Kia – you are the one we need, for reasons I'm not at liberty to go into now. But you will find out, and it won't be too long before you do."

"How do I get back? My mum will be expecting me downstairs in less than an hour – what do you want me to do?"

Betsy wrinkled her brow, thinking hard.

"I'm sorry," she said. "I'm explaining this very badly. I was told that you would be here for many days – you need to be trained and battle-ready."

Kia looked up at her in horror.

"But what will happen back home – I have exams to prepare for. School to go to. And my parents..." she began to rise from the sofa as she spoke, her voice getting more frantic, "...they'll bust a gut if I'm missing for an hour or two – I dread to think what they'll do if I disappear off the face of the planet for days on end. I..." Betsy had raised her hand, and she interrupted.

"Calm, calm," she said. "You don't understand. The time here is different from the time in your world. As far as your world goes, you will be missing for a fraction of a second, however much time passes here. Please sit down, there is so much more to tell you."

Kia shook her head in confusion and finally sank doubtfully back onto the sofa. She sipped tentatively from the glass, but she needn't have been cautious – the drink was delicious, far nicer than the drinks she was used to. She felt better almost right away.

"What is it you want me to do?" she asked again. "And what do you mean by 'battle-ready'?"

Max was sitting on the bench at the top of Durin's Hill, sending a message to his mum. At almost the same time that Kia arrived in Arelard Castle's ballroom, Max felt a jolt from his phone and appeared on the roof of the castle. The familiar view over his home town had disappeared, and he could see the unfamiliar country of Anasius stretching off into the distance, between the battlements just in front of him. He was sitting on a stone bench, with his back to a wall, and there was an occasional breeze blowing from his right, which was making him feel chilly. He stood up in a hurry, bemused, dazed, and trying to make sense of his surroundings.

He knew he was on the roof of a large castle. He could see towering vertical cliffs either side, topped with ice and snow, leading to even higher mountains, although cloud covered the tops of most of them. Foothills and uplands lay before the castle, with a river running, it seemed, right under the castle itself and meandering its way off into the distance. He was standing inside a sort of roofed tower which seemed to be in the centre of the front wall of the castle. Paved footways ran out from each side of his tower reaching to higher towers on the front corners of the castle. In front of these pathways ran battlements, behind them was a low wall, and then a drop of about two metres down to a slate-roof which covered virtually the entire castle.

Then he noticed that walking towards him from his left was a young man, perhaps only two or three years older than himself. He was smiling and extending his hand in a welcoming gesture. He invited Max to sit back down and then proceeded to explain about Anasius and extraction. They stared out over the battlements as he talked. To Max, it was all rather surreal. He began to wonder whether he was dreaming, but the intermittent breeze that was making him shiver felt real enough. After an hour or so, his companion, whose name seemed to be Traika, rose and led him down the walkway to his left and then turned off through a low doorway to the top of some stairs. As they reached the bottom of the stairs, Max asked, "Where are we going?"

"After finding you some sensible clothes, rather than those strange things you're wearing, I'm going to show you the library. You'll be there for three weeks, and in that time you will sleep in the Parnegi quarter, eating with your compatriot and working in the library. You are free to go wherever you please in the castle, but you're here because of the library."

"Traika." He wasn't sure he was pronouncing the name correctly. "What am I supposed to do in the library?"

"Read, I expect. What do you normally do in a library?" Traika grinned at him. "Max, I don't know precisely why you're needed in the library, but you have been summoned for a specific reason, so perhaps the place to start is to assume you're doing research. Find out everything you can about our history, geography, politics, legal system, religion and so on. Whatever you unearth will, apparently, be useful to Anasius as we face coming war."

"War?" Max asked, suddenly worried. "You're at war?"

"Not yet – but war is coming. And we need your help."

Traika led Max down a wide corridor and then down a curved staircase that ended in a grand hallway which must have been, Max thought, somewhere near the centre of the castle. His brain was whirling.

"You mentioned something about a compatriot? Who is that?"

"You're about to find out," Traika grinned again, as they arrived at a pair of towering arched oak doors. He knocked and then opened the right-hand door.

As they walked into the room, Max noticed immediately an older, broad-shouldered woman standing near the fireplace. Then he saw movement on one of the chairs. A blonde-haired girl of his own age was sitting there, and as they entered, she turned in his direction. Their eyes met.

"Kia!"

"Max!"

They both had questions, and kept speaking at once, interrupting each other, and trying to make sense of the last two hours. Betsy and Traika watched with some amusement. Then Betsy spoke, "I think it's time to eat. You must both be hungry? Come this way." She led them through a door further down the ballroom, into a smaller room set up with a long, highly polished cedar table and heavy, padded chairs. The far end of the table was laid for two, with a large spread of breads, cheeses, pies, salad, fruit and other things neither Kia nor Max could identify. Suddenly they both were very hungry indeed. They sat down and began to eat.

Directly after their evening meal, Max changed into some new clothes, which Traika had given him, and then he was shown to the library. He spent some time idly pottering about, flicking open books here and there, and wondering why he was there. Under the section on history he had found an ancient, dusty book which turned out to be all about the history of Arelard Castle. In the second chapter he had found some plans, which he copied on a small piece of paper, folded up and then put in his back pocket. Over the following few days, he learned to navigate the whole castle without making a mistake.

The library was a dream for Max, who loved reading more than anything else. He was one of those unusual people who remembers virtually everything they read, which meant that over the course of the following two weeks, he learned and remembered more about Anasius than most of the students who had been studying in the Academy for the past two years. For Max, the library was fascinating.

It was housed in a purpose-built vault on the floor below the ballroom, with most of the walls lined with books. In the centre of the huge room was a large mahogany table, tastefully in keeping with the dark-wood shelving, the high-backed chairs, and the deep-green curtained windows with accompanying window-seats. When the curtains were open the whole room was flooded with natural light. In the evening, the curtains were drawn, and light was provided by soft-glow downlighters that hung from the ceiling, and from lamps that stood on tables around the room, making the library feel more cosy. One end of the table had drawers under it, which held pens, various stacks of blank paper, cards and so on. A log fire burned in the grate in the mornings and evenings, and three gloriously soft armchairs sat pulled not far from the grate, inviting visitors to sit and read, or to stare dreamily into the fire as Max found himself doing on occasion.

One wall was hung not with book-filled shelves, but with a number of huge paintings of Anasiun historical events. The crowning of Prince Jandon II; the celebration of the overthrow of the Handed Isles and the Western Land Exchange with Notalia; the tsunami in the reign of Prince Rancorn the Ravager; the first graduation from the Overlord Academy; and a magnificent eagle. A few metres away from the wall were two or three more armchairs, placed opposite the wall as if a person might wish to view the wall from a distance. This puzzled Max for a few days, until one morning when Traika came into the library and said, "May I interrupt for a few minutes?"

"Sure," Max responded, wondering what Traika wanted.

But Traika sat on an armchair and said loudly and suddenly, "Information on Notalian navy for the last five years."

Max's eyes widened as the paintings and panelling dissolved into a huge white screen and what appeared to be a documentary played on-screen, with the sound coming from all around the room. After the documentary, Traika said simply, "Thank you. Away," and the screen dissolved and the panelling and paintings reappeared.

Max and Kia had been discussing Anasius, a country whose technology in some respects was very primitive, but in other respects was far more advanced than their own. All their technology seemed to work in harmony with nature. Unobtrusive, behind-the-scenes technology which supported and enhanced their way of life without drawing attention to itself.

He had just witnessed the fact that Anasius had a way cooler Internet than the one he was used to – an Internet that intuited what was required and gave all the information in video-format. In Anasius, there is no scrolling through pages of meaningless rubbish to find what you need. After Traika left, Max tried it out and discovered much more information about Anasius in the process. He also discovered that the library housed first-edition books only, most of which had also been digitised.

As a result, when Max drifted back to his real academic

love of reading physical books, he took more care of them as he read. The longest wall of books was dedicated to the Scroll, something Max learned a good deal about very early on. One of the first five known copies of the original Scroll was housed under thick glass which formed part of a large coffee table between the armchairs. Electronic versions of the Scroll were carried by most Anasiuns in the form of a credit-card which unfolded to make a screen about the size of a piece of A4 paper.

Max himself had been given one by Traika, and he had read most of it by day four, reading through it in the evenings as he lay on the extravagantly comfortable bed in the room he had been assigned in the Parnegi quarter, a section of the castle reserved for visitors. Kia had a room there, too, just down the hallway, and whilst they didn't see much of each other during the day (Kia had a very busy training schedule, it turned out) they had got into the habit of comparing notes each evening before bed. Kia, too, was reading the Scroll.

Some of it was fascinating to read; other parts were very difficult to understand. The Scroll formed the basis for the political and legal systems of Anasius, as well as providing the moral code upon which all citizens were exhorted to stand. The Scroll included a number of legends (written as memorable stories to teach wisdom), prophesies (involving promises from Xcion about his own actions as well as predictions about future events) and songs (written to comfort, to encourage or to challenge). Historically, the people of Anasius flourished most when the Scroll was prominent in education and in the corridors of power; and the people suffered when the Scroll faded into the background. This seemed obvious from history, but it turned out that many of the people of Anasius today seemed predominantly blind to the fact.

On day five, back in the library, Max was working his way along the shelf of history books. He thumbed through the pages of book one of a trilogy on the defence of the southern mountains – it did not look in the least bit interesting – but as he was about to replace it, he noticed another much smaller book, hidden behind the trilogy. He removed a few other books and pulled out the small volume. It was a book all about the dungeons of Anasius, and as he opened this book and read his heart began to race with excitement.

That same day, Kia had an exciting adventure of her own. She had spent the last four days being trained in military strategy – something which previously she had known nothing about. She was a keen chess player, and so she was used to anticipating the moves of an opponent, but military strategy was on another level entirely. After she and Max had enjoyed their first meal in the dining room next to the ballroom, Betsy had taken her across to the southern part of the castle where another large room had a few small slit-like windows which peeped out onto the mountains beyond. The canyon in which the castle had been built narrowed rapidly, so that the castle was almost at the mouth of a sort of funnel, and surrounded on three sides by forbidding mountains and towering cliffs. The River Dagon ran through the bottom of the canyon, directly under Castle Arelard, and then over the dam and through the gorge in the southern uplands where it met Beggar's Tarn, another river which flowed down from the mines in the eastern mountains. The rivers met at Maynard Bridge, where the river became much wider, and it moved more slowly downstream under Finiston Bridge at the city of Tsarn and then past Port Diblane and out through the estuary into Mannasa Sound. A good deal of shipping came up and down the river, delivering goods to and from the Handed Isles, the Northern Territories of Drism, or even further afield. South of Maynard Bridge, though, the river carried very little traffic, and very few people attempted to traverse the rapids below the dam in the gorge north of the castle.

Kia knew none of this when she went into the room, though. It was what lay inside the room that grabbed her attention. There was a background hum of noise – quiet conversations, people speaking into microphones, and so on. A number of people were sitting at large desks, working on computers and holding conversations. The wall opposite the windows was taken up with a huge screen, subdivided into a large central picture, with other smaller sections all around it. Each section was running in real-time, showing high-quality video of shipping on the river, a large fleet moored in a harbour, the entrance to the mines, some treehouse type buildings in a forest, and so on. The large screen in the middle was displaying an auditorium with perhaps 150 people in attendance, and a man was standing at the podium speaking. Kia realised that just above the noise of the room, the man's voice could be heard reading from the Scroll.

"Now Kia," Betsy was saying as they moved across the room past the busy desks, "you have been brought to Arelard Castle in order to help us with our intelligence gathering and military strategy. You have a great deal to learn in the next few weeks, and I will guide you through the process.

"Anasius has been in slow decline despite the best efforts of the king. Studying the Scroll has become less and less common across much of the country, and amongst some groups the Scroll is increasingly considered antiquated and irrelevant. The progressives are arguing for a new way of life in Anasius, with a new moral and legal code to support it, abandoning the path of life which Xcion the Sovereign has laid out for us. In our view here at the Xcion Strategic High Command, it is no surprise that we are facing veiled threats from Notalia to the west and antagonism from the Northern Territories as well. The Scroll is clear – reject the ways of Xcion the Sovereign at your peril. We are facing an increasing threat every day, and we suspect war is not too many months away, a war for which we remain ill-prepared and ill-equipped. Your role is to work here with us as we seek to bring together a three-pronged strategy. First, we are continuing to try to find a diplomatic route to resolve, or at least ease, international tension. Second, we are trying to shore up Anasiun defence in the event of war. Third, we are putting together a battle-plan for a war fought on our own territory. This third will be your prime focus, although you will have sight of the other two as well."

Kia was almost breathless. She was a school kid! What did she know about strategy and tactics and politics? She knew virtually nothing about Anasius, and until a few hours ago she didn't know it even existed. Now they were asking her for help with their national security. It was nuts. She voiced her concern, "Betsy – I'm fourteen years old. You have people here who are three or four times my age. How can I possibly be of any use at all?"

Betsy smiled. "You can be useful for a number of reasons. First, there are an increasing number of Anasiuns who have been seduced by promises of wealth and power from Notalia. We have traitors in our midst, and the one thing we know about you is that you have had no contact with the Notalians whatsoever and therefore can divulge secrets to no-one. You are clean. Second, the very fact that you recognise your limitations and your inability makes you an excellent candidate for the task. You will not be tempted to rely on your own resources, or bluster your way, or pretend you know best. You will be deeply collaborative, because you will have to be. Third, young people are much better at creative thinking. Many of us here have been around too long to think a long way outside the box, and you might be just what we need to develop and execute a different kind of strategy."

Kia responded wryly, "So you want me because you think I have no axe to grind, I don't know anything of any use, and I'm young and impressionable?"

Betsy laughed. "Another reason is that you can be relied upon to say what you think. Yes – I think you understand.

Now let's get down to work."

And what a work it was. She was given not an empty desk in the corner of the communication centre, but rather a small, much more cosy room of her own, just one door away. On that first day she was introduced to the Anasiun version of the Internet, and watched eighteen documentaries on the societal structure of Anasius – the legal system, the political system, treaties between Anasius and other countries, the construction and workings of the Overlord Academy, Anasiun policies on the balance between technology and the natural world, the training and infrastructure of the Xcion fleet and the Xcion battalions. In the midst of this marathon, someone arrived with a stack of seventeen books from the library on military strategy, all of which she was expected to read. As a highly intelligent student destined for great things, Kia thoroughly enjoyed all of it, and was beginning to relish the task ahead.

For Kia, though, it was the start of her communication training on day five – the same day that Max discovered the small book tucked away in the bookshelf – that really got her heart pounding with excitement.

9

Undercover Work

Following his first extraction, Joe had trained and graduated from the Overlord Academy before Zak had even arrived, so he was unaware of Zak's extraction three months later. When Joe was extracted for the second time, he was sent almost immediately on a mission just west of Ducal City, working as a junior labourer at a building site. The purpose of his mission was very simple – to keep his ears open and report anything unusual back to Xcion Strategic High Command. The first mission for any new graduate was always a strictly non-combat eyes-and-ears mission, seeking to gather intelligence. The site was at the border crossing between Anasius and Notalia on the Ducal / Crask turnpike, and the build involved improving security. Before his arrival at the checkpoint, this was all Joe knew.

It sounded like it was going to be a fascinating job, gaining an insight into how the border-crossing worked and how Anasius arranged its security without restricting the movement of its citizens. Technologically, Joe knew, the border-crossing was far beyond any security he had ever witnessed, but apparently the High Command had ordered an update of its infrastructure due to increased concern about a possible Notalian invasion.

This infrastructure update was not only technological, however. It also included a rebuild programme for the physical barrier. Back in the year 13, following the overthrow of the Handed Isles and the Western Land Exchange, the PAN treaty was signed. In that treaty, Anasius and Notalia agreed to a physical border to separate themselves, with two manned border crossings – one on the Crask / Ducal turnpike, and the other up at Parson's Edge on the northern slopes of the Arelard mountains.

Most of the 200-mile border comprised a high-spec, electrified chain-link fence. More recently, the fence had been rebuilt, and the new design included a thick concrete footing three metres below ground, and then the upgraded reinforced fence running from the footing, up through the ground to a height of three metres above ground. The fence wire had pin-prick cameras and sensors built into it, and it was electrified at a much higher current than before. It also housed vertical lasers which fired at anything crossing the airspace. However, instead of the usual bright grey or dull silver colour that Joe would have expected from a chain-link fence, in fact it was vary-coloured in dark green and dark brown. The result was that at any distance greater than twenty metres, the fence was quite hard to see. The ground to the east of the fence rose gently towards the southern uplands, so that unless the fence was nearby, a person standing towards the western edge of Anasius could see across the fence for many miles out into Notalian territory.

Joe found himself working on an extended site, digging deep trenches, building the concrete footings, erecting the pre-fabricated fencing, and then back-filling the holes once the concrete was dry. Mixing concrete and pouring footings was hard, physical labour, and whilst Joe was a keen athlete back in England, he found these days in Anasius long and exhausting. For most of his time, he was working with three other men who spent their time discussing either the late Spring Festival or their own exploits in the taverns of Ducal. They were rough men with little time for Joe, so he mostly worked and listened.

They always returned to the border checkpoint for lunch, and Joe had the freedom to eat where he wished. Generally, he sat at the outside tables of the border café, where he listened to the conversations going on around him, and he watched the freight traffic on the turnpike below. However hard he tried, though, he heard nothing that he thought would be of the slightest interest to the Xcion Strategic High Command until one day when an older couple sat at the table next to his own and began to converse in low tones.

For once, Joe had not been trying to hear their conversation, but he pricked up his ears when he overheard the woman saying something about "the overthrow of Anasius". He was sitting on the opposite side of the table from the couple, so it was difficult to hear everything they were saying. He didn't look at them, but he leant forward in his chair, over the table, and rested his chin on his knuckles and stared intently out of the window. This had the effect of bringing his head a good metre closer to them, and their conversation was now just about discernible. He watched the turnpike, pretending to be lost in thought. The woman was still speaking.

"It would be virtually impossible to get enough troops through Ducal City without being noticed, and with little idea of the size of the Anasiun army, this might be a foolish choice. The marshes are still unnavigable last I heard, so it seems to me that the only route is through Taston Forest, although it is easy to get lost there, and I'm not sure how we'll cross the border in the first place. We'll need to move fast, though, because fence security is being upgraded and they've moved south of Ducal City already."

"I'm sure General Qong has an idea," the man responded. "And we wouldn't attack unless we had a watertight plan. The story goes that the Anasiuns have a secret weapon, but no-one seems to know what it is. We need someone on the inside to infiltrate their Strategic High Command."

"That is a tall order. They vet all their personnel so carefully. It would take years to get a suitable candidate through the system, and we don't have that long."

The conversation paused for a moment as the woman sipped her coffee. Joe adjusted his position in his chair and tried to lean even closer. She began again.

"I'm not sure I believe the 'secret weapon' theory. And isn't it true that back in the year 8, the Western Land Exchange resulted in Anasius giving up fifty square miles of its land to us and then setting this border in place? Their supposed secret weapon did not help them then, did it?"

The man nodded. "Yes – that's why the prison complex of Crask still contains a number of Anasiun buildings. Crask was Anasiun way before the WLE was written."

"There you are," the woman said triumphantly. "And if we took land from them back then, we can do the same now. But now we'll take it all." She was smiling cruelly. "We need more information for a final plan, but we have enough agents in Anasius. If we apply some pressure on them, we'll discover the size of their army and navy without too much trouble. Discovering their current defence system and possible tactical responses will be more difficult, especially because the indications are that they're expecting conflict."

Joe's staring-into-space routine was becoming harder to pull off, and unbeknown to him, he was leaning a little too obviously to his left as he strained to hear the woman and she had noticed his attention. Joe still refused to look at the couple and pretended to be fascinated by a long low-loader that was approaching the crossing from Ducal City.

The woman winked to the man and nodded at Joe as she continued speaking.

"I wonder how many of the Anasiun people are aware of the extent of our infiltration?"

Joe became aware that the woman was getting up from the table, and her voice was getting clearer.

"They know of a few of our operatives," she said, "but I wonder how aware they are that we know of their operatives?" As she finished speaking, she appeared right in his line of sight opposite his table, and she was staring directly at him. "And you're one of them, yes?" she asked in a steely, uncompromising voice.

Joe's instinct was to run, but as he tried to rise, a heavy hand pushed him back down.

"No you don't," the older man said. He had moved directly behind Joe, and Joe was surprised how strong he was. "You will sit, and we will explain what happens next."

At that moment Joe realised he had given himself away. He couldn't believe he had been so stupid. He wondered about running but even as the thought came into his head, the tip of a knife appeared at his throat and his neck was held in an iron grip. His heart was in his mouth and he dared not move. The woman was smiling cruelly. "Don't hurt him yet, Musgrove – he's going to be useful to us." She turned to Joe.

"Now, in your training at Overlord Academy, you will have learned about communication, weapons training, history, and even something about Notalia." Joe was shocked that she knew about the Academy.

He nodded slowly – he did not want that blade cutting his throat. The woman continued in her low, menacing voice.

"You'll know that Notalia is a mighty nation hardly checked anymore by the PAN treaty, and keen to expand and bring technological and economic progress to this backward country and its dependence on an ancient and irrelevant text. Your temptation would be to pass the information you just overheard back to Anasius. In fact, maybe you've already done that?"

She was challenging him.

Joe shook his head carefully, still petrified by the blade that pressed against his skin.

"Of course," the woman shrugged, "killing you would be the simplest way to deal with you. Musgrove is quite handy with a knife. You wouldn't make a sound, and we'd be on our way before anyone noticed. But I have an alternative idea. You've finished your training. The Anasiun Strategic High Command trust you. You already have an idea of how things work in Anasius, so perhaps you could work for us now."

Joe almost spat the response, "You mean, you want me to be a traitor?"

The woman smiled again, but not with her eyes. "What are you doing here at the border-crossing?" she asked smoothly.

"I'm helping to replace the fence," Joe said, wondering why she was asking.

"So – the Anasiun Strategic High Command have spent three months training you. Then you graduated and now, rather than noting your considerable talents, the High Command have sent you on a back-breaking and tedious mission for the prime purpose of using you as muscle to get a job done. They trained you and then dumped you on the border to pour concrete. Cheap manual labour, yes? I'm fairly certain they're not paying you for your efforts?"

"No, they're not. But..." Joe trailed off.

The woman continued, "So they're not showing you any appreciation for all your training and intelligence, are they?"

"Well, I, errr..." Joe did not know how to respond. It

certainly felt like a dead-end job and a waste of his time, but they must have a reason for giving him the job. Mustn't they? He was beginning to wonder.

She asked, "How long will you work here for? Until the fence is finished – that'll take months? Think how exhausted you'll be by then. And you'll have forgotten most of your training as well. Seems like a waste to me. They don't know a good thing when they see it."

She was silver-tongued, that much was obvious. She changed tack.

"Anasius is a dying nation. They refuse progress, they depend upon some long-forgotten text written by people who have no understanding of the modern age. Notalia is looking for progress. We've already expanded our western border. We have the largest academy in all the southern territories. Our armed forces are large and greatly feared. Why not use your intelligence and training to help a stronger nation establish a better future? We'll make it worth your while. When Notalia is victorious over Anasius, you'll be a Colonel in General Qong's army with all the power and wealth that accompanies that rank, and you'll have a seat at the top table as we plan for the future of our great and expanding nation."

Her dull-grey eyes were boring into Joe's soul. His throat was dry. He wasn't sure what to do. He couldn't think straight with the blade pushing into his neck.

"It seems to me," she said, "that your choice is a pretty obvious one. We kill you, which does seem a bit of a waste, or you report to us every week and work for a brighter future. You're an intelligent young man. Which is it to be?" She asked it as if she didn't really care whether he agreed to her terms or died at the hands of the man at his side.

"...I'll help you," he managed to say eventually. And he didn't really believe he could have done anything else.

At the end of the week, he was transported back to the Overlord Academy for a weekly debrief. As before, he was quick to say that the building was progressing as planned, but there was nothing to report otherwise. Although he was physically very tired, as was usual on a Friday evening, he slept fitfully.

As the weeks went by Joe became increasingly frustrated with his exhausting work at the border. Initially, he was forced to meet the couple in the café every Monday morning, and always he was coerced to tell them every piece of information he knew, however small. As time went by, though, he went to see them voluntarily on Mondays – he had begun to believe they were right. Or, at least, he had talked himself into accepting their logic, for the most part. The Anasiuns were simply using him as cheap labour. So, for Joe, a position of power in Notalia seemed increasingly more attractive.

On Saturdays, his usual routine was to rise late, eat a large brunch and then practise his navigation, camouflage or tracking skills. This Saturday, he situated himself in the V-shaped fork of a large tree, just inside the treeline on the eastern-most part of Ruscorn Forest. He settled himself in for a couple of hours of observation. He was dressed from head to toe in a dark coloured cloak which blended perfectly with the tree. He had the hood of his cloak up and was wearing a dark face cloth so that the only part of him uncovered was his eyes. He used the binoculars to scan the few vehicles on the Ducal-Tsarn Highway. Joe had watched as a Notalian officer and his dog hunkered down into a clump of bushes, 500 metres or so from his own position, watching the highway. He had almost laughed at the officer's attempts at camouflage – whilst camouflage paint and carefully placed bits of brush would keep him hidden from anyone below or at his level, anyone looking down from higher ground could hardly fail to see him.

Apart from the occasional truck on the road, nothing happened for over an hour. Then, not 200 metres from the officer, an older woman and a young man came into view over a rise, hurrying along beside a stream. As he watched through his non-reflective binoculars, he realised three things almost simultaneously. First, the dog had not yet caught the scent of the unlikely couple, but it was going to happen any moment. Second, the woman had seen the dog and the officer. Third, the young man she was with was, in fact, Zak.

Joe's jaw dropped in surprise, and he nearly cried out and gave himself away. Zak! He watched as a small silver sword appeared in the woman's hand and she waved it about. He watched Zak race towards the forest and the woman run zig-zagging, silently towards the officer. He watched as the dog suddenly raised its nose and looked at the woman. He watched the officer turning to face her and lifting his bow with an arrow on the string. He watched as a sudden flash of light sparked from the tip of the woman's sword and shot across the intervening space, hitting the dog somewhere above its eye. He watched as the dog slumped to the ground to rise no more. He watched as the arrow from the officer's bow hit the woman's shoulder, and checked her step. But she was upon the officer before he could release a second arrow, and much to Joe's surprise, she somehow managed to knock the officer out rather than kill him. In a few moments, she had tied him up like a Christmas turkey and left him lying in the bushes, next to his dead dog. Then she was moving back towards Zak, clutching at her bleeding shoulder. And, through his binoculars, he watched as she opened the large tree and they entered.

Now Joe knew what no Notalian knew – there was an entrance to the subway system under Ruscorn Forest. Now he had some information for the couple at the café – information that was really worth something.

10

Ancient Discoveries

Max sat before the fire, reading the little book he had found with its enigmatic title *Anasius Beneath*. He knew he had free run of the castle, and he knew his prime purpose involved spending time in the library, but as he read he began to wonder whether he had been meant to find this book. He was only into the second chapter when he discovered not only that Arelard Castle held secrets, but that Anasius as a whole might well be inter-connected in a way long-since forgotten.

The book opened by describing the unusual geography of the Arelard mountains. They ran for over 100 miles and formed almost the entire southern border between Juntaou and Anasius. For most of that 100 miles, the mountains rose higher and higher to the north, culminating in vertical cliff faces which dropped nearly a mile from the snowy ice-capped razor-edged peaks directly down to the sloping foothills of southern Anasius. The only access from Juntaou to Anasius, then, was not via the mountains – no-one could scale those cliffs. Rather, it was via the Tenarial Gorge, at the bottom of which ran the Dagon river. For the last mile of the gorge the mountains again rose vertically on either side, reaching up to the sharp corners of the Tancon and Harfleet mountains on its east and west banks. The result of this strange geography was that the best way to defend Anasius from southern attack was to build Arelard Castle not at the top of the mountains, as is usual, but rather to build it pinned between the vertical cliffs of Harfleet's east-face and Tancon's west-face. Assault from above would be impossible and Arelard Castle could then provide a defence of the river.

Building the castle was complicated. The fast-flowing River Dagon filled the bottom of the gorge, and the castle was to stand over the water. The engineers sunk some deep pilings into the rocky river bed, and then with some carefully designed steel beams, they completed the first stages of a ground floor. Then the builders constructed some broad steps up to the huge front door. At the base of the steps, they built a wide, curving road which led away from the castle, nearer to Harfleet than Tancon and then sank steadily down towards the uplands. The River Dagon flowed out nearer to Tancon so that the river and the road divided at the foot of the castle and then came together perhaps half a mile or so downstream where they ran nearly parallel for a mile. Then the road reached up around the shoulder of Harfleet and began the long run across to Tsarn, whilst the river plunged over a dam and then raged through a second long gorge before widening out as it met Beggar's Tarn just south of the Maynard Bridge.

For the castle itself, though, the early engineers designed and built something else – something none of the current generation seemed to know about. At the beginning of their construction, they built a stone passageway spanning the gorge just above the river, and then they built tall stone pillars in front of the passageway to support the front of the castle. But the passageway was built with an unusual feature. If you had looked down on the castle from the air at this point in its construction, you would have noticed that the roof of the passageway had a wide channel running from south to north. At the north end, a gently-sloping stone gulley ran northward for some way and then stopped just above the river. The builders then constructed a completely level floor for the dungeons over the top of this passageway, its channel and the gulley, so that no-one would have suspected the channel or gulley existed. This level floor was supported by the pillars at the front and the passageway at the back. Next, the builders excavated a tunnel from each end of the east-west passageway, deep into the mountains. The spoil from that excavation they dropped down into the river and the gorge both behind and in front of the passageway, and below the dungeon floor between the supporting pillars. The result was simple. The river bed was raised by a few metres, resulting in the river being re-routed through the channel below the dungeon floor. In other words, the river did not run under the castle as everyone supposed. Instead, the river now ran through the castle, down the gulley and then dropped back to the original river level a few metres in front of the castle.

Some of the construction details were hard to follow, and it seemed that even the author was reluctant to reveal everything. But as Max read, he discovered that in the corridors outside the dungeons, there were two carefully concealed access points to the tunnels below. From one corridor, it was possible to get into the east-west passageway that led out from the castle into the Harfleet and Tancon mountains either side. From the other corridor, a person could move directly down into the channel through which the river flowed. In the early spring, with all the melting snow from the mountains, this would be suicide. But in the summer and autumn with less water flowing through, it might be possible to swim down the river and leave the castle undetected.

As Max read, he became increasingly excited. He tried to work out exactly where the access points might be, but the text was tricky to decipher and some of the language was hard to understand. As he read on, it became increasingly clear that not only did Castle Arelard have secrets, but that the tunnel system ran out from the castle for some distance into Anasius. How far did it go? Where did it reach? He needed to explore.

Kia completed most of her required reading late at night on day four, so when day five dawned, her communication training began in earnest. For the first part of the day, she was given a briefing by a middle-aged gentleman by the name of Rantukkan. He spoke with a soft, lilting voice which she could have listened to for hours.

"In the early 200s, technology was threatening to take precedence over environmental issues. Our forests were being cut down to make way for masts and transmitters and electrical substations and power plants. Our people were becoming more insular, wanting to travel on their own, access our education system remotely, have personal communication devices connecting them to whomever they wished whenever they wished, and so on. By the year 205, Anasius had come to a bit of a crossroads in the development of its communications technology. King Jandon III, after consulting with the leadership of the time, made a two-fold ruling. First, he ruled that we would strive to be connected relationally as well as informationally. Second, he ruled that all our technological advancements must be in harmony with the world in which we live, not against it. Before that point, Anasius had an individualised transport system with roads full of vehicles polluting the atmosphere chemically and audibly. On a personal level, everyone's Internet device had interactive and informational capability, but also resulted in many hours wasted through online gaming, gambling and worse."

Kia was thinking about the structure of life in England – his words resonated strongly with her. But how could a nation do anything about any of it? That was just how it was. The soft voice continued.

"As a result, there were some major changes to our infrastructure and way of life. In order to promote networking and genuine relationships, we wanted to provide every opportunity for people to interact face-to-face. Many things can be a hindrance to building relationships, so we put things in place to help guard against them.

All private transport was banned overnight. Apart from electric goods-delivery vehicles, the only available means of transport for the general public was the tram or the train. If you did not wish to use public transport, then you had to walk. Incidentally, this had a massive impact on improving the health of the nation, but that conversation is for another time. People complained about their "loss of freedom" and "right to choose" and so on, and they tried to oust the king, but he stood firm, and his government with him. It was a rocky couple of years, but the benefits were so obvious that it was not long before the country as a whole came to support the king and began to move forward once again.

"Early on, King Jandon III launched a huge three-way investment project, focusing on transport and power generation. On the transport front, within fifteen years all the railway lines in the country ran on electricity and ran underground to reduce the environmental impact, both of noise and of air pollution. The spoil from that huge tunnel network was used in part to build a hydro-electric plant at the top of the gorge on the River Dagon. Our scientists had invented electric vehicles many years earlier, but now that personal vehicles were abolished, this new technology was put to use in redesigning all our vehicles to run on battery alone. The result is that our naval fleet is extremely quiet and has very little environmental impact. A fully-electrical tram system was built for each city, too, so that transport around the city is both quiet and efficient.

"Following these major infrastructure improvements, and some carefully directed research and development, we replanted our forests, so that we have more trees now than we did back then. All our masts and substations were removed and replaced using new technology. Our scientists discovered a way to use real trees as radio masts, so that if an area of the country needs to boost its coverage, the solution is now simple: plant new trees. Trees became important for another reason, too. Rather than putting up large unsightly turbines to harness the wind, our scientists found a way to use the trees themselves to harness that wind power. In fact, nowadays more power is generated through our forests than through both the Dagon Dam and the tidal power plant off the coast of the Handed Isles.

"As for personal Internet devices, whilst communication and information are still possible, devices no longer have capability for gaming, gambling and the like. Furthermore, using them in public is only permitted if a person is alone. Our expectation is that if there are people around you, you will communicate with them face-to-face, or you will be quiet. In our experience, most people talk. This means that the vast majority of our citizens are very connected people, involved in each other's lives. Loneliness is an unusual phenomenon. Almost universally now our personal communication devices are known in shorthand as Scrolls."

At this point, Rantukkan unclipped the black credit-card from his cloak and handed it to Kia. It seemed to be no more than a rectangle of black plastic, but she knew there must be more to it than that. Rantukkan began to speak again.

"It is called a Scroll because primarily it is an electronic version of the actual Scroll and the library attached to it. But these devices are also a means for communicating with others and for accessing information. They hardly ever make any noise, so they do not intrude on any conversation."

Kia was confused. "But if the device rarely makes any noise, how do you hear anything?"

Rantukkan nodded, as if expecting the question. "Decades ago, people wore an earpiece which received sound signals from a gold ring." He fingered the ring around his ear as he explained. "And funnelled those sounds into the ear. The personal devices also contained a microphone through which a person could speak to communicate. They have come a long way since those days."

Rantukkan reached over and put his thumb on one corner of the small rectangle of thin black plastic. A small green light blinked three times, and then the card unfolded. It was black, firm, and extremely thin, and the fold-lines were undetectable. A moment later, apart from a thin black border around the edge, the whole surface turned white. Two icons appeared on the screen. One was a scroll and the other was a spiral-bound notebook. Rantukkan spoke again.

"The Scroll, upon which our society is built, is fully contained in that scroll icon. The text itself is front and foremost, but there are also huge numbers of reference texts, documentaries, movies, lectures, Academy notes, and so on which help the reader to understand, explain and interpret the text of the Scroll. The second icon, Notes, takes the reader to any information they require about anything at all, from a simple method for finding a compass bearing when you are walking the hills to how to make a decent Saturday lunch. If you need to know about anything at all, Notes provides the answers."

He placed his thumb in the corner of the screen again, and the whole page went black and then folded up by itself until it was credit-card-sized once more. He clipped it back onto his cape.

"So the Scroll, or the personal communication device as it is more properly known, is carried by all citizens. Now take a look at the ring." Rantukkan removed the gold ring from around his right ear, and gave it to Kia. "What do you make of this?"

Kia examined it carefully. It was a thin band of gold, thicker in the middle than at the edges. It contained what looked like two thin rows of four tiny holes on opposite edges, but apart from that it looked like an oversized wedding ring. It seemed to glow a little more brightly than was natural.

"I'm not sure," she said. "No-one in my country would wear jewellery quite like that."

"Let me explain," Rantukkan's soft voice continued. "You hear things because sound waves in the air are collected by the bit of your ear which you can see, and funnelled down your ear canal and onto your eardrum, making the drum vibrate. In a similar way, radio signals are both transmitted and received by satellite dishes and then converted into a format the user requires. Our scientists realised some time ago that the part of the human ear you see is like a satellite dish, receiving sound waves and funnelling them into the ear. So why could it not be used to receive other signals? Indeed, why could it not be used to send signals, too? So they developed a method of receiving and sending waves, whether sound waves or radio waves, using this gold ring as a booster and converter. At birth, our citizens are given two tiny implants just behind the tragus of the outer ear – the bit of cartilage that forms a lump half-way down the ear, attached to the head."

He pointed to his own ear as he explained.

"The gold ring converts radio signals received by the ear into auditory signals which it then transmits to the implant which, in turn, sends those signals as sound waves onto the eardrum. In other words, if I want to speak to one of my colleagues in the Academy, I direct a communication to them, and if they answer then they will hear my voice as if I were standing in front of them. They have control over the volume of what they hear, but nobody else around them will be able to hear what I am saying.

"More impressively, the gold ring contains a highly sophisticated microphone which senses the sounds made by the vocal chords and then transmits them back to the caller. This microphone took twelve years to develop at our research facility on the edge of the eastern desert.

"Now, if you're going to do your job effectively, you will need a Scroll, a ring and implants. The first two I have for you here. The third is straightforward – a painless procedure that we have performed millions of times and takes seven seconds on a bad day. Come with me."

Rantukkan led Kia across the hallway and into a small room that looked a bit like a doctor's waiting room. Kia felt very nervous. The incredible technology Rantukkan was trying to describe to her was significantly more advanced than any she knew about. And implants – that was a medical procedure. Surely they needed permission from her parents? She couldn't just decide to have it done and not tell anyone. When she returned home, she would still have implants in her ears. What if she were travelling and they set off the airport security? How could she explain that? What if one of them malfunctioned in her world – no-one would have a clue what was happening, and if she tried to explain, they wouldn't believe her. Or they would find the implant and remove it and examine it and try to mimic the technology...all kinds of things might happen. She was not going to agree to having any implants right now. At the very least, she needed to discuss it with Max.

But she had misunderstood Rantukkan. He was not intending to give her implants at that moment. Rather, he wanted her to understand the procedure and what it involved. So he took her to the implant room and invited her to sit on the deep, high-backed couch that sat opposite a blank wall. He touched a button next to the door and the screen came to life, sound filled the room and Kia was given all the details of the implant – its construction, its development, its purpose, the method of implantation and so on. There was even explanation about how one of the implant machines worked. Despite herself and her own worries, Kia found it fascinating.

After it had finished, Rantukkan led her from the implant room back along the corridor to the communications room she had seen on her first day. He took her slowly around the room, explaining what was happening at each desk. She met a dozen or so people as they moved from desk to desk, and while she struggled to remember everything she was being told she eventually got the gist. In essence, half the desks were devoted to information processing and response, and the other half monitored the Anasiun fleet, the army, the Academy, the infrastructure and Parliament.

There was so much to take in, she couldn't wait to tell Max everything. When she met up with Max that evening, he told her about the tunnels under the dungeons. All her interest in communication training was superseded by excitement and a sudden urge to explore.

11

Graduation

Marcia was tempted to close her eyes tight as the warriors approached. She wasn't sure she was brave enough to meet death head-on. But she did not want to be known as a coward either, so she gritted her teeth, blinked and tried to stop shaking with cold and fear. She didn't know what to do. She tried to speak again.

"I...I..." she stammered. "Where am I...? What...?"

To her surprise, rather than two thunder-faced warriors binding her arms and putting the point of a knife to her throat, the first person to reach her was a short lady who responded to her terror with, "Hello. My name's Gloria. Are you Marcia?"

"Err, yes."

"Come out of the rain. Those clothes of yours are hopeless for here, but the trees provide good cover. You look like a drowned rat." She put her hand on Marcia's arm. "Don't worry, dear, we'll get you warm and find you some dry clothes." She turned towards the group. "Friends, do not fear. This is Xcion's work. I knew Marcia was coming today, although I expected her at the Overlord Academy, not out here in the pouring rain."

The two warriors nearest to her relaxed and sheathed their weapons. Many in the group were still eyeing Marcia doubtfully, but then most of them had never seen an extraction first-hand, and it is   a bit unsettling. Gloria smiled to herself as she remembered the first time she had seen one. She had been crossing Maynards Bridge when someone was extracted directly in front of her. It was unnerving, and worse when you weren't even expecting it. At least Gloria had warning. She looked at the people in the group.

"Marcia is from a different world, and she has been extracted here by Xcion the Sovereign. In some way, she is going to help us in the dark days ahead. The instructions from Xci1 are simple – we have to teach her as much as we can for the time she is here, and we're to begin at the Academy."

Marcia listened to all this without really taking it in. She was nonplussed. She had no idea where she was, and she had no idea how Gloria knew her name. She was so wet and cold that she was beginning to shiver violently, and this made it hard to think about anything else. Her long brown hair was sticking to her face and making rivers run down her back, her clothes were soaked, and her make-up was a disaster. Gloria steered her through the throng of people, who were starting to look at her in a more friendly way, and on into the forest. It was much drier there, which was a good thing, but it was also much darker. Her jeans stuck to her legs and her canvas shoes were hopeless for walking on the slippery roots.

Gloria seemed to be talking to herself for a few minutes as she led Marcia up to a particularly big tree, with thick vines hanging down on one side of it. She told Marcia to put her arms and legs through some loops in the vine and then almost before she knew it, she and Gloria were whisked up the tree and onto the same wooden bridge that Trey had stood on a month earlier.

She did not like heights, so she was concentrating on not looking down. But Gloria led her straight ahead through an arched doorway and into a room with large windows out onto the forest. The room felt so solid and secure that Marcia almost forgot she was up a huge tree. Another lady was there, and she offered Marcia a towel and a little pile of clothes and then ushered her into a smaller side-room.

"Get yourself changed and dried off," she suggested in a soft homely sort of voice. "When you're done, I'll have some food fixed for you." The lady backed out and closed the door behind her.

Impossibly, the small room turned out to be a bathroom, and a very clean and ultra-modern bathroom at that. The almost perfectly oval sink stuck out from the wall and had a large mirror hung above it. Marcia looked at herself. Ugh, she thought, great first impression.

Then she began to think back to what had happened. She had been walking down the road on her phone. Then, all of a sudden, she appeared here. Coming here was something to do with her phone she realised, but she couldn't figure out what. And now her phone was gone, and quite what everyone at home would make of her sudden disappearance, she couldn't fathom. How could she ever get back, she worried. She pushed the rising panic back down, but a wave of nausea came over her and she rushed to the toilet. A very unpleasant few minutes ensued and she began to shed a few tears, but she stopped herself before the floods really broke. In this place, she knew no-one, so losing it was not going to help her. Somehow, she needed to hold it together.

She decided to be practical. She got out of her sopping wet clothes and got herself dry and changed as best she could. She tried to sort her hair out, but wasn't sure she made any progress, and the mirror was unkind. The clothes she had been given were a bit unfamiliar, and she had no idea what to do with the large piece of black material with the silver hook. She found herself hoping that when and if she ever returned home, she would still be wearing her clean and dry jeans and shoes. She draped the black material over her shoulder, took one final despairing look at the mirror, and then opened the door. What in the world lay ahead, she wondered to herself.

In the following three weeks, Marcia was educated in Anasiun history, politics and geography. She had taken the subway to Xanver and then ridden the electric tram around Xanver Naval Base, taking in the huge administration building, the arsenal, the barracks, the communications HQ and the Forward Command Centre. She had toured the fleet lying at anchor in the harbour, examined the guard-posts on the breakwaters and explored the forts that stood on the clifftops either side of the harbour. She had visited Tsarn, taken the ferry across the River Dagon to Port Diblaine where she inspected the garrison there, and then rode to Ruwark and down to the eastern desert before turning back south west to the Arelard mountains. From there she moved north again, crossed Finiston Bridge and then took the subway back to Runcorn Forest.

Then she was introduced to the Overlord Academy programme. She was not trained at the Academy herself, but she observed training sessions there. Her observation role included learning the layout of the Academy, the logistics of how the Academy was run, and its purpose and connection with Anasiun Strategic High Command. She was introduced to Xci2 and Xci3 (although occasionally even now she got confused as to which was which), along with a host of graduates who now worked at the Academy. Appearing in Ruscorn Forest was her first big shock. The second shock came whilst she was here at the Academy. She was asked to observe a group of students as they trained for their final examinations in fitness, martial arts and close-quarter combat. The fitness course required, amongst other things, that they complete the Academy assault course (nicknamed the "agony assault course") in under nine minutes. Some of the students were already able to do this, but all of them continued training on the assault course until the final examination, hoping at least to pass or, for some, to beat the assault course record.

Two training officers arrived, leading the first eight

students, and Marcia stared in disbelief. One of the officers doing the training looked exactly like Zak from Raynesborough County School. He saw her at about the same moment and grinned at her.

"I thought I might see you," he called out as he ran over to her, as if being in Anasius was the most natural thing in the world. "How long have you been here?"

Marcia was lost for words. She opened her mouth, but nothing came out, so she shut it again.

"Marcia," Zak said, running his hand over the back of his short hair. "You look like a goldfish. It's me – Zak. I know I should have told you before, but you would never have believed me. And I know you weren't expecting to see me, but someone mentioned that a 'Marcia' had been extracted and I wondered whether it was you." He grinned again. "I've never known Marcia to be lost for words!"

Marcia's pale cheeks reddened. "Zak – how? What? How come you're here?"

"Sorry Marcia – I need to get these guys through their pre-exam training. Let's meet in Treetop Café at dinner."

"Yes...of course," Marcia managed to say.

Zak called the students to order and then began to time them through the assault course. Marcia watched him giving commands to the whole group, encouraging a student struggling on the high wall, reprimanding a student for not having the right boots. This was a Zak she did not know. Her mind was a blur.

At the Treetop Café that evening, they were joined by Gloria, who showed a great interest in them both and had a number of questions for them, too. First, though, Marcia insisted on Zak telling his story.

Gloria listened with an ever-widening smile. When he had finished, she said, "Well – that's a different Zak from the one whom I met on the bridge all those weeks ago."

"Different good or different bad?" asked Zak.

"Good. But your storytelling is a bit off. You missed out some important things."

"I can't tell her every detail, Gloria – it would take too long – and I want to find out what Marcia's been doing," Zak said in response.

But Gloria insisted. "What Zak has failed to tell you is that he is the second of only two people ever to have graduated from Overlord Academy in six weeks. The first was the father of the current king. Zak also failed to tell you that he is now the holder of the fastest time ever on the agony assault course, having completed it in seven minutes forty-nine seconds. He failed to mention that he came top of his graduating class in almost all courses. And he failed to say that he was selected from the top twenty students to be the First Training Officer for the Academy going forwards."

Zak went red as she talked. He shook his head, looking a bit sheepish. "To be honest," he said, "when I realised how much I had failed to step up to the plate at school, both in lessons and in terms of just going along with the crowd, I decided I was actually going to make an effort and see how well I could do if I really tried. As someone who enjoys the great outdoors, I really enjoyed the physical aspect of all the training, but I found the classroom work much more difficult. With some help from Trey, though, I somehow managed to get into an academic rhythm after a while, and I even found myself enjoying history! Most of the credit goes to Gloria here for sticking by me, and for Trey helping me back at home. Without them, I'd never have got anywhere."

Marcia was fast understanding why Zak had grown up so much over the past six months or so. And she realised that his friendship with Trey had a good deal to do with it. She wondered what Trey would make of all this.

"Now, Marcia, you've heard my side. What about you – when did you arrive, and what have you been doing?"

Marcia suddenly felt very inadequate. Zak had been training and studying as hard as he possibly could, but she had just been travelling all over the country. She had seen all kinds of interesting things, but none of it had been remotely like working. She told him briefly what she had been up to, but she was embarrassed.

"So," Zak said with his cheeky smile, "basically, you've been on one long holiday."

Gloria killed the joke. "No Zak. She has been preparing for war." Her words were just as much a surprise to Marcia as they were to Zak.

"No I haven't," Marcia countered. "Zak's right. I've not achieved anything at all."

"Marcia," Gloria replied, "you have now travelled every major road in Anasius. You know your way around Xanver Naval Base, Forts Tula and Boan, Tranton, Tsarn, Port Diblaine, Maycross, Ruwark, the mines, the subway and Ducal City. You have walked all the paths in Taston Forest.

You have travelled every major track through Ruscorn Forest and you know every detail of the workings of Overlord Academy. You could navigate anywhere from any point west of the desert. Not only have you been taught about the Anasiun fleet, you have inspected every boat we sail. You have not just read about the Empress Ferry and the building of Finiston Bridge – you have been there and experienced them for yourself. You know where the hills rise and fall, where the uplands give way to the western marshes, and the main route to Arelard Castle. You have boated through Lake Agula and seen the border crossing at Parson's Edge. If I gave you a blank piece of paper and asked you to map out the whole of Anasius, you could do it."

"Well, yes," Marcia agreed. "I guess I could. But I'm not at all sure I..."

Gloria interrupted her. "You have a vital job to do in the coming war – the prince told me so himself. This 'one long holiday', as your friend has tauntingly described it, has been training of a very different sort. If you're in a tight spot and need a highly-trained operative in combat, then Zak is your man. If you're commanding platoons and planning attack and defence routes through Anasius, then you are a far better person for the job. You would not be planning on the basis of maps and plans and theory, like Zak would be. You will speak from experience." Gloria changed tack. "Now there is more to discuss, I know, but the graduation ceremony for the current students is next week, and they have exams for the next four days from now. Zak has much to do in preparation for those exams, starting early tomorrow morning, so we need to wrap this up for now. And we have much to do in preparing for graduation, too, Marcia. You will be attending the ceremony with Zak and me."

"You mean I can actually come to graduation? Really?" Marcia asked, her eyes wide. "I thought Overlord Academy graduations were for VIPs only?"

"They are. And now that Zak is a uniformed officer, and you have completed your first round of training, both of you are expected to attend." Gloria was smiling broadly. She knew it was an occasion to look forward to.

Graduation ceremonies at the Xcion Overlord Academy were amazing affairs, full of tradition and excellent food, and designed to be a celebration of success. A huge high-ceilinged marquee was erected in the clearing where Marcia had first met Gloria, and five or six smaller tepees, open on one side, were scattered around it. Half of the marquee was filled with big circular tables and chairs with room for about eighty guests. The chairs were soft and draped in white linen. Balloons floated above the table, anchored by long strings tied to the bottom of the chair legs. Tables were laid with thick white cloths, and adorned with shining silverware and sparkling glasses, ready for the five-course banquet that the Overlord Academy chefs were preparing in the Academy kitchens. There were bottles of something sparkling, jugs of water, and the centrepiece for each table was a large glass vase, with a second vase suspended inside it. Goldfish swam happily in the outer vase, and a tall, elegant flower arrangement rose from the inner vase and provided a striking and contrasting structure against the white and silver of the tableware. The table was scattered with tiny silver stars, and each place-setting included a starched white napkin folded into the shape of a swan, carrying assorted sweets on its back.

A hardwood floor was laid in the other half of the marquee, with a low platform at one end to carry the band, podium and microphones. A giant version of the goldfish and flowers table centrepieces provided a striking backdrop to the stage and also in keeping with the table decorations were the silver and white lights which hung from the ceiling and around the doorways. Large heaters stood about in case the evening got cold later on.

Marcia and Gloria arrived shortly before the start, and the marquee was already buzzing with people. The band was in place and playing some light background music that reminded Marcia of the smooth jazz she had heard on a street corner when her family were on holiday in New Orleans, except that the band was more like a small orchestra, with perhaps thirty musicians dressed in bright white and seated in two semi-circles to the left of the podium.

Each graduate was permitted to bring three guests, and the senior staff at the Academy always attended, mostly with a spouse or with their betrothed. Everyone was immaculately dressed, wearing traditional Anasiun formal wear, and the place was filled with smiling faces and happy laughter. Officially, the president of the Academy along with Xci4 (the most senior professor) sat on the top table. After the initial toast, however, tradition dictated that they separate and eat at a different table for each course of the meal, conversing with graduates and their families. For this reason, whilst all places at the tables were named, each table had an empty place which would be occupied for one of the courses by either Xci4 or the president.

Marcia studied the seating plan, looking for her name. She found it, and then drew in a quick breath as she read the other names on her table. She checked again. There was no mistake. Not only was Zak sitting opposite her, but two other names also appeared at her table. Jason Reeves and Trey Osborn from Raynesborough County School. Their names were printed clearly on the seating plan, right next to her own. Her mind whirled. So it wasn't just Zak who had been extracted alongside her. Trey and Jason were both extracted, too. Furthermore, they were both at the graduation ceremony and they were all seated together. She turned towards Gloria and saw that she was smiling broadly.

"How long have you known the four of us are all here in Anasius at the same time?" she demanded.

Gloria laughed. "Well, I've known for quite some time," she admitted. "But I was looking forward to tonight when you'd be together."

"But why didn't you tell me before?" Marcia asked, annoyed. "We could have supported one another, compared notes, talked about home stuff – been friends like back home. Why did you keep it a secret?" As she asked the question, Marcia scanned the room, looking for any sign of Zak or Trey or Jason, but she couldn't see any of them.

"You'll need to ask Xci4 that question," Gloria responded. "It was decreed by the king from the very beginning – none of you were permitted to know about the others until the time was right. For you four, this evening is the allocated time."

"But why?" Marcia still didn't understand. People were moving towards the tables now and the chairs were filling quickly.

"I'm not completely sure," Gloria responded, "but I think it was to do with wanting to train each of you without you being distracted by one another. We needed your complete focus upon your training, and maybe they thought that putting you together before now would have broken that focus. As I say, you'll need to ask Xci4 or the president. For now, though, we need to get ready for the procession." As she talked, she was guiding Marcia towards their table.

"Procession?" Marcia quizzed as they found their places and sat down.

"Yes, the Overlord Academy graduates process in, led by their training officers. The band play the 'Eagle's Egress' from the Scroll and we stand to welcome them. The president will then say a few words before the meal is served." Even as she was finishing speaking, the band drew the music to a close. The president walked on stage to the podium, and the room quickly became hushed. There was a happy and expectant silence.

"Ladies and Gentlemen of Anasius." The president spoke in a deep, authoritative voice. "I welcome you to the forty-third graduation ceremony of the Academy, in the name of the king, under the authority of Xcion the Sovereign who reigns over all. Please rise to receive the honoured."

Everyone stood, and a lone trumpeter played the long, sonorous note that began the "Eagle's Egress", an evocative tune that managed to be both majestic and deeply emotive. As a musician herself, the melodic and achingly beautiful sound brought tears to Marcia's face. The music seared into her heart and she felt like she never wanted it to end.

As the music unfolded, two commanding officers in their striking red and black colours led the graduates onto the stage. One of them was Zak. Then, as the graduates came into view, Marcia spotted first of all Jason, and then Trey, processing with the others from the right of the stage, down the steps and onto the hardwood floor, where they assembled into two lines of six facing one another and spaced about three metres apart. Finally, the music came to an end, finishing again on one long note on the trumpet. The two lines of graduates bowed to one another, then turned a quarter turn, and somehow became one line, facing the guests.

The president spoke again. "I present to you the honoured graduates of the Academy, prepared and in service of Xcion the Sovereign for the good of Anasius. Graduates, we receive you with gratitude. Let us celebrate this graduation feast together, joyful that, once again, Xcion blesses us all, the honoured for His honour and all of us in His service."

When he had finished the traditional call to celebration, the graduates broke rank and moved across to their respective tables for the meal.

At Marcia's table there was a joyful reunion of the four friends, each excited to learn of the others. It was only the night before, when the graduates had their final briefing, that Jason and Trey had discovered they were both in Anasius and graduating together. Trey had known Zak was in Anasius simply because Zak had been training him. But neither Jason nor Trey knew about Marcia, so it was a surprise to meet here at the graduation ceremony. The food was spectacular and the conversation flowed easily. They were four friends, united in an unfolding story, unaware of the double tragedy about to strike.

12

Failure at Arelard

It did not take long for Max and Kia to get down to the dungeons. On their second day, Betsy had said that part of their training was to know the layout of Arelard Castle and memorise the plans Max had found. So when they told Betsy on the sixth day that they were going to spend a whole day familiarising themselves with the castle, she was happy to let them do so. No-one but Traika would contemplate interfering with their training, and he was meeting Xci3 at Maycross for the day, discussing improvements to the national defences at Ruwark and especially at the Summer Palace. He left early and would not return until late into the evening. As a result, Max and Kia knew they could spend the whole day touring Arelard.

"I re-read the book early this morning," Max said to Kia as they walked down the wide sweeping staircase to the ground floor. "I think that this tunnel system runs not only outwards from the castle to the mountains, I think it also provides a route perhaps even as far as Tsarn."

"If it does, and war is coming, then it might prove to be

very useful indeed," Kia responded. "But if tunnels run as far as Tsarn, then it would take us hours to walk them. There's no way we could explore fully without someone getting suspicious and wondering where we've gone."

Max nodded slowly. "Yes, that's true. Let's not worry about that until we've found the access points. If we can't get in, then we won't have any exploring to do at all. If we can get in, then we have time to figure out how to get ourselves more time. But whatever the case, this tunnel system must be a close-kept secret. No-one in Anasius today seems to know anything about it. Let's keep it that way for now, it might give us the edge if it comes to all-out war."

"Agreed," Kia said. "The access points must be really hard to find, though, otherwise someone would have found them in the past, surely. Do you know what they look like?"

"No," said Max. "I thought that if we examine the stones then maybe we'll find a ring or a hidden catch or something."

"Mmm, maybe," Kia said doubtfully. "If the dungeons span the whole basement of the castle, then I'm beginning to think that finding an access point is going to be like looking for a needle in a haystack."

"There is one positive thing I guess," Max said. "At least we know there is a needle in the haystack."

"Great," Kia responded sarcastically.

Unlike the small, dark and dingy corridors they were expecting, though, the dungeons were well-lit, with the same soft-glow downlighters as those found in the library. They comprised a large open dining area with two long dark-wood tables and benches towards one end. Through an archway at that end was a small kitchen and pantry. Off to the left lay three bathrooms with showers followed by a corridor that led to the cells. The corridor was, in effect, a sort of figure-of-eight, with four cells in each half and the corridor wrapping around the back of the cells so you could walk all around each group of four cells. The ceiling and walls were built in light grey stone, and the floor comprised large, dark grey flagstones, laid wall to wall. It was cool, but not unpleasantly cold. Because the dungeons were windowless, air was supplied from the main castle via twelve evenly spaced small air-vents, eight in the open space and four in the central corridor between the cells.

Max and Kia spent half-an-hour exploring the dungeons, learning their way around and checking for possible rings or openings, but none could be found. During this time, Kia described her experiences in communications training, and especially the gold rings and implants and how they worked.

"Sounds cool," Max said. "Do we get implants?"

"Max," Kia protested, "we don't know how safe this process is – we'd be putting ourselves at the mercy of a robot. And imagine what would happen if we got an infection or it went wrong or something. How in the world would we explain that back at home? I don't think we're going to be here long, so maybe we won't need them."

"But I thought we were meant to be here to help defend Anasius in a possible coming war? We'll need to communicate with Xcion Strategic High Command if that happens," Max pointed out. "Seems to me like we have no choice. Anyway, I'd love to experience it for myself. It must be pretty safe if everyone in the Academy gets one."

"That's what Rantukkan said," Kia sighed. "But he would say that, wouldn't he? I mean he wants us to get implants, that much is clear, and he's hardly going to do anything to put us off. I wonder how often the robot gets it wrong or messes up or damages someone's hearing. We need to find out more, at least, before going through with an operation."

"You worry too much," Max said, slightly annoyed. "But yeah, sure. I mean, if you could find out if it has ever gone wrong then maybe you'd convince me. Maybe there are some deaf Anasiuns because of implant-error."

In essence, Kia thought to herself after Max had finished speaking, when it comes to making a mature decision, he was useless.

At the end of the half-hour, they began to examine the air-vents. Apart from the downlighters, there was nothing to break the even pattern of slate-grey flagstones and light grey stones that made up the walls and ceiling. The vents were situated two metres above the floor, just a foot below the ceiling, so they had to drag a bench from the open dining area to stand on. The benches weighed a ton, and it took a lot of puffing and straining to move the bench from one vent to the next. Kia and Max were both sweating, but neither cared.

The vents each had a square cross-section of about ten centimetres across, and two perfectly-spaced iron bars formed a horizontal barrier at each opening. Whilst standing on the bench, they pulled and twisted and looked for secret catches or switches or bits to push or bits to knock. By the end of over an hour examining each vent in turn, they were convinced of one thing, the vents were simply vents, identical in construction, and designed to circulate air from the castle to the dungeons and back again. Nothing more, nothing less. They had achieved no more than bruising their fingers, exhausting themselves by moving heavy furniture, and getting aching arms and feet from standing on tiptoe and reaching up to examine the vents.

Max got down from the last vent in the central corridor and sat on the bench, his back against the wall separating the cells behind him, recovering from the physical exertion. As he sat there, he stared into the cells in front of him. They all looked the same – bare but for a small sink and a metal-framed bed. The ceiling, walls and floor were constructed of the same stone as everywhere else. There was nothing interesting about them whatsoever.

"I'm thirsty," he announced. "Have you got a drink?"

"No," Kia replied, "but we might find one in that kitchen maybe? In fact, we haven't looked in there at all yet."

"I did," Max said. "It's not really a kitchen at all – just a sink and some cupboards."

"What's in the cupboards?" Kia asked.

"Err, I don't know. I didn't really check."

"So you haven't examined it at all then, have you?" Kia said testily. "I'm going to check it out. You coming?"

"Yeah, yeah," Max responded wearily, getting up off the bench.

They traipsed out of the main corridor, leaving the bench there for the moment, and padded over to the kitchen. Max was right – there was no cooker or fridge or anything, just a long counter down one wall with cupboards underneath it, and a stone sink at the end fed by a water pipe that ran vertically upwards and disappeared into the ceiling. They tried the cupboards and to their surprise found that they all opened easily enough. They were all empty except for the one nearest to the sink. In it, they found a stack of metal plates, a metal pitcher and three metal tumblers. Kia took the tumblers out and eyed them suspiciously. They felt dusty, and she wasn't at all sure they were clean inside. Max had no such concerns, though. He grabbed one and turned on the tap.

The water came out slightly brown initially, but after running the tap for a bit the water cleared. Max filled his tumbler and drank it all, almost in one gulp.

"Is it all right?" Kia asked doubtfully.

"Fine," Max said. "Tastes a bit...a bit..." he clutched at his throat and slumped, making gurgling noises that sounded like he was struggling to breathe.

"Max!" Kia shouted as she tried to support him. But she needn't have bothered. Max exploded in laughter.

Kia was annoyed. "Max – that's not funny."

"No," he agreed. "It's hilarious." And he fell about laughing again.

Kia ran the tap again, cleaned out a second tumbler, and poured herself a drink. "Why don't boys ever grow up?" she wondered aloud.

Kia and Max drifted from the kitchen, through the open area and back to the bench in the corridor.

Max started to think aloud. "Perhaps we're approaching this the wrong way? What if, instead of looking everywhere, we think about where would be the best place to put a secret entrance into the tunnel? I mean, you wouldn't put it in this corridor where any prisoner would be able to see..."

Kia interrupted, "And not in the open area, either, where anyone might walk in and see you going in or coming out. The bathrooms seem like a weird idea, and the kitchen is a pretty public space..."

"...which leaves the corridor behind the far cells," Max finished.

They looked at each other, and then both ran to the corridor at the back. They had already walked through it a few times, but this time they scrutinised it. They spent over an hour working slowly, staring at the ceiling, the walls, the floor. They dragged the bench all the way over and studied the ceiling carefully, especially around the lights. But there was nothing out of the ordinary.

Finally Max leant against the nearest wall and sighed. "It looks no different from anywhere else down here. And yet..."

"And yet what?" Kia demanded.

"Well, I think something is different, but I can't place it. We've searched everywhere. And I'm very hungry and getting chilly. Let's go up and eat and do another tour of the whole castle. Maybe we'll have an idea."

Kia agreed. "We've tried hard. Maybe we can look again tomorrow."

With much puffing and panting, they dragged the bench

146

back to its place by the table in the open area. Then they went back up the narrow staircase into the main body of the castle. It was the middle of the night before Max suddenly stirred from his broken sleep and sat up. He knew what was different about the corridor.

First thing in the morning, as early as he dared, he got dressed and left his room. He knocked on Kia's door, but there was no response, so he knocked more loudly and whispered,

"Kia! Kia – wake up!"

He heard a groan, then a shuffling of bed sheets, then nothing.

"Kia!" he called again, urgently.

Another groan and more shuffling, then the door opened a crack. "What is it?" she complained.

"I know what was different," Max said excitedly.

"What are you talking about? What time is it?"

"It's early. But it doesn't matter. You know when we were in the dungeon and I said something was different? I know what it was. I can't explain why yet, but we need to go there and find out."

"Now? It can't be time to get up yet. And why not after breakfast?" She sounded irritated.

"You're having another training day with Rantukkan today, so if you want to do this with me then we have to go now. Otherwise, I'll go by myself." He was insistent.

"Okay, okay. Wait a minute." The door closed.

Max paced the corridor impatiently. By his reckoning they only had an hour or so before they'd be expected at breakfast. Five minutes went by and he was getting more and more agitated. He banged on the door again, "Kia – hurry up!"

"I'm coming," she responded. "One moment."

Max bit his tongue and continued pacing. A minute later, Kia emerged. She had showered and dressed and done her hair, but this just annoyed Max. Precious time wasted, he thought.

"Come on," he said impatiently, and marched off.

Kia hurried after him and asked, "So what is it? We didn't find anything yesterday, what makes you think this morning is any different?"

"It's the temperature," Max said. "The reason the corridor was different was that it was colder than the rest of the dungeons. But the air in the dungeons is brought through the air-vents from the main castle, so it should be all the same temperature down there. Somehow, cold air is getting into the corridor. We need to find where it's coming from."

Kia understood right away. "So if we can find where the air is coming in, that will indicate the access point to the tunnel."

"That's the idea," Max said as they approached the narrow staircase.

"Hey, hang on a moment," Kia said suddenly, and dashed off towards the castle kitchens.

"Where're you going?" Max shouted, but she was already gone. He groaned. "We're never going to find it at this rate," he complained to no-one in particular. "What are you doing now?" But he knew Kia knew where he was going so he went down the stairs without her.

As he reached the bottom, though, he heard her running feet.

"I'm here," she panted as she caught up with him in the wide area with the tables and benches.

"What on earth were you doing?" Max demanded.

"Getting this," she said and held up a bag of icing sugar.

"Sugar?" Max was flummoxed. "There's no time to make a cake, you know," he said sarcastically.

"You'll see," she said mysteriously, as they crossed the open space and headed down the corridor. In a minute they were standing in the back corridor, and right away they both knew that Max was right. It was colder here. So where was the cold air coming from?

They decided to start at one end and move slowly down the corridor trying to locate the coldest part, but it proved quite difficult and they didn't entirely agree.

"Let me try the icing sugar," Kia said. "It'll be messy, but it might work."

She made Max sit right at the end of the corridor nearest to the open area. Then she moved to the middle of the corridor and opened the bag of icing sugar. She gave it a hefty squeeze, and then jumped backwards. A huge cloud of fine sugar particles rushed up into the air. Quite a lot of the icing sugar landed on Kia and on the floor around the bag, but not all of it. The finest particles were still in the air and they formed a big cloud. They watched hopefully for signs of an air-current, but there were none. Kia moved further down the corridor away from Max and tried again.

But the result was the same. She tried a few more times, getting progressively more covered in icing sugar herself, but it was no use. Even right back at Max's end, the only air-movement seemed to be the colder air from the corridor moving out into the large open dining area. They were both stumped. Suddenly Kia jumped up in a hurry.

"What time is it?" she gasped. "We've been too long, I'm sure. I must be really late – I was meant to be meeting Rantukkan first thing this morning – I need to run."

"Go!" Max said as she got up. "I can clear this lot up later." He looked worriedly at the mess covering the floor. "See you at dinner," he called after Kia.

Kia went to her meeting, but Max went in search of something else. His top priority now was breakfast!

An hour later, he located a device that looked a bit like a vacuum cleaner, and he thought it would probably do the job of clearing up the icing sugar in the dungeons. He almost succeeded in giving the game away on his way past the ballroom door. Traika was at the foot of the main staircase and asked Max what he was doing.

"Is this a vacuum?" Max asked, but Traika looked at him blankly. Clearly he had no idea what Max was talking about. Max tried again,

"Will this clean things up if they're spilt on the floor?"

"Oh yes," Traika responded. "Mud, food spills, liquids... the Xtric should do the job. But what have you spilt?"

"Oh, nothing major," Max quickly reassured him. "I just had a bit of an accident with my breakfast. Do you think it's okay for me to borrow it?"

"I'm sure it is, although our janitor usually does the cleaning so you could leave it to him."

"No, it's all right. I'll do it quickly and then return it."

Max hurried off, going past the staircase that led down to the dungeons and disappeared around the corner. He waited silently, with his heart in his mouth, hoping his explanation was good enough. Then he heard Traika ascending the main stairs and he breathed a sigh of relief. He waited a bit longer and then tiptoed to the staircase and then down to the dungeons, carrying the vacuum-thing with him.

I hope it's not too noisy, he thought to himself, otherwise someone's sure to come looking. But he needn't have worried. It was so quiet that he wasn't entirely sure he had turned it on. But it's sucking power was amazing.

He began working his way down the corridor fairly systematically, and it was working really well. He stopped for a minute and looked back at the clean part. He'd missed a spot, so he retraced his steps. When he turned back and looked down the corridor again, suddenly he noticed something.

The dark grey flagstones on the floor had a thin line of cement in between them. The icing sugar had created a very thin layer of white over the stones and the cement, except for around two of the stones, where it had fallen right to their edges but not at all on the cement between them. He rushed over to examine the nearest one as soon as he spotted it. And then he realised where the cold air was coming from. The reason the icing sugar had not landed on the cement in between the flagstones was very simple –

there was no cement. Instead, there was a very thin gap. When the icing sugar was cleaned up, the flagstone looked exactly like all the others, with a thin black line separating it from those around it, but for those two stones, instead of the black line being made of cement, it was a line of shadow. One of the stones was about ten paces from one end of the corridor, and the other stone was ten paces from the other end of the corridor – they mirrored each other exactly.

Max forgot all about cleaning up and busied himself trying to work out how to lift the flagstone. It adjoined the inside wall of the corridor, and it was actually only a half-flagstone because of the pattern the stones made on the floor. This meant that even if he could lift the whole thing out, the gap left would only be about one metre long and half-a-metre wide. He searched for a ring or something, but there was no sign of any means of lifting the stone at all. He tried stamping on it and jumping on it, but it moved no more than the stones around it. It was maddening to know that he was standing on one of the access points but had no idea how to open it. So near yet so far.

He returned to cleaning, making careful note of the location of the two important flagstones as he did so. Then he decided to take the Xtric back to its cupboard and find some more food.

He wanted to examine the little book again and see if he had missed anything. He carried the Xtric out of the dungeons with him, and managed to return it to its cupboard without anyone else seeing him. Then he went by the kitchens on his way to the library and grabbed a box of fruit crackers.

That's what he and Kia had decided to call them – they looked a bit like ice-cream wafers, but they tasted amazing – a bit like summer fruits, cookies and cream all rolled into one. Back in the library, he found the little book in its hiding place and settled into one of the deep, comfy chairs to read it. As he re-read the now familiar words, absent-mindedly he munched his way through the entire box of crackers.

13
Specialist Training

Zika wasn't extracted until late January of Year 10, and when he discovered all that had happened over the previous year, he felt like he was rather late to the party. At the same time, he was glad to be included, and his training at the Xcion Overlord Academy was mind-blowing. Out of the eight friends, Zika had no idea how he could possibly be of any use. Anasius had trained a few hundred agents over the previous year in anticipation of war, and most were significantly more capable than he was in terms of mental agility and physicality. Zika only just managed to complete the agony assault course on the day of his examinations, and even then he finished only two seconds inside the nine minute cut-off time.

At his graduation celebration, though, Xci4 had joined their table for the third course and had spent most of this time talking to Zika in particular. Immediately following the celebration, Xci4 invited Zika into a world very few people ever saw – the Underlord Academy. The Underlord Academy is not famed for anything. In fact, its existence is almost entirely unknown. Each year, one or two graduates from the Overlord Academy may get selected for further training under the radar. Sometimes this was a top-flight graduate who had scored way ahead of their classmates. But sometimes a person was chosen for a very different reason – the criteria for selection was shrouded in secrecy.

Xci4 motioned Zika to be silent and then led him out of the marquee and north through the forest. Zika felt both excited and apprehensive. He did not know where he was going or what awaited him there, but he did know that Xci4 was the most senior officer in the Academy. Something huge was coming – he could feel it in his stomach. Leaving the marquee and the grass clearing far behind, they came to some of the enormous redwood trees he had spotted just after he had arrived. They stopped before one of the trees and Xci4 removed his sword. If Zak had been there, he would have remembered Gloria's use of a similar silver sword to get him into the subway, but Zak was absent. In fact, Zak had only just discovered that Zika had been extracted.

Xci4 pushed the tip of the sword into a knot in the wood of the tree, two parallel lines appeared and before long a four-foot wide gap was filled with a gleaming metal door. Zika was wide-eyed, but somehow he knew not to speak. This was a secret entrance to somewhere. They stepped into the elevator and Xci4 tapped five times on the door. The door slid smoothly upwards and the elevator sank into the forest floor. Outside, the tree regained is usual appearance, and this time there was no-one watching.

Most people who took the subway used one of two access points, one of which stood not far south of the clearing in Ruscorn Forest, and both required a Scroll for entry. When Zak was with Gloria, however, they had taken a secret elevator directly into the subway train, and the result of that shortcut was later to prove disastrous.

But when Zika and Xci4 entered this second secret elevator, it continued down far below where the subway system lay, and arrived finally in a large, well-lit corridor deep underground. There were doors at identical intervals along the corridor, like you might find in a cheap hotel, and the doors were labelled A-group, B-group, C-group, and so on. Zika was taken directly to K-group and was never told anything about any of the other groups. Xci4 delivered Zika to the desk just inside the K-group door and then disappeared.

The room was roughly the size of Raynesborough County school hall, and contained three people. One was clearly training under the tutelage of a much older woman. The third person had risen to his feet behind a large desk and extended his hand to Zika.

"Welcome to K-group," he said. "We've not had a new recruit in over a year, so we're excited to welcome you."

"Why am I here?" Zika asked. "Who are you? What do you do?"

"You're here to train, obviously. We don't do names, ever. And K-group is all about micro-protonic combat." He answered each question in turn.

"Micro-prot...what?"

"We have a lot to do. Please sign here." The man pushed a document towards him and offered him a heavy silver pen.

"What's this?" asked Zika.

"It's the Anasiun non-disclosure act. It means that you promise not only never to reveal what you learned in K-group, but also never to reveal the existence of the Underlord Academy at all." Zika felt a surge of excitement. This was like the official secrets act. Only more secret! He signed his name, whilst the man looked deliberately away and then pushed the paper into a large envelope without reading Zika's signature. "As I said," he murmured, "I don't wish to know your name."

He posted the envelope through a slot in the wall and it disappeared. And then Zika's training began.

Zika was introduced to the training officer, as the younger student disappeared through a door at the far end of the room.

"Greetings," she said in a harsh, gravelly voice as if she'd spent her life chain-smoking. "Your first lesson is to observe carefully." As she spoke, she tapped on her Scroll and a picture of a forest scene flashed into view on the right-hand wall. Then she stepped back a few paces, removed a silver sword from her cape and pointed it at a rabbit in the picture. She seemed to be murmuring to herself as she twisted her wrist back and forth and then jabbed her sword forwards. Suddenly, a tiny spark of electricity shot from the end of her sword and hit the wall where the rabbit was. Zika had never seen anything like it.

"Cool! What in the world is that?"

"That," the woman responded, "was a micro-protonic pulse – an MPP. You're here to be trained in how to use them."

Even more cool, Zika thought, but he didn't say anything.

"How is your swordsmanship?" the woman asked.

Zika was uncertain how to responded. Should he tell her that he came bottom of his class at Overlord Academy?

"By the look on your face, I'm guessing it's fairly useless," she said starkly. "We'll need to change that. There is no way you can use a MPP accurately if your swordsmanship is poor. We'll spend the first two weeks improving it. Following that, you'll be studying the Scroll in depth alongside your MPP training. The study of the Scroll is vital to your usefulness in battle, and the Scroll is where the real power lies."

Zika did not understand. "If you say so," he said, utterly unconvinced. Quite how reading an ancient document had anything to do with electric sparks from the end of a sword was quite beyond him.

"I do," she said emphatically. "What is more, the best combatants in Anasius are those with the deepest understanding of the Scroll, whether or not they use the MPP. You are going to get a crash course in diving deeper."

"Diving deeper? I'm not a very good swimmer. Where are we diving?"

Zika would discover later that she never smiled, as far as anyone knew, but her lips twitched at his comments.

She responded, "Nothing to do with water. You'll be diving deeper into the Scroll. You'll learn the basic tools for interpreting what you read and you'll have some practice at applying them. There'll be some memorisation, but the most important thing is Xcion Himself. He is Xcion the Sovereign, and He is the one who supplies the strength you will need not only to learn how to use a micro-protonic pulse effectively, but also to learn to recognise a situation where the MPP is the only appropriate weapon."

By the third day of training, Zika's legs ached horribly, and he was extremely tired. The training was relentless. Apparently, one reason that his swordsmanship was so poor was that his footwork was completely wrong. So he had to spend hours learning how to move during combat, where to put his feet, how to turn without exposing his side, how to keep his head up and watch for vulnerabilities. Learning to get all the footwork right was the first thing, but then you had to be able to do all the correct footwork without thinking about it at all. He spent hours in the evenings studying video-footage of expert swordsmen and studying diagrams of different situations. Then he was up early, spending all morning and all afternoon trying to replicate those movements in the practice room. This footwork training continued mercilessly for eight days before he even saw an actual sword.

During the second week, as he began his sword-stroke training, he realised that the strokes required for the short silver sword were not at all as he had thought. He could not understand how he had managed to pass the swordsmanship element of his Overlord Academy training – it was obvious to him now that when it came to using a sword, he had no idea what he was doing. Sword training was equally as intense as his footwork training. And half-way through his first day using a sword, he forgot all about his feet and returned to his old habits. As a result, the sword was removed and he had to spend another two days on his footwork. At the end of the first two weeks, Zika was completely exhausted, and the training officer decided to give him a day of complete physical rest.

It wasn't mental rest, though. During this day, Zika had the first of many diving deeper sessions. He sat through eight hour-long interactive video lectures, played on the right-hand wall of the main room. For each hour lecture, you could highlight sections, copy slides, animate pictures and so on, a novelty Zika never tired of. For each lecture he was required to take notes and then give a five-minute summary to his trainer before he moved on to the next video.

Through this mentally gruelling day, he learned a good deal about the Scroll. The second lecture was all about the authorship of the Scroll. He learned about the people who wrote different parts of it: their background, the timeframe during which they wrote, their historical and political setting, their character, their triumphs and tragedies, and so on. He was fascinated to realise that knowledge of these background details helped enormously in coming to understand the words that were written. The authorship was interesting in another way, too. All fourteen authors were separated geographically by over 250 miles, chronologically by 140 years, and experientially in numerous ways. Nevertheless, their writings came together and expressed the same purpose, the same ideas, the same values and the same goal, albeit in many different forms. The reason for this, the Anasiuns believed, was that

Xcion the Sovereign was the true author behind what the writers wrote. Whether writers were describing historical events, penning songs, telling stories, or prophesying about the future, all that they wrote had the same trajectory, coming from the same convictions and driving to the same destination. As someone who loved both language and history, Zika found it completely fascinating.

The later lectures began the process of unpacking different parts of the Scroll. For example, Zika discovered that the way to read and understand the legends is to recognise that they are not just interesting stories, but rather they were written for a purpose, to teach certain things about Anasius, the wider world, people, and ultimately about Xcion the Sovereign. For the songs, the introductions tell you important background information so that you know the purpose of the song and how it can be used. The songs themselves give insight into the life of the writers, and how they responded to various difficulties and joys they experienced in life.

Zika had been required to read the whole Scroll for his Overlord Academy examinations, but he'd found some of that reading long, difficult and, frankly, boring. Now, though, as these lectures unfolded, he grew slowly to love reading it, partly because he understood a bit more about the sorts of things he was reading.

There were many more videos to go, but after supper his trainer urged him to have a shower and get to bed. "The remaining videos you will need to complete during the evenings in the coming week – there will be no time to fit them in during the day. Tomorrow, your micro-protonic pulse training begins in earnest. And that will require all your energy and all your attention. This evening, though, you need to rest."

Zika did exactly as suggested – he couldn't remember a time when he felt so exhausted. He was given an excellent meal, after which he collapsed into bed and was asleep within ten minutes. In fact, he did not wake up for eighteen hours, and on instruction from Xci4, no-one disturbed him. When he finally awoke, it was already mid-afternoon – little time for an intense training session on using an MPP. But for the few hours that were left, he began to realise why he had been chosen by Xci4. When it came to using an MPP, he was a natural.

Zika was three weeks into his training at the Underlord Academy before he discovered the truth about the MMP. He had thought it was something magical, like an ancient mystical spell which made the electricity spark from the end of the sword. This is what Zak had thought, too, when he'd seen it in action over a year previously. But he and Zika were both wrong.

In fact, what was required to use the MPP was the silver sword and a Scroll. Whilst the sword itself contained the technology to direct an MPP from its tip, that technology was unlocked only by the physical proximity of a Scroll. The Scroll held the piece of code necessary for the MPP to work. And that code transfer to the sword was possible only if the Scroll and the sword were physically in contact with one another.

From this point forward, whilst half of Zika's training involved learning how to alter the direction, intensity and timing of the MPP, the other half involved learning the sleight of hand required to get the Scroll from the lapel of the cape and onto the sword and then back again. These manoeuvres had to be completed without any observer having the least idea of them, regardless of where they were standing. In effect, not only was Zika learning to be an outstanding swordsman, he was also training to be an expert at the conjuror's art of sleight of hand and misdirection. In his fourth and fifth week, he spent a total of 150 hours practising and repeating the same sleight of hand manoeuvre over and over again. At the end, it felt almost as natural to him as walking.

The secret of the sword was extremely closely guarded, and very few people knew about it. In fact, aside from Xci1, Xci4, and the trainer in the Academy, only eight people had been trained in the use of the MPP over the past ten years. In other words, Zika was only the twelfth in this prestigious group in the whole of Anasius. And, like the other eleven, he had been sworn to utter secrecy. He could tell no-one, anywhere, ever.

14

Crask

At last, and dog-tired, Trey had excused himself from the graduation party and wandered across the clearing towards the trees with the vines. He was walking mechanically and thinking only of his bed waiting for him up at the Academy. Perhaps that was why he did not notice the little group of hooded men standing in deep shadow just outside the clearing. He didn't even notice when one of them raised an arm and pointed in his direction. He felt the dart hit his neck, but apart from getting his hand up to it, the anaesthetic worked far too quickly for him to do anything else. He teetered and then would have crashed to the ground, had not swift hands caught him, shrouded him and carried him off silently south through the forest.

It was a good half-hour to the edge of Ruscorn Forest, and another ten minutes before he was in the fruit truck. And it was an hour later still before he began to stir. They were approaching the border-crossing on the Tsarn / Crask Highway, and he realised quickly that the gag on his mouth was firmly fixed, and his hands and feet were firmly and efficiently tied with white cord which also looped around his chest. He was trussed up like a turkey, and secured to something like a table with a thick white tablecloth over it, unable to make a sound and unable to move. His arms and legs ached, the rope was chafing his wrists and his weapon was gone. A man with long black hair and his signature sharp sickle swung menacingly at his side was seated across from him. He discovered later that his name was Qinoda – a young but key member of the Notalian Liberation Army. As they drove through the crossing into Notalia, Qinoda was grinning from ear to ear, an evil grin full of malice.

"The great Trey awakes," he mocked. "I trust you will enjoy your holiday in the dungeons of Crask."

Trey shook his head to try and clear the fuzziness, but the drug had not quite worn off, and it only made him nauseous. He considered his situation as best he could. His friends thought he had gone to bed, and wouldn't try to disturb him until late the following morning. Even then, they would have no reason to suppose anything had happened to him. It could be a couple of days before anyone got concerned, and they would have no reason to suspect he had been abducted. Such a thing had never happened before, as far as he knew. So now he was on his own, with no help or rescue any time soon. Moreover, Crask was synonymous with one thing only: pain. And here he was, a fifteen-year-old boy facing unimaginable torment with no hope of escape. His head was pounding and his nausea deepened rapidly. In sum, he was terrified.

The city of Crask looked little different from any other

city, as far as Trey could tell as he craned his neck to look through the cracks between the crates in the truck in which he travelled. The crates were full of fruit, and he realised that the Notalian method for moving quickly and secretly both into and out of Anasius was to travel inside freight trucks – trucks which legally were permitted to carry goods across the border. The truck in which he was imprisoned looked from the outside like a farm-loader, piled high with crates of apples, pears and mangoes. However, the crates did not fill the truck. Inside, below the truck's rim and inside an outer layer of fruit crates, was an open space, large enough to carry perhaps ten people at once. From the outside, you would never know the space was there. But from within, not only could you see out through the myriad little cracks here and there between crates, you could also ascertain any hostile attention and use appropriate weaponry through the gaps to ward it off if absolutely necessary.

For Trey and Qinoda, though, there was plenty of space, even with Trey being trussed to a table. Qinoda was explaining all about their torture methods in Crask, originally designed to illicit information from people, of course, although Trey got the horrible impression that Qinoda would torture people just for the fun of it. He was trying desperately not to listen and instead to watch where they were going, but it was hard to focus, and he could only see the road and buildings as they moved away from them, not the road ahead. He saw high-rise buildings, new metal-built Notalian houses, office blocks, shopping malls – all the usual things you would expect in a city. The truck slowed and stopped and he heard a few words exchanged. Then they travelled into a large compound and some iron gates clanged shut behind them. They had arrived at Crask Compound, known for its penitentiary, its hospital, its morgue, and, above all, its dungeons.

As the truck came to a halt, helping hands removed the crates from the back and Qinoda got out.

Trey's table was pulled out, and Trey discovered that it was on wheels like a hospital bed. Someone threw a sheet over him making it even harder to breathe, and he was wheeled off into a building. He realised that, from the outside, he probably looked like a dead body brought back to the morgue. Although he wasn't sure why anyone there would care – they knew what the dungeons were for – but clearly Qinoda wanted to be certain that no-one interfered with the work that he was planning.

It seemed an age before his trolley came to a stop and he was untied and told to stand. After being strapped to the table for hours, Trey had lost all the circulation in his hands and feet, and the skin was bleeding from the chafing of the ropes. He tried to stand, but fell hard onto the dark grey flagstone floor. He noticed the floor as he tried to get up and, almost impossibly, he felt a tiny little warming in his heart. This might be the Crask Compound, but it was an Anasiun built building – of that, he was certain. No-one else built floors like this. Suddenly, despite his pain and exhaustion, he felt a brief pang of comfort.

Two burly, six-foot tall and unshaven guards held his upper arms in a vice-like grip. They half-dragged him down three flights of stairs to the dungeons, which turned out to be a number of stone built cells running either side of a long corridor. Over the smell of sweat, urine and human excrement, rose one unmistakeable stench: fear. Three or four of the cells had occupants, one per cell. They looked like they had been human once. Now they cowered, whimpered, bled and festered, beyond caring. They were wretched. And Trey was now prisoner number four.

The guards pulled off his gag and threw him into an empty cell which contained nothing but a bucket toilet, and then the heavy door clanged shut behind him. He hit the floor with a crash and rolled into the bucket. It had not been emptied. He retched involuntarily at the smell. His arms throbbed from the treatment of the guards, his wrists and ankles were painful from rope burns, and the side of his head swam from hitting it on the stone floor. When he rubbed his head, he realised without interest that it was bleeding. All this alongside the horrific state of his fellow-prisoners and the knowledge of what was in store for him caused him to retch once again.

Back at the graduation ceremony dinner, Marcia, Zak and Jason watched Trey leave. They looked at one another and grinned.

"He's really part of our group now, isn't he?" Zak said.

"I still can't quite believe how horrid we were to him when he first arrived," Jason lamented. "I don't know how he put up with it, really."

"I wasn't horrid to him," Marcia contradicted. "But I

didn't really try to befriend him either. It must have been hard, coming to a new country and a new school in the middle of the year. I never really thought about that. He's very determined, isn't he?"

Zak smiled. "You should have seen him tackle the agony assault course," he laughed. "On the first attempt, he spent twenty minutes trying to climb the high wall, and he refused to give up until he had nailed it. He worked harder than anyone else I've ever seen in training." His mind drifted. Then his smile broadened.

"Oh look," he said pointing. "Here comes another person who's graduated from the Overlord Academy." Marcia and Jason looked up and followed Zak's gaze.

"Joe!" they shouted simultaneously. Joe was looking a bit sheepish.

"Hi," he said. "I didn't realise graduation was today, or I'd have tried to wangle an invite. I was on assignment. Errr, I thought Trey was here, too?"

"You've just missed him," Zak said. "He's really tired and so headed off to bed. I've been wondering about something for a while – maybe you guys have some idea."

"What's that?" asked Jason, and they looked at Zak expectantly. "Well, it's just that all five of us have been extracted."

"What do you mean?" Joe questioned.

"In our friendship group, there are basically eight of us, yes? The five of us, plus Zika, Max and Kia. There are billions of people in our world, but none of them have been extracted as far as I know. Just five out of eight friends. What are the chances of that?" They were silent as they digested what Zak was saying.

Marcia spoke first, "You mean, it's not an accident at all? Someone wanted us all to be extracted?"

"Yes. I think Xcion the Sovereign has planned this all out. And for some reason, He wanted some of our particular group of friends."

"Maybe the others will be extracted, too," Zak wondered aloud.

"Yeah, right," Joe scoffed. "We're perfect candidates for changing the course of history – kids from a state secondary school in England. Who better?"

"No, wait Joe," Jason said. "Zak might be right. I mean... Zak graduated top of his class in record time – clearly he was meant for his role. You're already working a non-combat assignment, even though you've only been here a few months. Marcia has insight into the entire geographical, military and political landscape and has a photographic memory so she'll never forget it. And I start a non-combat role tomorrow. Zak may have a point."

"But we're just a bunch of kids," Joe argued. "How can we make a difference when war comes?"

Marcia looked at him. "*If* war comes, Joe. We don't know yet that war is coming. Maybe we'll have a role in preventing it? I don't know, but it's worth considering."

Zak was pleased his idea hadn't been thrown out entirely, well not by Marcia and Jason, anyway. Joe was always a bit more thick-headed. He sighed.

"Well, no doubt we'll know when we need to know,"

he said. "I vote we get some sleep and reconvene in the morning before Jason heads off."

"Sure," said Jason. "I need to sleep anyway. That food was delicious, but I have a serious post-Sunday-lunch feeling!" The friends drifted back to their quarters and within half-an-hour, almost all of them were sleeping soundly.

But Joe was not. He was thinking about everything he'd learned about the Anasiun defence, and wondering whether he should pass it on to Qinoda. The fact is, he thought to himself, this war just needs to happen and be over with. Then Notalia can rise and make the world a better place. I know these guys won't like it, but the sooner it's done, the better. He had convinced himself that the couple's offer back at the café was real. In a triumphant Notalia, Joe could have a top military job. And he found that idea highly attractive.

Trey had finally fallen asleep on the stone floor in the corner opposite the bucket. He was exhausted, cold, aching, hungry, thirsty and scared. His sleep was fitful. Every noise jarred him awake. He could hear the other prisoners scuffling or using the bucket toilets or occasionally whimpering. It was a pitiful night. The next morning he heard guards coming down the stairs. He sat up slowly, groaned and tried to focus. He heard them unlocking one of the other cells and dragging a prisoner out. They passed his cell, taking the whimpering prisoner somewhere, and it wasn't long before the prisoner began to scream – guttural, animal-like, tortured screams that went on and on and on. But Trey had little time to think about them because then the guards reappeared and began to unlock his own cell.

He was dragged along the corridor through a big open area, and into a small room within which was a dirty metal table, a comfortable chair and an array of tools. In the chair sat a middle-aged bearded man who looked like he had never smiled in his life. He watched as Trey was dragged in and heaved unceremoniously onto the table. Mercifully, they gave him a bottle of water, which he drank greedily. Then the guards forced him into a kneeling position and tied his wrists together behind his back. Next they tied his ankles tightly together, the ropes cutting into his already grazed skin, causing Trey to yell in pain.

Next, the man rose from the chair, crossed the room, and took another length of cord from a hook on the wall. He slowly and deliberately made the end of it into a noose. Trey wondered if the intention was to kill him then and there. But the reality was almost worse. The bearded man put the noose over Trey's head and around his neck and then tightened it to the point where it was uncomfortable. Then he took the end of the rope which hung down Trey's back and looped it through the rope around his ankles, before slowly tightening it. The rope from his neck to his ankles forced him to kneel up straight in order to be able to breathe. The man adjusted the length and tied it off at Trey's ankles. His work was quick and sickeningly efficient. Then he sat down on the armchair and closed his eyes. He never said a word. And all the while, from the room just next door, the screaming went on and on.

As the hours passed, Trey began to realise the genius of

his bonds. If he fell over sideways, he would fall off the table altogether and probably break his neck. If he tried to relax, then the rope would tighten on his throat and he wouldn't be able to breathe. So he had to kneel upwards on the metal surface of the table without moving. He was already weak, having not eaten for twenty-four hours, and the muscles in his thighs ached horribly. The screams of the prisoner rang in his head and dulled his ability to think. And as the hours dragged on, not only did he hurt more and more, he became increasingly desperate for the bathroom. Eventually he spoke, in a strange raspy voice that he didn't recognise.

"Please, could I use the bathroom?"

The man in the armchair opened his eyes and looked at him disinterestedly.

"XSHC," he said. "Where is it located?" Trey shook his head and didn't reply.

"This gets easier the moment you give us information," the man said. "I repeat – where is Xcion Strategic High Command located?"

Trey was really desperate for the toilet now. "If I could use the bathroom...?" he asked.

The man rose from his armchair, crossed the room to a sink in the corner and turned the tap on. It ran and splashed and gurgled down the plughole, tormenting Trey. His bladder was hurting and demanding release.

"The XSHC," the man repeated. But Trey gritted his teeth and didn't respond. The man left the tap running and returned to his armchair. Trey realised now why the guards had been so happy to give him a drink. They wanted his utter torment and humiliation. Trey was in agony. His determination was steely, but within an hour he had lost control of his bladder.

As the afternoon wore on, Trey began to get very lightheaded. His muscles were seizing. His wrists and ankles felt like they were on fire. His throat was chafed. He was faint from hunger and thirst. He was beginning to have trouble breathing. He knew that it wouldn't be long before he couldn't hold himself up any longer and he would crash off the table. And he was beginning to think that it would be a welcome relief to do so.

But before it happened, the guards reappeared, cut the ropes, dragged him back to his cell and threw him inside. "Maybe you'll talk tomorrow," they said. The screaming continued for another hour before it died away. When the guards dragged the prisoner back past Trey's cell, Trey could not help but notice the blood. It left a streak down the hallway as they dragged him. Trey was surprised the man had survived. And he was terrified that he was facing similar agonies in days to come. He dragged himself to the wall opposite the cell door and propped himself up. It was there that he noticed a difference.

Just by his left arm on the floor was a stirring of cold air. A movement of air that should not have been there. Why he noticed it, Trey didn't know, but notice it he did. He turned around to look at the floor, but forgetting his bruises as he tried to kneel down, he almost cried out. Eventually he found the least painful way to examine the floor was to lie face down and prop himself on his elbows. It was far from comfortable, but it was not agony. He examined the flagstones where he had previously been sitting.

He noticed the dark cement between the stones. Like Max in the dungeons at Arelard Castle, he noticed the half-flagstone with no cement around it at all. The movement of air had been a slight updraft through those tiny cracks. Despite his squalor, his battered body, his ravenous hunger, his rasping need for water, his tortured tomorrows, a little flame of hope kindled in his soul. It was enough to get him thinking, trying to work out how to remove the stone. It felt solid in every way. Jumping on it proved useless and was so painful that the exhausted Trey bit his lip to avoid crying out. He tried pressing and pushing the flagstone and those around it. He tried blowing down the crack. Eventually, he sat back against the wall again and tried to think. He stared around his cell. The bare ceiling with its single downlighter. The grey rock walls and metal-grate door. The bucket toilet, now almost overflowing. His cape crumpled in one corner.

A sort of idea dawned on him as he looked at his cape. He went over to it and felt it over. Yes – the guards had forgotten his Scroll. It was still clipped to the upper lapel. He unclipped it and slowly made his way back to the flagstone. The Scroll was just thin enough to push into the crack. He held the end of it tightly – he did not wish to lose it down the crack. Then he pushed it carefully into the crack on one side of the flagstone and pulled it right across to the end, dislodging some dirt and grime that had accumulated. He lifted his Scroll out again and wiped it on the sleeve of his shirt. Xci1 would be extremely unimpressed with the way he was treating it, he thought to himself. Then he pushed it into the second edge and began to slide it along there, too. He had not moved it far, though, when he heard a soft click. To his complete surprise, the half-flagstone dropped away towards the left-hand wall and left a gap in the floor. He dropped his Scroll in shock and heard it thud to the floor some way below him. He peered down into the darkness. And then he noticed a ladder, running down from the long edge opposite the hanging flagstone.

It was at this moment that he heard the guards descending the last few steps into the basement. As best he could, the highly weakened Trey scrabbled across to the opposite corner, grabbed his cape and rushing back desperately to try and hide the gaping hole in the floor. He spread his cape out, sat on one end and stretched the rest across the hole. He put his hand down on the far side of the hole seemingly to support his own weight, but really to hold the cape in place. He leaned back slightly against the wall and pretended to doze. The guards passed his cell a second later. With only a brief glance inside, they entered the cell next to his own and then Trey heard a slight exclamation. A minute or two later, they came back passed his cell, and Trey noticed through his half-closed eyes that one of them was carrying the prisoner in a fireman's lift. Trey didn't need to look for long – it was obvious that the prisoner was dead. The guards disappeared again, and shortly after that the lights dimmed for the night.

Trey got to work right away. He took off most of his soiled clothes and rolled them up as best he could. He arranged them in the corner furthest from the door and spread his cape over them. He carefully moved the overflowing bucket near to the same corner to hide some of the clothing. It was a disgusting job because he had to carry it close to his chest; it was full of human filth and it stank to high heaven. He retched as he moved it, but there was no vomit left in him.

When he had finished his task, he hoped that a quick glance into the gloom might just convince a guard that Trey was asleep against the wall under his cape behind the bucket. Then, shivering with cold, and wearing only his socks and boxers, Trey tried to climb down the ladder. It was agony on his wrists, but the desire for escape was overpowering. When he had climbed down a couple of rungs, he spent a good ten minutes trying to lift the hinged flagstone back into place.

Eventually, using every ounce of strength he possessed, he managed to push it up and heard a click as it locked into position. He breathed a sigh of relief, and half-climbed and half-fell the remaining distance to the floor. Then, standing in his soiled boxers, he looked around him and tried to take stock of his situation. He was in a straight corridor, lit only by the occasional downlighter, that came to an abrupt halt at a blank wall about ten feet from him. In the other direction, though, the tunnel disappeared around a corner off into the distance. Painfully he started to walk.

Then, all at once, ahead of him appeared a little golden zero. As he approached, it grew and grew and, as Trey stepped through it, he found himself standing once again in his bedroom at home, exactly where he had been when he was extracted for the second time. Trey had been re-inserted.

He was a sweaty, bloodied and exhausted mess. He was shivering violently from the cold. He stank. He was hurting. He was starving and he was gasping for a drink. Carefully, he crossed the hall to the bathroom and locked the door. Then he took a long drink from the tap and ran a hot bath. He knew he wasn't meant to drink from the tap, but he didn't care. He drizzled some shampoo into the tub and bubbles began to build up.

How was he going to keep all this from his mum? He couldn't possibly tell her the truth – she simply wouldn't believe him. But he didn't want to lie to her – what would he say, anyway? He was struggling to think straight, and he couldn't stop shivering. He began to realise that he needed help, and soon.

He messaged Zak: "In trouble. Please come. Mum out. Front door unlocked." He was shaking so much that it took him a while to type the message, and as soon as he'd sent it, he wished he hadn't. He hadn't been friends with Zak for that long – he couldn't expect him to drop everything and come over. Even less could he expect Zak to shoulder this burden. But Trey's mind see-sawed between the horrors of Crask, the bullying at school, the training and graduation from Overlord Academy, and then back to his current pain, round and round and round. It was too much. He slid to the bathroom floor and wept. His body heaved.

Underneath everything else, he simply couldn't understand why he had not been re-inserted earlier. Why did he have to go through all that pain? Xcion the Sovereign must have lost control. And that was almost more unsettling than anything else.

After a while, though, his sobbing subsided, he roused himself and tried to get into the bath. He was still shivering, and he cried out with the intense pain of the water on his wounds. But he knew he needed to warm up, so he gritted his teeth and steeled himself and climbed in. Slowly, the pain subsided and he sat down and then lay back in the bath.

Then he heard the doorbell. Zak had arrived. He couldn't shout – his voice didn't really work properly, and his hands were wet. He reached out for the towel and his phone and then messaged Zak again, although not before another ring on the doorbell. "In bathroom, but out soon. Could you come in and fix me some food? Sorry." He heard Zak open the door and come in.

"Hi," Zak called up the stairs. "Are you okay?"

Trey messaged again. "Sorry, can't really speak – please could you grab me a sandwich from the kitchen and bring it up to my room? I'll explain soon."

He waited to see if the message worked, then Zak called up, "Okay – sure. I want to know what's going on, though."

Trey lay back in the bathtub and realised there was great relief in getting warm again.

Within a few minutes, he was no longer shivering, and a few minutes later he managed to get himself mostly clean. He got painfully out of the bath and pulled the plug.

Drying himself was another agonising experience, and

the huge towel seemed adept at finding new bruises and broken skin. Eventually, though, wrapped carefully in the towel, he returned to his bedroom to find Zak sitting at his desk with a sandwich and a can of coke, playing on his phone. Zak swivelled around on his chair as he heard Trey come out of the bathroom, but when he saw Trey, he gasped in horror.

"Trey – what on earth...?"

Trey sat on his bed with the sandwich and the coke. He hurt all over, his head ached and he was still feeling faint from hunger. He didn't respond to Zak yet. Instead, he took a bite of the sandwich, chewed it and swallowed. He closed his eyes briefly. It was his first food for thirty-six hours. He took another bite and reached for the coke. After a few more mouthfuls, though, he wasn't sure if he wanted to eat any more just yet. His stomach was pretending to be a washing machine.

"Trey," Zak demanded. "What happened to you?"

Trey tried to respond. "I've only just been...re-inserted," he said. He was struggling to speak because there was a lump in his throat, and he didn't want to cry in front of Zak. He swallowed and tried again. "I was in Crask...They..." But he couldn't hold it in. And even as Zak was staring at him, the tears came again. He buried his head in his hands. He was dressed only in a towel, crying and acutely embarrassed. What would Zak think of him now?

Zak was looking horrified, and had given a huge intake of breath when Trey said "Crask". He repeated, deeply concerned, "Crask? How? What did they do to you?" His head was whirling. Crask, the place of torture, pain and death? How had Trey ended up there? What had happened to him? What terrors had he experienced? It was in this moment, as his friend sobbed on his bed, that Zak finally realised the seriousness of the situation in Anasius. This other world was not some fun adventure between a few of his friends. This was real, with real enemies, real pain, real torture, real death. He felt sick to the stomach. He had no idea what to say to Trey. He just sat there waiting for Trey to recover himself.

After a while, Trey got a hold of himself again and calmed down a bit. Over the course of the next hour he managed to tell Zak the story of his abduction, his treatment in Crask, and then his re-insertion, although he didn't mention the flagstone and the tunnel. His story was interspersed with tears, returning to the bathroom to get into some clean clothes, and with eating more of his sandwich and drinking more coke. By the end of it, Trey was feeling a bit more human. Suddenly, he asked Zak, "What time is it?"

"7:30," Zak responded shortly.

"Oh no. I don't know what to do. Mum's home in under an hour. How can I keep her from finding out about this? I'm supposed to have cooked dinner, but I don't know if I can. I really need to sleep."

"Marcia will help," Zak said shortly. Trey tried to protest. "No, Trey. This is a time when you let us sort it out. You're always so strong and take whatever comes and never give up and never give in. Well not this time. You need help, and we're going to supply it." Zak was still upset about his failure to stand up for Trey back at school. So now, he thought, here was an opportunity to do something positive for him, to make it up to him a bit if he could. Zak was messaging even as he spoke to Trey. "You lie down in bed. Let me know if you need anything, anything at all. I'm going to sit here until Marcia comes, and then we'll sort food for your mum. What were you going to cook?"

Trey tried to think. "Lasagne, I think. But there's no time now."

"Stop," Zak cut him off. "Don't you worry about it – we'll figure it out and find a way to placate your mum. You just need to get some sleep."

Trey didn't try to argue any more. He sank down gratefully into his bed, rested his head on his pillow and was asleep within five minutes. Zak was messaging rapid-fire, and Marcia was already on her way.

15

Council of War

It was early evening on 10 June. Trey was at his computer attempting his biology homework. Zak was on his games console. Zika was watching a video about how to fix the back wheel of a bike when it goes wobbly. Jason was watching random YouTube videos on his phone. Joe was watching a movie on his iPad. Marcia was messaging Kia about her maths homework. Max was emailing his Latin teacher for some help on something called the "vocative". Suddenly, at virtually an identical moment, all of them felt a familiar pulse and found themselves extracted.

The library at Arelard Castle was a very familiar place for Max, so when he found himself there on extraction, he moved naturally to his favourite armchair and sat down. Kia appeared at the same time, but whilst she also started moving towards a comfy chair, she noticed Xci4 standing in front of the wall with the oil-paintings, and then she saw Xci1, Prince of Anasius and heir to the throne. She did not know Xci4, but she recognised the prince from her research and training. She curtsied clumsily.

"Hello Kia," Xci1 said in a deep, sonorous voice. Max jumped up from his chair in a hurry, embarrassed that he had not noticed them. "And hello Max," Xci1 continued. Max felt his cheeks begin to turn red at his social faux-pas, but his embarrassment was quickly forgotten, because even as the prince finished speaking, the other friends appeared. First Jason, a minute later Joe, Trey and Marcia virtually simultaneously, and finally Zak and Zika. They stared at one another in surprise – surprise at having been extracted, but more surprise at the fact that all the other seven had been extracted as well. The last six friends to arrive were even more bewildered, because they had no idea where they were. They looked around, taking in their surroundings, noting the walls lined with books, the window seats, the wall with the oil-paintings, the large mahogany table and chairs, the plush carpet and the three men standing by the paintings.

After a minute or two, Zak said, "Zika. I had no idea you had been to Anasius..."

"Me neither," Jason chimed in. Some others were nodding.

"Apart from Max, I didn't know any of you had been to Anasius," Kia said.

"I..." began Max, but Xci4 coughed loudly, and the eight friends stopped talking and turned towards him

"I am sorry to intrude," he said. "And I know you all feel you have a good deal to catch up on, but we have very little time. Please come and sit at the table. And please pass around these cards and pens as you do so – everyone will

184

need one." As he spoke, they obeyed, pulling out the heavy dark-wood chairs with their padded dark green upholstery which turned out to be extremely comfortable. Xci4 continued to speak as they got organised.

"May I take the liberty of summarising where you all stand? Joe was extracted first, trained at the Overlord Academy and was then sent as a non-combat informer to the Tsarn / Crask border. Zak was extracted next, graduated in record time, was designated Outer Warrior One, and was selected to be a training officer in Overlord Academy. Trey was extracted at about the same time and graduated later, alongside Jason. Jason was partly trained by Zak, and graduated alongside Trey. He also had a non-combat informer role, but this time on the outskirts of Ruscorn Forest. Marcia was extracted at the same time as Jason, but her training was of a different kind. Kia and Max were extracted here, to Arelard Castle, at the same time. They have both been fully trained in their separate disciplines. Zika was extracted last of all and graduated from Overlord Academy two months ago. Following that he has been training as a special recruit."

As he spoke, the friends looked at one another, learning things about each other they had not known until now. They were going to have a lot to talk about later, but Zika noticed he did not speak about the Underlord Academy.

Xci4 continued, "Now, though, we are meeting for one major reason. The prince, under the authority of the king, has called all of you to this Council of War. That is why you're all here. On Jason's latest assignment, he gathered information suggesting that the Notalians are planning to invade Anasius just nineteen days from now. There is much to prepare. Jason – please tell us what happened as you lay on the Ruscorn Forest floor two evenings ago."

Jason re-lived as accurately as he could his experience as he had lain in the woods, trying to hide under his camouflage cape. He described the conversation between General Qong, Qinoda and the Notalian prince.

"So, in essence," Jason concluded, "the Notalian plan is to bring troops from Crask, cross the border somehow and then move through Ducal City and up into Ruscorn Forest. From there, they would travel east and take Tranton, after which they would move swiftly further east to Tsarn. Then, using the ferry to take some early fighters across in disguise, they would take Port Diblaine by storm."

Kia remarked, "I don't see how they can defeat Anasius without taking our naval base at Xanver. But from what you've said, we have no information about their plans for that. Perhaps they plan to use Tranton as a base and send some troops northwest to Xanver as well as other troops to Tsarn? Or perhaps they're planning for some of their troops to attack Xanver from the southwest by coming at it from the edge of Ruscorn Forest? Whatever their plan, though, if they manage to take Xanver, Tsarn and Port Diblaine, then the Notalians will hold Anasius by the scruff of the neck."

The friends looked at her in amazement. How did she know about all those places? And since when did Kia know anything about military strategy? She saw their quizzical looks and tried to explain.

"I trained here in Arelard Castle," she said. "I spent three months studying Anasiun history, politics, military tactics and strategy, which included a good deal of geography."

Marcia chimed in, "From a geographical perspective," she said, "Kia is exactly right. Most of our military might is centred at Xanver, Port Diblaine and Tsarn. Without taking all three, the Notalians have no hope of a successful invasion. It's a shame Jason did not hear more – we really need to know their plans for Xanver." Realising that everyone was now staring at her, she added, "And I have visited and inspected all our naval capability and defences, and toured all the major routes through Anasius from Ducal City across to the eastern desert, and from the coast right down south to the foothills of the Arelard mountains where we are right now. So I should know."

Zak said, "So the big question is, how do we stop them? What can we do to improve our defences and repel potentially thousands of Notalian warriors?"

"And," Xci1 said, "therein lies the problem. Most of our population seem more interested in pleasure-seeking than national defence, although we do have a good number of trained troops. Around 1500 have graduated from Overlord Academy in the past twelve years, most of whom are now sleeper-agents who have reintegrated into society. All are loyal and would activate if called upon. We have 2000 troops operating Xanver Naval Base. Our special forces unit comprises sixty-three troops who have been particularly highly trained, with specialisms in sabotage, electronics, intelligence and so on. Those sixty-three will need carefully coordinated deployment."

The eight friends stared at each other, unsure what to say.

Xci4 said, "Your Majesty, my idea was for each of us to take some time to think and record our ideas on these cards. I know we could use our Scrolls, but electronic communication can be hacked, so we're going old school. Then we can go around the table and use our collective wisdom to formulate a plan. Let's take about ten minutes for silent thinking, and may Xcion the Sovereign help us."

For most of them, the following ten minutes involved frowning, scribbling ideas, then crossing them out and scribbling other ideas. For Marcia and Trey, it was ten minutes of staring at a blank card and having no ideas whatsoever.

When the time was up, Xci4 called them to order. "As the one who has been here the longest, Joe, I wonder whether we might start with you?" he queried.

Joe began uncertainly. "If the Notalians are bringing 20,000 troops, then we are seriously outnumbered, so we need to fight smart. The border fence between Notalia and Anasius is virtually impregnable now it has been upgraded – I should know, I was laying a good deal of it. Not only is it founded ten-foot underground in concrete, but the fence itself runs with a fatally high electric current, and the lasers mounted on its top fire up at anything larger than an eagle that crosses the air-space. So it seems to me that the only way the Notalians can bring so many troops across the border would be to take out the border-crossing itself.

Therefore, we need to increase significantly our troop presence there. Of course, they could use the southern crossing, but that's a long way from Ruscorn Forest and they would then need to cross the marsh and the southern uplands before ever reaching Ducal. It doesn't sound like that's where they were thinking of invading."

"No," Jason returned. "I agree with that. But how many troops do we deploy to the Tsarn / Crask turnpike crossing? I mean, we could increase the physical defences there, for sure, but couldn't we just close the crossing for the moment?"

Xci4 thought for a moment. "I think we could, but I think the problems would outweigh the benefits. Under the terms of the PAN treaty, we have oversight of both sides of the crossing. But it is jointly-manned, so that closing the crossing would involve sending Notalian workers home as well as our own. Whilst the virtually unused steel barricades would come into place immediately, a determined army could get through them in a matter of days. More importantly, closing the crossing would send a clear message to the Notalians that we know that war is coming. We would lose the element of surprise from our inside knowledge from Jason. I suspect that once they knew the crossing was being closed, they would throw a few hundred more troops and heavy equipment at the crossing and it would fall even more quickly.

On the other hand, I think the idea of improving border defences is a good one. We can do that from our side without arousing suspicion. We already have a busy building site at the crossing, as Joe well knows, so we could do quite a lot before it became obvious that we were putting in further defence measures. As well as improving the technological defence, we should be able to reinforce with physical barriers and tighten road crossing security, at least. Let's leave Joe and Marcia to work on the details."

Trey suggested, "I think we need to bolster our defences at Xanver, especially on the approach from Ruscorn Forest and from Tranton. Can we send some of the Overlord Academy graduates there? I mean, I think we'll need to activate all of them, and some for the border crossing of course, but we'll need some at Xanver and also at Port Diblaine, won't we?"

"What about the Overlord Academy itself? Does Notalia know about it?" Kia wondered aloud.

"Yes," Trey said shortly. She looked at him, but he did not elaborate.

She moved on.

"What about the subway? Can we utilise that to move our troops around?"

"That's a good idea," Zika said. "That way they won't arrive exhausted from travel."

Kia interrupted, "And we can coordinate troop movements from here at Arelard. I can do that with the team upstairs."

Zak was hesitant. "Okay, guys, this is all very interesting and everything, but we're a bunch of school kids. What we're discussing here is serious. Really serious, I mean. People will get hurt. People will die. We could get hurt." He looked at

Trey. "And if something happens to us here, how does that work out back home? If someone dies here, do they die at home? Do we really want to get involved in a foreign war with all the dangers that accompany it?"

Joe looked at him. "You're scared," he taunted.

"Frankly, yes," Zak responded. "And I think we should all be." He was still looking at Trey. "You should have seen..." But he stopped talking when he saw Trey shaking his head at him.

Zak started again. "How could we explain to a parent that one of us was seriously injured or even died here in Anasius? There would be no body – we would just have disappeared. They wouldn't believe us. There'd be hell to pay. This war could have very serious consequences." He was pleading. He was re-living those two hours with Trey after his incarceration in Crask, and he didn't want that to happen ever again.

Marcia nodded. "You're right, Zak. I know you are. But our training was for this purpose. We have been put together to get this job done. I don't know why it's us. I don't know what the outcome is to be. But Anasius needs us. Xcion the Sovereign has brought this about. Now we need to step up to the plate and take whatever comes our way."

Zak looked at Trey for help. Trey realised and said, "More than any of you, I know that Zak is right. This is dangerous and deadly and if anyone thinks this is just a little adventure, then they should go home now. But Marcia is right as well. If there's one thing I know from my training, it is this: all things happen for a reason. The fact that the eight of us sit here together is proof enough for me that we need to see this thing through. Whatever it takes. I'm in." The others slowly nodded their agreement.

Finally Zak spoke again. "Okay, I'm in, too. But please be careful. We don't want to lose anyone."

Xci1 had listened to the interchange. He smiled faintly. "I am continually impressed with you all," he said. "Don't let people look down on you because you are young. You may not have huge amounts of experience, but you are committed to doing what is right, to trusting in the oversight of Xcion the Sovereign, and to looking out for one another. Our people could learn a thing or two from all of you. And, on behalf of the king, I thank you for your willingness to serve. Frankly, without you we would be lost – of that I am certain."

Xci4 spoke again, "Okay, so we've got that sorted. What other ideas do we have?"

Jason asked, "In terms of Xanver, what troops do we have at Fort Tula and Fort Boan?"

Xci4 responded immediately. "100 troops living in each, all between twenty-five and forty years of age. The two forts would be easy to overrun – their defences are not strong."

Zak said, "In that case, why not give a show of increasing the defences and increasing the military presence there? Why not take seeming truck-loads of troops in, but in fact secretly take all troops out and lay traps in each fort entirely? We could install speakers and remotely controlled lights to suggest troop movements, but once the Notalians approach to take the forts we could deploy the traps and use that as a way of removing at least some Notalian troops. Then we could use the troops in the forts as part of the defence of Xanver."

Xci4 grinned. "That's a genius idea," he said. "I don't like the idea of losing the forts, but if it helps us defeat the Notalian army, then it'll be worthwhile. What do you think, Your Majesty?"

Xci1 agreed. "I'll hate to lose 300-year-old buildings, but it does seem like a good plan. Now, Xci4, I think we need to give these folks some freedom for a few hours to discuss further plans, and we have one or two things to see to up in XSHC." He declared a pause in the Council of War, and then he and Xci4 left the library, and the friends looked at one another. Now they had to figure out how to defend a whole country from an attacking army.

They talked for a bit longer as a big group, but after a while, they split up to figure out and then record the various parts of their collective plans. Then they handed their ideas to Kia who seemed to be the one coordinating the strategy.

Joe and Marcia's ideas about the border were the first to be handed over. As Kia took their card, Joe asked, "Sorry to be boring, but where is the bathroom?" Max showed him the way and he hurried out. Kia read what they had written, "We could extend the electrification of the barrier fence right into the crossing itself, and construct large reinforced concrete barriers across much of our side of the crossing. The Notalians would have no idea it had happened. We could even divert traffic to a secondary carriageway for a couple of days on some pretext, install stronger steel barriers below the main turnpike on our side, and then return the traffic to the turnpike. If we then complete concrete barriers right up to the road, then by the time the Notalians try to cross the border and move large troop numbers through, they would be funnelled towards the same narrow gap. Then we could raise the new steel barriers which would take them some time to breach."

"Excellent ideas," she said to Marcia. "How many people will be needed?" she asked.

"Well," Marcia said, "the good thing about it is that most of the work can be done by labourers – very few troops would be needed until the border is actually closed."

"That's true and very helpful, knowing how few troops we have," Kia responded.

The others brought their ideas to Kia and all of them were discussed. It was about an hour later when, in the middle of a discussion about how they could use the subway, Kia suddenly asked, "Why hasn't Joe returned?" They tried to think what might have happened, but apart from Zika's stupid idea that Joe had fallen into the toilet, no-one knew.

Jason went off to find him, but returned a few minutes later looking worried.

"Joe has left the Castle. Traika noticed him closing the main door and watched him take off down the road to Tsarn at speed."

"Perhaps he's meeting someone who has some information for us," Max suggested. "Although I'm not sure who it could possibly be, or why he'd not tell us where he was going."

"And we can't track him," Kia said, "because he's not equipped. He's been to Anasius before any of us, though – do you know what he did back then, Zak?"

"No," Zak said. "He graduated before my time, and he was on the non-combat mission to the border-crossing for quite a lengthy period of time. Do you think he knows something we don't?"

"The biggest worry," Trey said quietly, "is how much he heard of our plans before he betrays us to the Notalians."

"Trey," Marcia reprimanded him. "Joe wouldn't betray us." But her tone revealed a hint of uncertainty. Zak was also unconvinced, and he knew better than any of them. He mused aloud, "Joe is one of my best mates, and we've known each other since we were seven. He's always up for a laugh, doesn't take life too seriously and, of course, he loves parkour. But he doesn't always make good decisions. He knows that – he felt bad about the way he treated you, Trey, and he promised me he would be civil to you in the future, which I think he has been. But if he were pushed in the right way, betrayal would not be impossible for Joe. Anyway, why else would he run off without saying where he was going?" Try as they might, none of the seven friends could think of a better explanation.

"Okay," said Marcia. "We know he left as soon as he and I gave you our thoughts about the border crossing. Anything we've discussed since then has been in his absence."

"Not if he hung around outside the door," Max argued. "He could have been there for ages."

Jason spoke up, "No, Traika said that Joe left almost an

195

hour ago. So Marcia is right – he left right after Max directed him to the toilet."

"So that means that he knows the plans for the border crossing, and the plans for the traps in the forts," Zika groaned.

"But he doesn't know our ideas for Tsarn, the ferry or Port Diblaine," Kia responded. "It's annoying about the forts, though – that idea was inspired. I have no clue how you thought of it, Zak, but it's genius!"

"To be honest," Zak said, "I was thinking about a parable from the Scroll, and the idea sort of suggested itself."

"Clearly I need to read the Scroll more closely," Jason commented. "Anyway – can I suggest we put all our other plans together so that we can forward our thoughts to the prince and Xci4?"

Then Max spoke, "Yes, but I also have another idea, an idea which I can't quite figure out yet..."

"I know what you're thinking about," Kia said, "but can you hold that thought in your head until after we've spoken to Xci1 and Xci4? I think we need to do some more research before we discuss it." She looked at him intensely. He realised that she did not want to bring hope to everyone else about a possible tunnel system until they could be sure about it.

"Sure – it can wait," he said shortly.

When Xci1 and Xci4 returned, Kia explained their progress. "We have begun to compile a full strategy for defence and for defeating the Notalian Liberation Army if they do invade in under three weeks' time. We have activation plans involving all Overlord Academy graduates, and we have written assignments for some key players. We will also require around thirty manual labourers to complete the reinforcement works at the Tsarn / Crask border crossing." She paused and chose her next words carefully. "We also have a plan for all current troops at Xanver and Port Diblaine, but we need some time for two of us to do some research before we finalise that plan. The research might take a few hours. Completing these assignment lists will also take some time. Finally, although we all have Scrolls, we will require rings and implants."

Zika protested. "Implants? No – how will we explain that back home?"

"It's okay," Kia responded. "I've been thinking about that. When we have re-entry, our Scrolls disappear, even if we've been holding them in our hands. I'm convinced that technology from Anasius cannot survive re-entry and so we shouldn't have a problem back at home."

Xci4 was grinning. "She's amazing," he said to Xci1. "Yes – we have thought this for some time. Implants here will disappear on re-entry, as will gold rings and Scrolls. This means that whenever you are extracted, you need new Scrolls, rings and implants when you return. And yes, Kia, we can sort rings and implants for you all very easily – it'll take less than five minutes."

Since some of the others knew nothing about implants, they were at a loss, but Kia stopped their questions, "There is no time now for those explanations. I will tell you later. Your Majesty." She turned to Xci1. "May we have a few more hours?"

"Yes, that will be possible," Xci1 said. "How many people do you need to help with your research?"

"None," Kia said shortly. "I need Max and Marcia to do the research alone, if that's okay?"

"Me?" Marcia asked incredulously.

"Yes, you and Max. You'll see why later. Please just trust me on this one, okay?"

"Okay," said Marcia meekly. She decided she may as well be useful for something, even if she had no idea what it was going to be.

"And I'll sanction it," Xci1 said. "But please be careful. There are Notalian spies everywhere these days." He looked around at the friends. "And where's Joe?" he asked.

"We don't know," said Zika shortly. "He left, but we don't know where."

Xci1 and Xci4 looked at each other. There was an awkward silence. Then Xci4 said, "Okay, we'll find him. In the meantime, food is being sent down here in about fifteen minutes. Once you've eaten, perhaps Max and Marcia can start their research?"

"Yes," said Kia. "And the rest of us may be required to help later on. Is that okay with everyone?"

There were nods all around, then Xci4 said, "All right, we'll be in the communications room if you need us. Some encrypted messages are arriving as we speak, and we need to know their content."

Xci1 and Xci4 left again, but before the food was delivered, a small golden circle appeared and grew rapidly. All seven of them were re-inserted.

16

Treachery

As soon as Max returned to the library, Joe ignored the toilets and tiptoed about looking for an exit door. He found the main entrance on the floor above the library and slipped out. Having descended the wide stairs at the front of the castle, he found himself on the long, curving road that ran all the way to Tsarn. He started jogging. He thought he had left unnoticed, but Traika happened to be coming down the main staircase by the ballroom, and he saw the front door close. He went to a window, peered out, and saw a boy jogging down the road. He knew trouble was afoot.

For Joe, though, he simply jogged. Whilst he knew that Tsarn was a long way off, he was a good athlete and even with the evening half gone, he should be able at least to get to Maynard Bridge. There he hoped to find a passing Notalian goods vehicle. If so, he might get a ride to Tsarn, or even Ducal City and then onwards to the Crask / Tsarn border. He needed to report his discoveries – surely they would be enough to cement him a place at the table of a triumphant Notalian army.

After two hours of jogging, in which the territory did not change a great deal, he dropped back to walking. He was thirsty, hungry and getting tired. The sun was sinking in the western sky, throwing his long shadow on the ground to his right, and he judged it would soon be dark. He had reached the place where the road ran atop a gorge, in which nestled the Dagon Dam and the hydro-electric power plant. Fifteen minutes later, he could hear the Dagon River flowing fast and treacherously through the rapids beneath the dam far below. He was walking well-away from the edge of the gorge, but he found the sound of running water increasingly maddening because he was so thirsty. Another hour and the sun dropped below the horizon. The road was growing darker by the minute, Joe was exhausted, and he began to worry that he might slip down the gorge if he didn't stay focused. He was walking on the far left-hand edge of the road now, and he reckoned he was still quite a distance from Maynard Bridge. He realised he had seriously underestimated the distance he needed to travel.

Not until it was quite dark and the stars were out did he come across a long low building, looming up on his left. He skirted around it cautiously, his eyes quite accustomed to the dark now, but he saw and heard nothing. He crept around it to the far side. There he discovered three closed doors, each padlocked, a number of dark windows and then, at the far end, a barn-style door, hinged across the middle. The top half stood invitingly open. Everything was still and quiet, there was no light shining anywhere, and the whole place appeared deserted, both inside and out. Just before he ventured inside, he noticed a tap on the outside wall by the door. He bent down to it, turned it on very slowly so as to make as little noise as possible, and then drank greedily from it. It was ice cold and very refreshing. All he needed now was a bit of rest, then he could get going again.

He turned back to the half-door, could not find the bolt to the bottom half and so climbed wearily over it, and then found a rough blanket over a chair just inside the door. Apart from the space near the open doorway, it was so dark inside that it was almost impossible to see anything at all. He padded about, feeling his way, and eventually discovered that the shapeless mound to his right was, in fact, a large stack of hay bales. He grabbed the blanket from the chair, shifted some of the hay aside, and then climbed up and in amongst the bales. He lay down on the hay with some of the blanket underneath him to stop the hay sticking into him, and the other half pulled over the top of him to keep the cold of the night out. It was far from the most comfortable bed he had ever had, but he was so tired, he didn't much care. In ten minutes he was sleeping soundly.

He stayed asleep when a pin-prick of light crept into the barn fifteen minutes later and swept the room. He stayed asleep when a long mean face appeared not one metre from his sleeping place and shone a small light on him briefly. He didn't wake up when, off in the distance, a low phone conversation ensued for three or four minutes. He didn't wake when a vehicle drew up alongside the barn half-an-hour later, and low voices conversed outside in the darkness of the night.

He woke only when it was too late. All of a sudden he was rudely awaked by a bright light in his face. His shoulders were pinned with an iron grip, his feet were secured together with a rope, a gag was stuffed into his mouth and he was lifted bodily from the hay and carried outside to the truck. Within moments he was wide awake, and he struggled violently, but to no avail. He was no match for the three men. They bundled him inside the truck and set off down the road towards Tsarn. Joe was extremely hungry, aching from his long jog and walk, and dazed from his abrupt awakening. There was nothing comfortable about having his hands and feet tied securely, a gag in his mouth, and then being forced to lie on the floor of a truck which appeared to have little suspension.

When they reached Tsarn an hour or so later, there were more inaudible voices and then he was transferred to a second truck. This time, though, there was only one guard with him plus an older man with the Notalian military insignia tattooed on his forehead, a thick mail-shirt and the usual uniform of the Notalian Liberation Army. A short dagger was strapped to his left calf, and he fingered it suggestively as they travelled.

Five minutes later, when they were out of the city, he took the dagger from his calf, stood up and came over to Joe. Joe was terrified. The man cut the gag from Joe's mouth in one swift movement, just nicking the side of Joe's neck with the blade.

"Ow," Joe complained,

The man interrupted immediately "Shhh. Any noise, and I'll silence you once and for all," he promised. Joe believed him. He continued. "Now, in a whisper only, what is your business, and why were you in Gramond's barn?" he asked.

Joe responded, his eyes never leaving the dagger. "I was coming from Arelard Castle. I have information for a Notalian couple who work at the Crask / Tsarn border crossing – information they will pass onto Qinoda."

The man with the dagger raised his eyebrows. "Information for Qinoda, eh?" he asked. "Information about what?"

"About Anasiun troop movements," Joe said. "It has to be for the couple directly."

"I see. So you want to go to the border?" he asked, smiling slightly.

"Yes, and quickly," Joe responded.

"As you wish," the man said. "We're heading that way now." He made no offer to untie Joe or make him more comfortable, and he made a new gag and put it in place. Joe was annoyed. He had vital news for the Notalian war effort, and this guy didn't seem to understand. This is no way to treat an informant, he thought. He was still thirsty and very hungry, but somehow the dagger stopped him from complaining. He tried not to think about it. Once he met with the couple, he thought, he could eat and drink then. He had important news. And maybe the couple would deal with these ignorant captors.

It was several hours later that the truck rolled to a stop, Joe's bonds were cut and he was ordered down from the truck. Finally, they had reached the border crossing. The couple from the café were standing beside the truck.

"Tell us your news," the woman demanded.

"First, a drink please," Joe managed to say.

"Shut up and answer the question," the man with the dagger replied.

But the woman shook her head with just a trace of a smile. "No, no, he is right. Musgrove, would you mind fetching our esteemed guest a drink?" She sounded sarcastic. Musgrove grinned at her.

"Of course," he said and disappeared up to the café. In the meantime, the woman looked him over.

"You look dishevelled," she commented. "You should look after yourself better, you know." Joe was angry, but contained it as he had been taught. She wasn't to know about his long jog and walk, his fitful sleep, and his treatment in the trucks.

He replied with, "I do apologise, I was in a hurry to get vital news from Arelard Castle to Qinoda."

"All in good time," she said mildly. "I suspect your news is not directly for Qinoda, but rather for Zvarak, and he'll be here presently. If you've left by then, well, we'll pass it on of course. Ah, here comes your drink."

Musgrove returned and offered Joe a bottle of water. He drank it quickly. Then he said, "The news is simple. They know Notalia is planning to invade Anasius. They know about some of the strategy plans, especially the travel through Ruscorn Forest and the aim to take Tranton, Tsarn and Diblaine."

Musgrove spoke up. "What about Xanver? Do they know about Xanver?"

Joe shook his head. "No. They are planning to reinforce

the border crossing and bring more troops here. They're guessing Xanver will be approached from Ruscorn Forest or from Tranton, but they don't know." He decided not to tell them the plans for the two forts.

"Anything else?" the woman asked.

"Well," Joe said, "I know a secret route into somewhere, although I'm not sure where." And he told them about the doorway in the tree. The woman's eyes narrowed.

"Very helpful," she growled sarcastically. "There are millions of trees in Ruscorn Forest. Any idea which one?"

"Yes," Joe said adamantly. "Show me photographs of the eastern edge of the forest, and I'll point it out. I know exactly which one it is, because I took careful note of it."

"I can do better," the woman said. She removed a card from her pocket and unfolded it. Exactly like a Scroll, it unfolded to become a large electronic tablet. She tapped at it for a few seconds and then handed it to Joe. "There's the edge of the forest," she said, pointing to a sideways photograph which, somehow, could be scrolled left and right to run the whole eastern flank.

Joe tapped the tablet for a few moments and then suddenly said, "Yes, that's it." He showed it to her. "This one here," he said, and pointed to it.

The woman drew a ring in red around the tree and then pinged the message off.

"Okay, anything else?"

"Not that I can think of," Joe said.

"Right," said the woman. "That's it then." She turned her back, and she and Musgrove walked back to the café. The men at his side grabbed his arms and bundled him back into the truck. Joe tried to shout his protest, but one of them clamped a hand firmly over his mouth. Before long he was tied up again with a gag in place. And then the truck moved across the border and onwards. The man with the dagger leaned forward to speak to him.

"Thank you for the information," he said in a silky voice. "Now we're taking you to Crask to see if you know anything else. I think you know what that means." The man sat back and started humming a little tune. Joe's eyes widened in terror.

Just half-an-hour later, the truck rolled into Crask Compound. Joe was dragged from the vehicle. Then they untied his ankles and frog-marched him through the main doors and through miles of corridor before he was forced down three flights of stairs. At the bottom of the stairs were a number of cells, and Joe was thrust unceremoniously into one of them. The door clanged shut, the lock rammed home and he was left in the dungeons of Crask to contemplate his situation.

He realised not only that he had been very foolish, but that he had betrayed his friends as a result. He had been utterly hoodwinked. There was no real offer of a seat at the table in a triumphant Notalia. Instead, the Notalians had used him as a pawn in their war effort, and now they were discarding him in the dungeons of Crask.

He looked at the bucket toilet, the stains on the floor, some of which looked suspiciously like dried blood. He was just beginning to despair of all hope, when a little gold circle appeared and grew rapidly in size. Joe was re-inserted, thinking that his ordeal was over. In fact, though, his nightmare was only just beginning.

17

Horror

Tim was at work when he had a call from Zika's mum. It was hard to understand her words through the crying, but he understood enough to have a quick chat to the pastor in the study across the hall, and then both of them left the church offices. Tim made a few calls on their way to the hospital, and then he called each of the group of friends and asked them to meet at the top of Durin's Hill in two hours' time.

Two hours later, the friends had gathered at the familiar bench next to the ancient oak. This was the bench where they had ended up after Zika's birthday dinner and played cards until midnight. This was the bench where they had spent hours listening to music and talking about movies. This was the bench where Kia, unknown to the rest of the group, had whispered to Marcia her infatuation with Jason. This was the bench where Joe had broken his arm two summers ago whilst trying to demonstrate his fledgling parkour skills. This was the bench where Max had been sitting the first time he was extracted. There were so many memories made at this bench. From now on, though, this bench would hold a much more vivid memory; a sadness that gripped the friends and tore at their hearts.

Tim had arrived first, greeting quietly each of the others as they arrived. Jason came by bike, dressed in jeans and a hoodie. He looked pale and uncertain, and disinclined to speak. Marcia and Kia arrived together, dropped off by Marcia's dad who spoke to Tim in low tones and then drove off. Marcia and Kia were arm-in-arm, tight-lipped and scared, leaning on one another for support. Trey and Max arrived separately but on foot, uncertain, stricken. Joe arrived last, jumping off his bike and looking angry. Zika and Zak didn't arrive at all, and they knew why. The friends had heard the worst of it already, but they weren't sure it was true. They didn't want it to be true.

Tim began to speak, "I wanted to see you together, to try and give some details. I know how tight you have become as a friendship group. I've just been talking to Zika's mum at the Royal Marnic Hospital." There was a slight tremor in his voice. He paused and swallowed. "This afternoon, Zak and Zika were cycling home from school. As they crossed the roundabout at Turner's End, a white van turning from Snyder Road did not see them and drove straight into them both. Zak..." He broke off and there was a moment's silence. "I'm sorry, I don't know how to do this." Tears built in his eyes, and he swallowed hard again. "Zika was thrown off the road into the hedge. Zak was thrown into a lamppost. He... He didn't..." Tim wiped his hand roughly across his eyes. "He didn't make it," he finally managed to say.

Tim stopped, wiped his face again and controlled himself.

"Zak died at the Turner's End roundabout. He died..." his voice cracked again, but he forced himself to carry on. "He died because the van didn't see them...Zak...I..." Tim couldn't continue.

For Marcia and Kia, the tears were falling freely. Jason was struggling to understand, shaking his head, an emotional blank. Max felt like he had been punched deep in the gut and he was struggling to breathe.

Joe blurted out, "Is this some sort of sick joke? Zak's fine. I caught him out in cricket this morning. We were planning a summer camping trip. He's meeting us on Friday for pizza. Zak's good. You're lying Tim. I don't believe you." His voice was defiant, but the others were eyeing him warily. Joe was their friend, but after what had just happened in Anasius...the whole thing was so impossible.

"I'm so sorry, Joe," Tim's voice began.

"No," Joe interrupted violently. "It can't be true. It can't be." He was almost shouting.

"Joe," Tim began again.

But Joe interrupted with a loud, angry obscenity, as harsh as it was unexpected. And then he stalked away, across the car park, kicking at a parked car as he went. He cried out again, a deep, guttural, animal noise reflecting his inner turmoil. They would never forget that noise. Tim didn't know what to do or say. Joe's shout echoed unanswered across the valley. The harshness of that cry seemed to drive the horror of the last couple of hours even deeper. Tim sank to the ground and propped his back against the arm of the bench. He gazed unseeing down the hill to the woods beyond. Kia was on the bench, crying with agonised sobs. Marcia, also with tears falling freely, was holding Kia. Neither attempted to speak. Max was running his hands through his blond hair, shaking his head, and slowly rocking backwards and forwards. He made no sound, but the tears were falling.

Jason was sitting on the ground, leaning back on the oak tree, face drawn but almost expressionless, head slowly shaking left and right. He couldn't cry. He just had this growing emptiness in the pit of his stomach. Zak who always beat him at chess. Zak who had helped Joe climb onto the gym roof and stuck a model of Mr Johnson to the drainpipe so that everyone saw it on their way into school. Zak who, on mufti day, had come into school dressed as Mrs Harkson the RE teacher. Zak whose dog had been renamed "Potato". And now Zak was gone. It was surreal. Horribly surreal. He didn't have anything to say. There was nothing to say. And the tears would not come.

Trey was sitting quietly on the other end of the bench, leaning forwards and cupping his face in his hands. His eyes were moist. He was trying to make sense of Tim's words. So many questions. What questions are okay to ask? He wanted to know details. How had it happened? What happened to the van driver? What state are the bikes in? Where was Zak now? Then, he knew what question to ask. Turning his head towards Tim, Trey inquired quietly, "What about Zika, Tim?" Tim was remembering the phone call from Zika's mum, two hours earlier. Her broken, sobbing voice asking the pastor to come to the hospital. Their rapid departure from the church, and their quiet but prayer-filled drive across to the Royal Marnic. Their heart-wrenching discovery about Zak, and their short-lived visit to Zika before he was whisked off for emergency surgery. He was remembering Zika's mum – her panic, her pain, her shaking. Their totally inadequate words as they prayed with her. The arrival of Zak's mum, wild-eyed, almost hysterical, utterly distraught. The doctor's clinical explanation that Zak had died before the ambulance crew even arrived, that he had almost certainly died instantly without any pain. Trey's voice interrupted his thoughts, repeating his question, "Zika, how is Zika?"

Tim shook his head clear and responded almost mechanically, "I don't really know. I saw him briefly before he went into surgery. He was sedated. Broken leg, broken arm, internal injuries. His mum's there, waiting, and Pastor John is with her. I think it's going to be a while before we know how Zika is...but Zak...Zak's mum is at the hospital, waiting for his dad to arrive, but..." He stopped speaking. He didn't need to continue. They all knew what he was going to say. There was nothing Zak's mum or anyone else could do. Zak was gone.

Trey's mind was racing. "Can we see Zika? Will they let us visit? What about Zak's parents? We can't just sit here. There must be something we can do?" The questions were tumbling through his mind. Then he noticed Joe. Joe was emerging from around the corner at the top of the car park, walking very slowly, hunched over with his head bent. He looked utterly devastated. Rudderless.

Despite Joe's treachery, Jason got up and moved towards him. Joe was one of his best mates, always positive, always fun. He was sporty, strong, always in control. But when Joe looked up briefly, his face was red; his eyes suspiciously moist. As Jason reached him, Joe said to him, "I'm sorry, I..." but he couldn't get further. He broke down. Jason held him. They stood there, at the end of the car park. Joe sobbing silently as Jason held him.

They had never seen Joe like this. Joe was never bothered about anything. He didn't cry when his leg was broken on summer camp. He made jokes and held a mock-funeral when his cat died. He was happy-go-lucky, fun-loving, risk-taking, outrageous Joe. And now, Joe was sobbing uncontrollably. Somehow, in the last two hours, the whole world had changed. The eight friends were broken forever. Seven friends, maybe even six if Zika didn't pull through. Max, Joe and the girls were crying. But Jason was filled with an aching yawning gulf. He could find no relief in tears. He and Joe were united in their torment. He didn't know how long they stood there, adrift. Time stood still. If God is real, he must have lost control, Jason thought wildly.

Eventually, Joe's sobbing subsided. Jason still held him. He wasn't sure what else to do. Then Joe began to regain control of himself   and slowly they drifted towards the bench – churned up, distraught, achingly empty.

Back at the bench, Trey was equally distressed. He felt so alone. The girls had known each other since they were babies. Jason, Joe, Max, Zak and Zika had been together for four years. But Trey had become part of this group only a year ago, and it was Zak who'd made it happen. Trey felt like he was an outsider – culturally and relationally. After the first three months of being snubbed and bullied in Year 9, these seven kids had accepted him into their friendship group. He loved spending time with them, he loved their banter, their openness, the way they spoke. But he never shook the idea that he was the new guy. He didn't have the deep ties they had. And now, seeing the deep grief of his new friends, he felt his own anguish was somehow unwarranted. If anyone had asked him who his closest friends were are school, Zak, Zika and Max would have been his instant response. He was just as grief-stricken as the girls looked, but he wasn't sure he had any right to be. Marcia and Kia were together on the bench. Jason and Joe were together in the car park. Tim was sitting on the other end of the bench alongside Max. Tim was a great guy and everything, and Trey enjoyed his leadership at church, but he felt he did not know him well.

So as this group of friends shared their agony, Trey didn't know how he was supposed to respond. Did Zak's death – the death of the one guy who had invited him into the group in the first place – now mean he was out of the group? Would this horrible churning knife stuck into his gut ever be removed? Suddenly, he yearned for his friends back in Charlotte. In his grief, Trey felt utterly alone.

Eventually, Jason and Joe reached the bench, walking side by side now, and saying nothing. Joe's face was red, but he didn't care anymore. Jason was tearless. The girls had quietened down, and Tim had composed himself and organised his thoughts. These kids needed to be together, but they also needed looking after, and they would need feeding. As he sat with them, he created a text group for their parents, and then sent messages explaining his plans. He promised they would all be home mid-evening. The parents were grateful for his help and readily agreed. Then he ordered pizza and drinks to the car park just above where they were sitting.

None of the six friends felt the least bit hungry, but when the delivery guy arrived half-an-hour later, having something to do together somehow helped a bit. And it wasn't long before they had devoured all the pizzas and were feeling a little better for it. They sat together, drinking coke and not knowing what to say. Sometimes, the tears of one person would start others crying again, but Jason remained tearless. Tim decided the time had come to talk a bit. His normal voice sounded harsh amidst the quiet horror of the evening.

"Okay," Tim said. "I know this is really hard, and I don't have any idea why this terrible thing has happened. But there are a few things I can help with. As far as the hospital goes, we can't visit today. There's nothing to be gained from visiting Zak's mum and dad, they will need lots of support and help, but that's for later. For now, they need space and time to be together in their grief. And Zika is in surgery and won't be out until tomorrow morning sometime, possibly later. Even then, he'll be sedated. Pastor John is there with Zika's mum, and they're just waiting and praying. She will not want interruptions from visitors today. Perhaps tomorrow – let's wait and see."

He stopped talking for a moment, giving time for the others to take in what he was saying.

"There's something else, too, though. I had a short conversation with Mr Mason earlier, and then a brief text conversation with him just before pizza. He says he would like to speak to you, Jason, if you're up to talking to him?"

Why me? Jason wondered to himself. He felt nothing – life seemed unreal, like watching things from outside himself as if he wasn't really a part of it. The change in Joe. Zika in surgery. Zak. He shook his head to clear it. It must be the shock, he thought to himself.

"You were one of Zak's closest friends," Tim explained. "Mr Mason has an idea about an assembly tomorrow at school, and he wants to tell you about it."

"Okay," said Jason in a flat mechanical tone. How could anyone think of going to school when this had just happened? Who could possibly study chemistry or Latin when Zika was in intensive care and Zak was dead? Tomorrow seemed a million miles away. School seemed further.

"Let me return his call," Tim replied.

He dialled the number, said a few words, and then handed his phone to Jason.

In a few seconds, Jason heard Mr Mason's familiar voice. "Is that you, Jason?"

"Yes, sir. Can I be on speaker phone so my friends can hear too?"

"Of course. That will probably make it easier all round. First of all, can I say how sorry I am. I cannot imagine the pain you are in right now."

Jason found Mr Mason's words weird – he'd only spoken to Mr Mason once, and that was when he had been caught climbing over the tennis-court fence. This Mr Mason was very different.

"Now, Jason, I know you don't want to think about this now, but I need to. Tomorrow morning, most of the kids from Raynesborough County will be back in school. Whether or not you and your friends choose to be in school in the morning is up to you and your parents – if you need a day or a few days out, that is fine by me – but whether or not you are there, the very first thing I need to do is speak with the whole school in a special assembly directly after registration tomorrow. Most students will have heard the news about Zak and Zika by then, but some will not. I will need to explain what has happened, and I will need to tell the students about the support we are putting in place for those who need it – extra counsellors, Pastor John, Tim and our school chaplain, as well as our tutors providing extra tutorial time during break and lunch. That support is, of course, available to you and your friends as well.

"I wanted to tell you about it because I don't want this assembly to make things harder for you. If you're in school, you may be excused from assembly if you wish, or you can be present and sit wherever you like, together as friends, or along with your tutor group as usual – whatever is easier for you. And then we're going to make an attempt to have a normal day. I know it won't feel normal, but we need to try. Does everyone understand what I'm saying?"

Jason looked at his friends. They didn't speak, but Max

and Trey both nodded. "Yes sir," Jason responded. Nothing would ever feel normal again, he was certain. He said, "To be honest, sir, I'm finding it hard to think about going back to school right now."

"Of course," Mr Mason said reassuringly. "You do whatever is best for you. Chat it over with your friends. I will be speaking with all your parents, so they're in the loop. And you may not believe this, but how you are now and how you are in the morning could be quite different. Perhaps the best thing to do is to see how it goes."

"Yes, sir. Thank you, sir," Jason managed to say.

"Please do whatever is best for you. The school will support you in any way it can."

"Yes sir. Thank you."

"I may see you tomorrow, and again may I express condolences on behalf of the whole staff team." Mr Mason hung up.

The group sat around quietly. Tim sat with them, sending the occasional text to reassure parents and respond to messages. Marcia was still crying, on and off. Joe had recovered himself. The time was coming to leave, but they didn't want to be apart and face the night alone. The trauma of the last few hours had driven them much closer together, and they weren't enjoying the prospect of facing their various families. So they sat at the bench, watching the sunset and wondering how they would get through the night. They thought of Zika in surgery. They thought of Zak. And tears flowed again.

18

Invasion

The Notalian offensive was not expected for another seventeen days, so when the Notalian army invaded two weeks early, Anasius was ill-prepared. It was just before 3 am that morning when messages came flooding into Arelard Castle. Xci1 was sleeping and Xci4, who seemed to sleep very rarely, was again sifting through the details of the defence plan which the eight friends had put together two nights previously. Work on the Crask / Tsarn border crossing had begun just fourteen hours ago along with various orders sent to Anasiun troop divisions stationed at the forts at Port Diblaine, Ducal City and at Xanver Naval Base.

Xci4 heard the shouts from the Communications Centre and moved swiftly from his study to find out what was happening. The big screen was providing live-feed using night-vision cameras. As he watched he became increasingly sickened. Somehow, Notalian troops were already at Xanver Naval Base, moving quickly, efficiently and with deadly force.

At Xanver, Anasiun troops had risen valiantly from their

sleep and rushed to put up the best fight they could, but they were horribly outnumbered and most were killed within the hour. Somehow, the Notalian troops had attacked from the sea. They had taken the breakwaters first, sunk more than half the fleet in the harbour, and invaded the naval base not from the south as had been expected, but from the north. Had the advanced radar and infrared screening of all craft within three miles of the harbour somehow failed to pick up on an invading Notalian army? At this juncture it was impossible to tell, but what was certain was that Xanver had fallen and Anasius was in trouble.

Some of the small screens were giving different views of Xanver, and some were reporting from other areas in Anasius, too. The camera feeds from Port Diblaine showed fifteen merchant ships docking, vessels which legally could carry only fresh produce and eight crew. Even as they watched, though, the ramps were lowered and, instead of crates of potatoes and vegetables, hundreds of Notalian troops swarmed out and moved swiftly into the city, killing everyone in their way and making for the barracks. Xci4 wasted no more time. He sounded the clarion. Within minutes, every Anasiun troop across the country knew that invasion was under way. They were dressing rapidly, logging into XSHC and awaiting information and orders. Arelard Castle moved from quiet calm to a place of feverish activity.

Xci1 arrived at the Communications Command Centre within four minutes of the alarm, dressed, wide-eyed and alert. He came directly to the command microphone, pressed the red upload button and said, "This unprecedented and unprovoked attack on our sovereignty is a clear act of war, sanctioned by the Notalian Royal Family and executed by the Notalian Liberation Army. I hereby authorise our troops across Anasius to proceed on a war footing. Follow your orders and may the might of Xcion the Sovereign save our nation from defeat." He released the button and looked around the communication centre.

Xci4 spoke up, "Your Royal Highness, I think we should activate extraction for the eight."

"I agree and so authorise. Extract them here, with immediate effect," Xci1 responded decisively.

Xci4 sat at a keyboard and fired off the relevant code.

On extraction, however, and much to the surprise of Xci1 and Xci4, only five of the group arrived in the communications hub of the Xcion Strategic High Command. Joe, Zika and Zak were absent – and the remaining five were clearly distraught.

Xci1 looked at them, unable to fathom why they looked so grief-stricken, and at a loss to know why the summons had not worked for all eight. He asked directly: "What is it? What's happened?" He guided them to some chairs and motioned for drinks to be brought.

Max explained. "Zak and Zika were in an accident yesterday. Zika is in intensive care following surgery." He swallowed. "Zak didn't make it." His eyes were moist, but he brushed his hand roughly across his face.

Xci1 went white. He sat down quickly. "Zak died?" he asked incredulously. "How can that be? He's so young. Why would Xcion take him now? And Zika? He plays a crucial role in Xcion's plan, of that I am sure. How did this happen? And what about Joe? Xcion has specific instructions for him. He should be here." His questions hung unanswered in the room. The friends looked at one another, and there would have been a long silence had it not been for the noise of the screens, the communication officers rushing about, the rapid-fire typing and the regular whispers into Xci4's ear. Despite their grief, and in spite of themselves, it was obvious to the five friends that something major was unfolding, and it looked bad.

Eventually Marcia asked, "Why are we here? How long is it since we were re-entered?"

Xci1 turned towards her. "Only forty-eight hours," he said. "And just over an hour ago the Notalian army invaded."

"But that's not possible," Jason protested. "They said three weeks."

"I know, Jason," it was Xci4 who spoke. "But I have it on good authority that the conversation you overheard was staged for you. Both General Qong and the Zagonite prince spotted you and, rather than capturing you and sending you to Crask, they elected for you to overhear a conversation which would give you entirely the wrong idea. You were deceived."

Jason went very red. "I'm so sorry. I had no idea."

"No, no," Xci4 was quick to reassure him. "You did everything exactly as you should have done. I was not scolding you. And, as you well know, everyone here in the command centre overheard everything just as you did, and they were taken in as well. But we have called you all here because we're in desperate need of help."

Xci4 went on quickly to detail what had happened in the past couple of hours, and the decision to extract them all. He wondered aloud briefly about why Joe was not extracted, but he didn't dwell on it and moved on to ask for help as they directed their troops. He turned to Jason.

"Jason, I am sorry to ask this of you, but Zak was Outer Warrior One, and he was lined up to lead the defence at Ruwark. With Zak not here, I need you to step up and fill his shoes." He knew this was a big ask, but he also had an idea that it might also help Jason, in some way. Jason still felt sickeningly empty. He still couldn't cry. The loss of Zak was too big, too awful to comprehend. But now Xci4 was asking him to step into Zak's shoes. How could he? Zak had graduated at the top of his class. Jason thought about the last twenty-four hours.

In that time, the friends had endured school assembly together. They had spent most of their out-of-school time together, too. Sometimes they had talked about Zak or Zika. Sometimes they cried. Sometimes they sat together silently. They had been due to visit Zika that evening, although last they heard, he was still asleep and they didn't know whether or not he was going to make it. Their world had fallen apart. And now, suddenly they were back at Arelard Castle. There was a crisis afoot. Anasius was on the brink of disaster, too. In a weird way, it seemed a fitting mirror to the distress of home.

Furthermore, here, they were not surrounded by those unaffected by trauma, by school students discussing their summer holidays, by quiet whispers and glances in their direction, or by people avoiding them completely because they didn't know what to say. They didn't find themselves on the bus surrounded by people who were carrying on with normal life. In short, at home the vast majority of people acted as if Zak's death didn't matter. Everyone seemed to think life could go on as it had before. They didn't understand that it couldn't, that nothing would ever be the same again. But here in Arelard Castle, everyone was upset. Everyone was facing trauma. In the past hour, everyone had watched neighbours, friends and relatives die. Everyone was affected. For these five friends, in some strange way being surrounded by this unfolding invasion and the horror of it somehow made their own grief easier.

Jason looked at Xci4. "You know as well as I do that Zak is..." He paused and corrected himself. "That Zak was a better man for the job than me. Outer Warrior One – I could never be that. I cannot possibly fill his shoes." He felt the raging emptiness in his stomach churn again. "But I am willing to do whatever I can to help. I will go where you direct me."

"Thank you," Xci4 responded. Another officer whispered in Xci4's ear. His eyes widened. "I need to tell you this," he looked at the friends. "As feared, Joe betrayed us, but the Notalians think he knows more than he's telling them, so they had taken him to Crask. He re-entered back home, as you know, but when we extracted him, for some reason it seems that he has been extracted back into the dungeons at Crask. I cannot fathom why."

Max, Jason and Kia all gave a sharp intake of breath. Marcia looked quickly at Trey, who said wearily, "Oh no, I know what that means."

Kia said, "We all know what that means. I..." but Marcia interrupted her.

"No, you don't, Kia. Trey really knows what that means."

Max, Kia and Jason looked at her and Trey, not understanding. "What do you mean? Trey?" Max asked the questions all three were thinking.

"I've been there," Trey said simply.

"What?" As Max blurted his question, the shock on his face was evident, and the others were equally stunned.

"At the end of my graduation, I was abducted and taken to Crask by Qinoda. They put me in a cell and I also spent a day in one of their torture rooms, an experience I'd like to forget but still have nightmares about. After my re-entry that evening, Zak and then Marcia came to help me." The tears were falling, but he managed to say, "In fact, Zak was the best friend anyone could ever hope for that evening. Without him, I don't know what I would have done. And now..." He couldn't go on. The tears were falling freely. But they all understood.

"Crask," Kia was almost speaking to herself. She was utterly horrified. "You were in Crask? And we never knew. How?" She trailed off. She was still opening and shutting her mouth, but no words came out. She had read about the dungeons of Crask and some of the horrific tortures done there. She had not been able to read it all, because it made her retch. And now her friend Trey was saying he himself had been tortured there? She could think of nothing to say, and neither could the others.

Trey, however, had managed to compose himself, and to the total surprise of everyone present, he said suddenly, "I'm leading a mission to rescue Joe from Crask."

"No," Xci4 responded. "That's suicide. We're losing enough people today. Joe is there because he betrayed us. He betrayed you – his friends. I absolutely forbid..." He trailed off because Xci1 had raised both his hands.

"Steady, Xci4," he said softly. He looked at Trey. "You have an idea, haven't you?" he asked.

"I think so," Trey said. "But it depends on secrecy." He spoke more quietly and they all leaned in to hear him. "What I have not told anyone is that when I was thrown back in my cell for the night, I landed by the wall at the back of the cell. For some reason I noticed that my arm was colder than everything else and I ended up examining the floor. It was made of dark grey flagstones, with some black cement or something filling the thin gaps around the stones."

"And?" Max interrupted. "You found that for the one half-flagstone under your arm, the gaps were not filled at all and the cold air was coming up through them."

Kia looked at him, "How come you didn't tell me that?" she asked, a bit too loudly, so that the nearest officer looked in their direction.

"Shhh, quieter," Trey said.

"I only worked it out later," Max explained, again in a low voice. Although, if he was honest with himself, he was really only telling a half-truth. He didn't know why he didn't tell

Kia. All he knew was that he wanted to keep it to himself for a while. "Sorry Trey, I interrupted you. What happened next?"

"Well, I did manage to open it, and there was a ladder I climbed down which ended at the floor of a long tunnel that disappeared into the distance. As I began to walk along it, the golden circle appeared and I was re-inserted."

"How did you open it?" Max asked excitedly.

"Wait a minute," Xci1 said. "Back up a bit. I'm not sure I know what you're talking about."

"I have no idea at all," Jason said, and Marcia nodded in agreement.

"Me neither," she said.

Max looked at them, and then explained in a voice not much louder than a whisper.

"As part of my study in the library, I came across an ancient book which described the construction, amongst other things, of Arelard Castle. The more I read, the more I realised that it was hinting at a tunnel system that ran from underneath Arelard Castle at least as far as Tsarn. It seemed that there are two access points into the tunnel from the dungeons below us. Kia and I went hunting for them, but had no success. We tried everything we could think of. Later, though completely accidentally, I discovered the access points, but I could not open them. It is a puzzle I could not solve (although it seems that Trey has solved it). What seems clear to me, though, is this: before the Western Land Exchange, Crask belonged to Anasius. If Trey made it into a secret tunnel in Crask, then it seems likely that the tunnels run all the way from here to Crask, and, therefore, perhaps also to Ruscorn Forest, Xanver, Tsarn and even Ruwark. We won't know until we've explored those tunnels."

Xci1 was shaking his head in wonder. "I have been studying Anasius all my life. I have travelled through all of it many times as part of my royal duties. I know its politics, its history and, I thought, all of its military secrets. And now, five youngsters from another world visit for a few weeks and discover things I know nothing about. Now I know why Xcion the Sovereign wanted you here."

Kia jumped in. "So if there is a tunnel system that underlies all of Anasius, and Trey knows how to access it, we might be able to insert troops at various key points without the Notalians knowing anything of our troop movements. That could change the tide of this invasion. It seems to me that exploration of the tunnel system is a top priority here."

"And," Trey said firmly, "I am running a mission to rescue Joe."

Xci4 hesitated. "I'm still not convinced that it's a good idea to lose you and whomever else to a mission unlikely to succeed right into enemy territory when we have just been invaded. We need all the help we can get."

Marcia rejoined. "And I don't see why you'd want to anyway. Joe was horrid to you and was suspended because of it. He's hardly your best mate."

"No, he's not. But he needs to be rescued as soon as possible, because what he's about to endure is something I would not wish on my worst enemy. More important than all that, though, is what you said, Your Royal Highness," Trey had turned to face Xci1, "you have specific instructions from Xcion for Joe, yes?"

"Well, yes, Trey. But..."

"Then we need to rescue him and give him those instructions. This is part of Xcion's plan, don't you see? If reading the Scroll has taught you anything, it is that Xcion the Sovereign is always in control. Always. So whatever we see happening on these screens, and out in Anasius, Xcion has not lost control. And part of his plan is for me to rescue Joe. So that's final." He folded his arms defiantly.

Xci1 nodded slowly. "Okay. The logic is good and fits with what we know to be true of Xcion. Thus, whilst I will need Kia and Marcia here to oversee XSHC strategy, I'm releasing you, Trey, along with Max to lead an exploration of those tunnels with almost immediate effect. I'll deploy six XSHC officers to assist you. As I have said, you, Jason, will be required to lead the defence at Ruwark, but we'll keep you here for another hour in case the exploration mission discovers that the tunnels run to Ruwark. If so, we'll send you that way, otherwise it'll be a road and subway trip which will be significantly more dangerous."

Kia spoke up. "Before anyone leaves, though, they need to be fully kitted for communication. I'll let you know how it works on our way. Is that okay?"

"Your thinking is flawless, as usual," Xci4 smiled. They followed Kia out of the room and Xci4 returned to a keypad in front of a large screen and continued sending orders and messages to the troop commanders.

Kia explained the communication system to them and

answered most of their questions.

Max asked, "Will those devices work underground?"

"I'm pretty confident they will because they work throughout the subway system, but we won't know until we try them. We need to get these implants as soon as possible – every minute lost is one more minute of Notalian savagery."

Jason looked around at them all. "What do you think, Max? Marcia? Trey?"

"I'm game," Max said simply.

"I guess so," Marcia was more hesitant.

"The let's get on with it," Trey said.

So they trooped into Rantukkan's study. He was already on his feet as they came in, and when Kia explained their purpose, he grinned.

"Of course," he said. "I knew you'd come around." He led them all to the little room Kia had been in a long time earlier, and then, one by one, each sat at the booth and the robot injected the implants. It was an operation that was virtually imperceptible. At the booth, each of them placed their chin on a pad and their forehead into a strap. Then, all at once, a little metal arm came from the side, touched their right ear, located the correct place, and injected the implant just below the skin. Then the same thing happened on the left ear. It hurt less than a scratch. And it took five seconds at most. Following the implants, each was given a gold ring which they put around their right ear. They had Scrolls clipped to the lapels of their new Anasius clothing, and then three of them returned to the XSHC whilst Trey and Max headed directly for the dungeons. They had a tunnel to explore.

At the communications centre, Kia and Marcia were allocated a desk and computer together. Kia pulled the tracking details for Max and Trey up on her screen right away.

"They're in the dungeons already," she said. "We need those six officers to catch them up directly. Please send them with torches. And Trey also requested a large pair of bolt-cutters."

The others looked at her. Whatever did he want those for? They shook their heads, but Xci4 gave the order, and six well-armed men set off at a run, with the torches and bolt-cutters as requested.

"Excellent," Kia said. "We'll be able to keep an eye on Max, Trey and the other six from right here. Since the tunnels are an extremely well-kept secret, I think it would be wise for no other computer in Anasius to have access to these tracking details. May I encrypt them for our eyes only?"

"Of course," Xci1 responded. "You're in charge of XSHC for now – I have a different job to do." He gave instructions to the remaining officers and then left the room.

With Jason hovering beside them, Kia and Marcia started the vital job of mapping out the progress of the invasion and where their new defences needed to be focused. For Jason, he spent the next hour studying the geography of Ruwark and trying to figure out how to defend it from the Notalian Liberation Army. It seemed an almost insurmountable problem.

19

The Underground

As they hurried down to the dungeons, Max asked, "How in the world did you open the access point? I tried everything I could think of!"

Trey grinned. "I used the Scroll!" he said simply.

"What do you mean?" Max asked as they headed down the steps. "I'll show you in a moment, assuming it works the same way as the one in Crask. We must do it before the officers arrive, so we don't give the secret away." When they got to the bottom of the steps, though, Trey's grin disappeared and he looked sick and scared.

"What is it?" Max asked. Something had brought a sudden change in Trey.

"It's this room. This layout. It's exactly the same as the dungeons of Crask. It brings those memories flooding back. The smell. The screaming."

"It's okay, Trey," Max said, trying to reassure him. "There is no-one down here at Arelard. Kia and I have spent some time here looking for entrances. And I've been here alone a couple of times, too. There's nothing to fear."

But Trey struggled to focus on the task. His mind was swirling with thoughts of the tortured prisoners, the overflowing bucket, the metal table where he knelt all day and wet himself. And then, somehow interwoven came the memory of Zak's death, looming over everything else like a thundercloud over the rain. His chest heaved. Tears fell again.

"Trey," Max said. "Trey!"

Trey shook his head to clear it and brushed his hand across his eyes. They were standing in the corridor close to the right-hand wall, just where Max had noticed the absence of icing sugar. Max spoke again, "Trey. I know it's awful – everything's awful. But we don't have time to dwell on it all now. We need to do our job." He pointed to the floor. "That's one of the flagstones we need – an access point to the tunnels. Now how do you open it?" They could hear the officers descending the stairs. Trey pushed the crowding thoughts from his mind. Swiftly, he removed his Scroll, guided it into the crack and slid it smoothly across. There was a soft click, the flagstone fell away, and Max shook his head in amazement as Trey replaced his Scroll onto his cape. The Scroll was only just back in place when the first of the six officers rounded the corner of the corridor and saw them standing there beside the hole in the floor.

"Well, would you look at that, Kenny," one of them said, astounded. "I've worked here all my adult life and thought I knew everything there was to know about Arelard. A secret access-point to a tunnel? Who'd have thought it?"

The officers made some comments, but Trey and Max

were already descending the ladder, and the officers followed quickly.

Within two minutes all eight of them were standing in a tunnel around three metres wide and over two metres high. It disappeared into the distance in both directions, east and west, and a double metal rail gleamed on the ceiling. Ahead of them was a large open archway, and standing within it was what looked like a carriage, connected to the rail at the top.

One of the officers gave a shout of recognition.

"Hey – that looks exactly like a tram from Tsarn," he said. "Except that it's powered from above rather than from below. I drove one of those for six years before being recruited by XSHC. Riding that should make our journey much faster, assuming it's fully charged. Come on, guys." They ran up to the vehicle and it did, indeed, look a bit like a tram. There were seats for perhaps fifty people inside, plus a driver's carriage at the front with space for three. The officer was speaking again. "Welcome aboard the secret tunnel tram of Arelard. I will be your captain today and you may call me 'Your Excellency'." He grinned and jumped into the driver's seat. The tram doors slid silently open.

"We'll call you Derek, just like always," another officer said gruffly, but they were all smiling as they climbed aboard.

Derek said, "Come on, you lot. Max and Trey – I need you guys up front. Be quick – we have a country to save!"

Within moments, and with hardly any noise at all, the tram doors closed and the tram moved in a smooth arc, out of the archway and towards the tunnel facing east. Then

Derek released the break and the tram took off.

The speed was difficult to ascertain, but the rapid acceleration was breathtaking and drove their heads back hard into the soft headrests. The tram must have been pretty fast. Max was looking concerned.

"Hey," Derek said, having seen Max's face, "Don't worry – it's pretty safe."

Max queried, "What if we meet something coming the other way?"

Derek laughed. "Yes, I guess that would be pretty terminal, wouldn't it? But we reckon this tunnel has been unknown throughout Anasius for three centuries, so the chances of meeting anything else in it are pretty titchy. Anyway, these trams have an excellent computer system that warns of any movement within two miles of us. Look," he pointed to the radar screen on the dashboard, "nothing!" Max relaxed a bit, but as someone who hated rollercoasters, this was not a journey he was enjoying.

Seven or eight minutes after their journey began, the tram slowed and came to a stop. Ahead was a black wall. To their left was a ladder, just like the one they had descended from Arelard.

"Check it out, Kenny, would you?"

"I can't," Kenny responded. "I don't know how to release the flagstone."

Trey pointed to the opposite wall. There was a sign that read simply, "Broward's Mine".

"Where's that?" Trey asked.

"Well now, how can that be?" Derek asked, wonderingly.

"Broward's Mine is miles east of Arelard Castle. No wonder it felt fast! I wonder whether this tunnel leads anywhere else?"

"We need to find out, and quickly," Trey said. "See if there's any other way to go, other than straight back to Arelard."

Max was tapping on his Scroll. "You getting this, Kia?" he asked. "Yes – what in the world happened? You suddenly disappeared off our screen, so I'm guessing the tracking doesn't work in the tunnels."

"We're on this electric tram which runs through the tunnel. We're at a place called Broward's Mine." He heard Marcia draw a breath.

"Broward's Mine?" Marcia questioned incredulously. "That's thirty miles east of here at least. Zoom out, Kia."

There was silence for a moment.

Then Kia said, "Pretty impressive tram. I calculate your average speed to have been somewhere around 220 miles-per-hour."

"Really?" Max responded. "I mean, it certainly felt fast."

"Never mind that," Marcia interrupted. "Were there any tunnels off to the north?"

"Hang on a second," Max said. He turned to the officer beside him. "Hey, Derek," he said. "Are there other routes from this tunnel? Does the map tell us?"

Derek tapped a few buttons and the result was a map of Anasius with a few arrow-straight lines in red over the top. "There you go," he said.

"I don't get it," Max responded.

"Those red lines. I reckon those are tunnel routes. We've certainly just travelled this one." He tapped one of the lines with his finger. Trey and Max scanned the map quickly. Then Max spoke to Kia again.

"The news is excellent," he said quickly. "It looks like this tunnel runs from Broward's Mine in the east, under Castle Arelard and across towards Parson's Edge on the Notalian border in the west. More importantly, from Arelard there is a line running north all the way to Tsarn. Tsarn looks like the main hub, from which lines run to Port Diblaine and on east to Ruwark, over to Tranton and on northwest to Xanver, and to Ruscorn Forest and on through Ducal City, finishing at Crask."

He heard Kia's breath of thanks she offered up as he spoke. She said, "So that means Jason can go to Ruwark and be there within the hour, our troops can move across the country at top-speed without being detected provided we can get them into the tunnel system in the first place, and then you and Trey can head to Crask to try and rescue Joe."

"Yes," Trey said. "But we can only transport around fifty at a time."

Derek interrupted. "Actually, if they're the same as the trams at Tsarn, and they certainly look and feel that way so far, then you can link an extra one or two cars behind this front carriage, so that you can transport up to 150 at once. It doesn't slow the thing much in Tsarn, but then we weren't travelling at this speed then, so I can't be sure. Perhaps there were extra cars behind this one when we left?"

"Find out," Kia instructed. "I'm calling our key troops to

gather at our safe-houses in Tsarn, Xanver, Ruscorn, Ducal and Ruwark. Plans will need to be executed as soon as you return. Derek, I'm wondering. Are there any others at XSHC who can drive a tram?"

Derek thought for a moment, "I don't think so."

"What about people not at Arelard, people also trained at Overlord Academy, I mean?"

"Sorry, I can't think of anyone."

Kia sighed. "I guess that means Derek's going to be doing a lot of driving for the rest of this battle."

Marcia looked at her. "I can drive," she said unexpectedly.

"What?" Kia looked at her, disbelievingly.

"For my training, I travelled through virtually all of Anasius, getting to know the geography as well as the history and political setting and so on. As part of those travels, I was trained on the subway trains, the royal yacht and the trams. I can drive all three with reasonable competence."

Trey whistled. "The royal yacht? I've never even seen it! One of these days, you need to tell us the details of your training," he said.

"Sure, but not now. Get back here asap," Kia ordered. "Marcia and Jason will meet you in the dungeons."

As they were talking, Derek had pressed a few buttons and the tram had reversed swiftly around a ninety degree curve and then moved forward around a second curve so that it was facing in the opposite direction. Within seconds, they had accelerated rapidly away from the mine and back towards Castle Arelard. It did not take long.

"This tram might just help turn back the invasion," Derek

said. "I've lost friends already to the marauding Notalians. They will never possess our country." The final sentence was said with a steely determination which Trey recognised. Derek was reciting a sentence from the Overlord Academy, "They may invade our land, they may take our possessions, but they will never possess our country."

When they alighted a few minutes later, they examined the side tunnel the tram had come from originally. What they discovered was even better than they had hoped. Not only did it contain more cars which would hook-up to the front carriage, there was also a second tram with its own two cars behind it. Once Marcia and Jason came down, they could move troops around at double speed, and the rescue of Joe could happen simultaneously.

They called up to the command centre and Kia told them Marcia was just above them. Derek and the other officers remained where they were, and shortly they were joined by twenty others, all battle-ready. They got themselves sorted out into the right trams, and Marcia took her place in the driving seat of the second tram. Jason, along with twelve officers, shot off down the north tunnel to Tsarn and on to Ruwark where they were to lead the defence of the royal city.

The remaining troops headed for Tsarn, Xanver and Ruscorn Forest. Various troops were to be collected and delivered en-route, as per Kia's instructions from the XSHC. But Trey, Max and Marcia were going on to Crask, along with the sixteen troops they were due to pick up in Ruscorn Forest – all recent graduates and students of the Overlord

Academy. One minute after Jason's departure, Marcia pressed a button and their tram shot off down the same road to Tsarn. It was 6 am, and their journey took an hour.

20

A Rescue Attempt

It had only been two hours since their arrival, but Kia was fully into her role of strategy commander. She had tied her hair up in a tight business-like bun on the back of her head, rolled up her sleeves and settled at the main desk in the communication hub. She had absorbed all the pertinent information coming into Arelard, and she was confident of a few things the Notalians would want to achieve next. She also discovered how the Anasiuns had been attacked by surprise from the sea. The strategic defence technology system beyond the breakwaters around the cliffs comprised radar, sonar and laser technology. It provided real-time data displayed both at Xanver HQ and also at XSHC. Any craft, large or small, naval, military or pleasure, would be logged and tracked as soon as it entered the three-mile zone.

No craft had been logged that night – the sea was quiet, as it usually was in the pre-dawn hours of summer. But the Notalian invasion had been cunning. They had run most of their vessels right around the Handed Islands and then south towards the shoreline. Half of these moved off east and into the harbour. The other half travelled in-shore and nestled right under Carliggan Cliffs, just outside the three-mile exclusion zone. The tide was high, and their boats were shallow-beamed, so they had floated only four or five metres off- shore. Then, kitted with carefully prepared grappling hooks, they had sent their elite naval task force to scale the cliffs and secure ladders for the remaining troops to climb.

Simultaneously, they had 8000 troops hidden inside cargo ships and heading for the docks at Port Diblaine. So with the 7000 troops standing atop Carliggan Cliffs, they then launched their offensive. In addition, a further 2000 troops, still undetected, had scaled Ralligan Cliffs to the west and were marching rapidly south towards Ruscorn Forest. The three-pronged attack from the north was a brilliant piece of military strategy, executed flawlessly in the dark, and it had taken the entire country by surprise.

Notalian troops were inside Fort Tula before anyone knew the invasion was under way, and by then it was too late. All ninety-seven Anasiun soldiers at Fort Tula were slaughtered, most of them in their sleep. It was brutal and sickeningly efficient. No-one survived long enough to raise an alarm.

Half-an-hour later, it took only twenty of their naval special forces to attack and overcome defence positions on the eastern breakwater, and again they succeeded without raising an alarm. So it was only when the main force of 5000 Notalian troops were marching southwest to Xanver that the alarm was raised. An hour later, they launched a full frontal attack on the naval base, with the Notalian soldiers killing mercilessly everyone they found. At the same time, their twenty naval special force troops on the eastern breakwater donned diving gear and quietly and systematically scuttled the Anasiun fleet as it rested at anchor in the harbour. Whilst the Notalians did take a number of casualties in their attack on Xanver, they did not lose many, and the Anasiun troops were horribly outnumbered. The result of the fighting was inevitable.

Kia watched all the events on the screens in the XSHC communication centre. She kept an eye on all the Anasiun soldiers via the tracking devices they carried, and on her personal screen, she paid careful attention to the progress of her friends in the tunnels beneath her. Within six hours of her arrival, Port Diblaine had almost completely fallen and Xanver was not going to hold out much longer.

Kia knew that whilst the taking of Xanver and Port Diblaine dealt a severe blow to Anasius, Tsarn was the heart of the country. Tsarn held the electrical power hub, distributing power from the Dagon Dam, the tidal power station off-shore from the Handed Isles and the power generated by Taston and Ruscorn forests. Tsarn held the Anasiun Supreme Court and judiciary, along with its correctional facilities and its dungeons. And Tsarn Tower was the seat of the Anasiun government, overseen by the Xcis and, ultimately, by the king himself. Arelard Castle held XSHC, and so it was a desirable target to be sure, but Arelard was remote and extremely well fortified. Tsarn was a bustling city full of civilians with a military presence only in the background, and Tsarn was the centre-point of Anasius geographically, too, with direct and multiple access points from the east, south, west and northwest. Holding Tsarn was the key to the survival of Anasius. If Tsarn fell, Anasius was overthrown.

As soon as Trey, Max, Marcia and Jason had taken off in the trams, Kia had been feverishly sending orders and updates to the Anasiun troop commanders, urging a convergence on Tsarn. One of Kia's first orders was for their troops to use the subway system in order that their movements might be invisible to the Notalian Liberation Army. She drew as many troops as possible from Ducal City, Ruscorn Forest, Tranton and the smaller towns and villages west of the River Dagon, leaving a much smaller force to repel any invasion of those places. But taking troops from Ruscorn Forest was a serious miscalculation.

At 10:30 am, Notalian troops arrived at the north end of Ruscorn Forest. They penetrated deep into the forest over the next hour until they arrived at the clearing by Xanver Overlord Academy. And there, with flamethrowers brought for the purpose, they made short work of setting the forest ablaze. The treehouses and training rooms and kitchens and living spaces were set alight, and Xci2 was killed as he tried to battle five Notalian officers armed with flamethrowers. He had no chance. The Notalian Liberation Army drove northwards, burning trees as they went.

Even worse, Joe's words to the couple at the border had been passed on to Zvarak and then Qinoda, with devastating result. A task force of twenty Notalians, riding in an adapted tanker, skirted the forest and approached it from the south, just above the Tsarn / Crask turnpike. They located the tree Joe had pointed out and proceeded to concentrate their flamethrowers on the base of it, burning through the outer layer of wood and revealing the elevator shaft down to the subway. Their tanker had two compartments of liquid. The first compartment was water, which they used to douse the flames and put out all the sparks. Following that, they emptied the second far larger compartment from the tanker straight down the shaft. That compartment contained petrol.

By 11 am, almost all the people of Ruscorn Forest, including the few who had escaped from the Overlord Academy, were sheltering in the subway, a position Kia had approved since the Notalians did not know about it. Marcia, Trey and Max had already picked up Xci3 and thirty-seven Overlord Academy officers on their way to Crask, but the others, like Xci2, were either trying to defend the forest or had recognised the futility of such action and descended to the subway for safety whilst awaiting further instructions. Those defending the forest were all dead within the hour.

At 11:15 am, a huge quantity of petrol had been poured down the subway shaft at the south end of the forest. And when a senior special forces officer directed his flamethrower a few metres from the shaft, it took less than a second for the petrol to ignite. With a ground-shattering explosion, the shaft collapsed, as did the subway for a few metres around its base. The burning petrol sucked the oxygen from the subway like a vacuum sucking up the dirt, and two-thirds of the subway became an instant death-zone. Of the 750 or so Anasiuns from the forest, only twenty-eight survived unscathed, with fifty-five more carrying various degrees of injury. From her seat in XSHC, Kia watched it all happen and wept.

The tram to Crask ran at lightning speed. They had stopped for three minutes in Tsarn, where they had explained to one or two senior officers the mechanism for opening the access points, but sworn them to secrecy. At Tsarn, there were three access points – two in the Tsarn Correctional Facility dungeons, exactly as at Arelard and Crask, the other in the basement of Tsarn Tower. Troops were dropped off in Tsarn, and Trey, Max and Marcia then headed west for Ruscorn Forest. It turned out that the entrance to the tunnel system at Ruscorn was immediately behind the B-group door in the Underlord Academy, a place known by only a handful of Anasiuns. Kia had provided the instructions to Xci3 who had mobilised the ten allocated officers from Overlord Academy and taken them down the secret elevator shaft to the Underlord Academy – a place only Xci3 had seen before. They were sworn to secrecy, joined by six Underlord Academy officers, and then set foot on the tram as soon as it arrived at Ruscorn. From there, they shot off to Crask, ignoring the platform at Ducal City.

By 10:30 am they were below the dungeons of Crask. Max and Trey instructed the men to wait down the tunnel for five minutes whilst they opened the access point and tried to ascertain the situation in the dungeons and the location of Joe.

"If we're not back in five minutes storm the dungeons," Max instructed.

Trey looked white, and the Academy officers did not know why, but Max did. Trey was remembering what lay above the flagstones. They tiptoed up the tunnel to the ladder, carrying the bolt-cutters with them, and Trey climbed it. He removed his Scroll and very gently slipped it into the crack, holding the flagstone up as he did so. There was a soft click, and he felt the weight of the stone on his hand. He lowered it slightly and felt the change in air temperature. He listened intently.

There was hardly any sound at all. He thought he could detect the sound of fitful breathing, but he was not sure. He lowered the flagstone to vertical and slowly lifted his head. This was the cell he had been in, but now it was empty and the door stood open. There was no sign of a guard, and no sound of torturing going on. He descended the ladder again.

Then he removed his shoes and motioned for Max to do the same. He knew that walking silently on a stone floor is difficult when wearing shoes, but in socks it was a different matter. Then he climbed the ladder again, risked a look into the cell, saw nothing and then hoisted himself up through the hole. He was now standing in the cell where he had been incarcerated not long before. The stench was overpowering. Horrific memories were flooding his mind. He shook his head and swallowed hard, forcing himself to breathe quietly. Max was right behind him and was almost knocked over by the stench, trying not to gag. They tiptoed to the door and took a quick look into the corridor. Nothing. They moved silently into the corridor of the dungeons of Crask, expecting any moment to be sprung upon by a devious prison guard. Now Trey was certain he could hear fitful breathing, and it was coming from one of the other cells. They tiptoed along the corridor, checking the cells as they went. And in the third one lay Joe, on his side with his back to the door, curled up and shivering. From behind, he looked reasonably healthy, but Trey was not fooled. Somehow he needed to get Joe's attention whilst, at the same time, stopping him from making a noise. Max tugged Trey's sleeve to get his attention. He motioned for them to return to the first cell. Trey followed and they moved back, through the first cell, down the hole and quietly to the foot of the ladder.

Then Max whispered right into Trey's ear words which he struggled to hear, even then. But he got the gist of it. Five minutes later, Joe started suddenly in his cell. He had heard a clink from his door behind him. He turned over slowly and saw no-one. But he did see a small slip of paper on the floor inside his cell. He picked it up and read it.

"Make no noise. We have come to rescue you. If you make any noise, all will be lost. We think we are safe for a few minutes. Be prepared to run. Your friends, Max and Trey." He read it again, incredulous.

Was this some kind of sick joke? he wondered. How could Max and Trey be outside my cell? The guards must be baiting me. And they've got it all wrong – Trey is hardly a friend of mine. I burned my bridges with him over a year ago. Yes, we're part of the same friendship group, but Trey doesn't want to know me, not really, not after how I treated him. And now I've added insult to injury and betrayed them all. No, this must be another attempt to break me, to humiliate me. And whatever the note said, I can't possibly run. Apart from my cloak, I'm pretty much naked, in bare feet, cold, and haven't eaten for nearly two days. I'm so thirsty, I could hardly make a noise if I wanted to, and I've never felt this weak.

He tried to block out the memory of yesterday, when he'd endured the screaming of a fellow prisoner for ten hours with no let-up as he sat helpless and shivering in this stinking cell full of tears, dried blood and human filth. He didn't want to think of it ever again, but it was seared into his brain like a branding is seared onto a cow. And he couldn't get his head around this note. It was undeniably real. He was holding it. But it was incomprehensible. Interrupting his thoughts, though, as if in some kind of twisted dream, Trey appeared in the doorway with a grin on his face and waving a pair of bolt-cutters. Max's hands appeared just below the padlock and Trey applied the cutters to the shackle. The two boys were almost silent, but Joe noticed one or two quiet straining noises from Trey as he heaved the handles of the bolt-cutters together. There was a distinct ping as the shackle broke, resulting in a tense wait in utter silence for two minutes.

When they were certain the coast was clear, the shackle was carefully removed and Joe's cell door swung open silently. In a moment, Max was at his side, helping him to his feet. Together, he and Trey supported Joe down the corridor and into the cell with the dropped flagstone at its end. Joe's eyes were wide with astonishment. Trey descended the ladder first. Then Joe went next, and he was so weak, he lost his footing and fell the rest of the way and landed on Trey. Trey tried to catch him, but found him too heavy and crumpled underneath him. Trey's right leg got bashed in the process, and he was almost entirely winded. For a second or two, Trey tried to untangle himself and Joe tried to get up, but then Anasiun officers were at their side, and strong hands got Joe and Trey back on their feet. Trey was rubbing his bruised leg, wincing and trying to get his breath back. Joe was trying to apologise, and Max's comment as he descended the ladder was a murmured, "You couldn't have been louder if you tried!" Within seconds they had a brief and silent reunion. And, thought Joe incredulously, Trey seemed genuinely happy to see him.

Max briefed the guards in whispers and they disappeared up the hole into the dungeons. Trey helped Joe towards the tram. Joe wondered whether this was some kind of strangely vivid dream. Rescuers had appeared like magic at his door, opened his cell door, led him down a hole in the floor into a tunnel beneath, and now he was getting into this weird vehicle, but the water Marcia handed him felt real enough and there seemed to be some kind of plan under way which he knew nothing about.

One of the officers returned from the dungeon and approached the tram. He spoke in a normal voice, and it sounded horribly loud after the near silence of the last fifteen minutes.

"There is no-one else on the dungeon level of the Crask Compound," he announced. He noticed Joe again, carefully keeping himself covered with his cloak, and said to him, "There are some clothes in the luggage rack above you." Then he continued, "Because it is so quiet in the dungeons, we're wondering whether the keepers of the compound have mostly been enlisted for the invasion of Anasius. If so, we might be able to take the compound and push east to the border. But the four of you will be needed back in Tsarn. And remember to stop at Ruscorn to pick up the remaining Overlord Academy officers."

Joe was looking increasingly sick. "Invasion? But that's not for another couple of weeks, isn't it? How?"

Trey was pulling his arm. "Not now. We can talk on the way. This officer needs to join his men."

"Indeed," the officer responded. "Just do what Kia instructs you, and I'm sure you'll learn more on your return journey. Oh, and there's food on the tram as well – Kia insisted on it being taken aboard at Tsarn."

"Come on," Marcia urged. "We have to go."

"I'm glad you're safe," said the officer, looking again at Joe. "One day I want to hear of your adventures. But now I must run." And with that he ran back to the ladder, climbed it swiftly and was gone. By the time they met again, there was far more to be told than any of them could have imagined.

Joe's voice cut through their thoughts. "I need to stay here," he announced.

"I beg your pardon?" Marcia questioned. "Trey put this mission together to rescue you. We travelled all the way here and infiltrated the Crask Compound, possibly the most dangerous place in Notalia. And we did it to rescue you. That was the whole point of the exercise. You're coming with us." Trey and Max were nodding their agreement.

"No," Joe contradicted. "I do not deserve rescue. Trey, I treated you like dirt at school, and I got suspended for it. Then, even worse, I betrayed all of you to the Notalians. The whole thing is my fault. The invasion, the fighting in Xanver, maybe the fall of Anasius itself. All because I..." He hesitated. "All because I wanted power and prestige in Notalia. I am a traitor. Traitors deserve punishment – torture, death. I belong in the dungeons of Crask. I need to stay."

Trey grabbed him by the shoulders and stared into his face. "Joe, look at me. The Notalians were planning to invade Anasius well before you ever came along. Don't be so pig-headed as to think that you brought that about. There was always going to be fighting in Xanver and lots of other places as Anasius sought to defend herself. None of that is on you. And yes – you were awful at school and I was afraid of you. I didn't like you and I didn't want to be anywhere near you. But then you were suspended and since then you've been a lot nicer. Here in Anasius, we all know you betrayed us. We figured it out when you failed to return to the Council of War and ran off down the road to Tsarn – Traika spotted you leaving. We knew you were going to betray us. So don't think we were unaware of your actions. But I, for one, don't believe your words to the Notalians will have made a huge difference to their war effort. And even if they did, we had to come to rescue you, Joe. No-one deserves what the Notalians do to people in Crask. No-one. I know it better than you might think. So you are coming with us, whether you like it or not."

Joe tried to protest, but the others would have none of it and he was too weak to fight, so he resigned himself to his fate and settled into his seat. Marcia started the tram up, and they pulled away from Crask. The rescue had taken just under thirty minutes, it was 11 am, and they were off.

21

Zika Awakes

Zika couldn't remember what day it was or what he'd been doing the day before or whether or not he needed to get up. Usually he felt groggy first thing in the morning, but this was different somehow. His room was brighter than usual, and more echoey. He tried to think, but his brain wasn't working properly. He became aware that he was aching all over, his left leg hurt a lot, he couldn't move his left arm and he seemed to be attached to something. He moaned, screwed up his face and tried to open his eyes. This was definitely not his bedroom. And here was his mum, right up in his face. She seemed to be crying. Why in the world was she there? He tried to sit up and shake the sleep from his head, but he gave up that idea almost as soon as he started – the pain was intense. He sank back into the pillow.

"Shhh, Zika. Don't move. Rest...not quick...worry..."

Zika drifted off. In the next few hours he drifted in and out of sleep. Slowly he began to have longer periods of wakefulness, if his mushy-brained painful episodes of consciousness could be described as being awake. He discovered that his mum wasn't always the only one in the room. Sometimes there were others – white-cloaked, speaking in low tones he couldn't hear. Occasionally he seemed alone. Sometimes he felt that he'd been asleep for quite a long time; at other times it was more like five minutes.

At one point early on when he woke up, he began to suspect things. Maybe the Notalians had discovered him. Perhaps the figure in the room wasn't his mum. Maybe they were experimenting on him. Perhaps the war had started. All kinds of conspiracies suggested themselves to him. He tried to move again, but the pain made his brain reel. Darkness returned and he slept again.

Each time he came around, he managed to stay awake a little longer and slowly he began to piece together what was going on. He figured out that he was in hospital and must have been in some kind of accident. Certainly he was in pain. He discovered that his left arm was in plaster and heard one doctor talking about surgery on a compound fracture of the ulna. His stomach hurt and he discovered a heavy bandage wrapped around his abdomen, but he didn't know what had happened for it to be there. And his left leg was tightly bandaged, too, and painful if he tried to move it. Try as he might, he could not remember what he had been doing before the accident.

And Zika had a crucial role to play in the war.

22

Trench Warfare

In the second tram, Derek, Jason and the officers with him raced to Tsarn where they picked up fourteen Overlord Academy graduates. From there, they hurtled under Maycross without stopping and arrived at Ruwark at around 8:45 am. There was only one access point in the city, and that was in the basement of the Summer Palace. The troops at Ruwark were expecting them and were awaiting further instructions.

Ruwark was more like a small town than a city, and there were very few fortifications. There was a good-sized guard-post immediately outside the city walls on the Maycross Highway, and there were some minor defences at the City Hall. But the only properly defended building was the Summer Palace itself, with its high walls topped with battlements, its top-grade electric-fence perimeter and its radar detection and laser defence system. Defending Ruwark as a whole was not going to be an easy task, especially since 180 troops had squashed in with Derek and taken the tunnel tram back to Tsarn to help with the defence effort there. He was thinking the best thing might be to retreat to the Palace and defend that alone, although if the Notalian Liberation Army took the city and surrounded the Palace, it would not be long before retreat back into the tunnels would be the only option. Jason elected to contact Kia back at XSHC before proceeding.

He came straight to the point. "Exactly how many troops do I have?"

Kia's response had devastatingly clarity. "143, including yourself."

"And how many troops from the NLA invaded Port Diblaine?"

"Just over 8000."

"So even if the vast majority of those 8000 focus on taking Tsarn, I could still be facing hundreds, if not one or two thousand?"

"I'm afraid so, yes. But I have already made some preparations for you which will help."

"With 143 troops, I will hardly have enough men to keep watch at the walls, let alone fill the guard post and do anything at all to defend City Hall. It seems to me that the only defendable building in Ruwark is the Summer Palace. We may be able to hold that, but otherwise this whole thing seems to be an exercise in suicide."

"Again, I'm sorry Jason. You don't know what it's like back here watching Anasiuns get slaughtered by the dozen and being unable to do anything about it. And we do have a plan, remember."

"I know, but it's pretty desperate. And it's all very well

for you to say, Kia. You're sitting safely in a castle directing people to their death. Out here, with 143 troops, we're going to get thrashed. I'm going to die, Kia." Jason was trying to make her understand.

"Jason, please. I don't have much time, but let me explain it to you. If Tsarn falls then Anasius is overthrown and unless we all get re-entry in time, we all die here. So I need to throw as many troops into Tsarn as possible. On the other hand, Xci1 is adamant both that you need to be at Ruwark and that you have a key role to play there in defending the city. The city, not just the Palace. So I've given you as many troops as I dare – more than I should have, really."

Jason sighed wearily. "When I die, I'm going to haunt you forever."

"Don't be ridiculous Jason," Kia responded. "And don't you dare die. I forbid it. Zak's death is more than we can hope to cope with. You dying would be..." she checked herself. "Would be unconquerable."

"You're nice, but totally deranged," Jason replied. "I'll try not to die, just for you."

"Just stick with the plan."

"Sure," Jason resigned himself. The plan was insane, with an impossibly short timeline for completion. He needed to get right to it.

Most of Ruwark's 11,000 citizens had already been given orders to go to the subway via the three well-known access points. Hundreds were already there, filling the benches, cafés and restaurants, and spilling out onto the station platform areas. Kia had also asked the citizens for some volunteers. She needed 700 citizens, 400 untrained and 300 trained manual labourers, competent with farm machinery or on building sites. Volunteers came thick and fast, and the troops in the subway had to prevent more citizens offering their services, for which Kia was very thankful.

The 400 citizens unskilled in warfare were deployed along the top of the city wall. Their instructions were simple: any sign of Notalian troops and they were to sound the alarm both to her and Jason, along with details of their location and speed. They were to stay on the walls as long as they dared, and then head down to the subway themselves where they would be safe from the marauding Notalians.

The 300 farm and construction workers were deployed within the city wall. It turned out that the plan for Ruwark had not changed since they'd prepared it forty-eight hours earlier. And since that night, every piece of heavy farm machinery, every vehicle built for excavation, and every machine designed for road construction had been in constant use. The achievements of the last forty-eight hours outside the city wall were staggering. The people of Ruwark and the surrounding farms had already dug up perhaps 100 metres of road, making a vertical-edged trench eight metres wide and almost four metres deep. This trench had then been lined in synthetic biodegradable sheeting – something the Anasiuns had developed over 100 years earlier. They had built a wooden roof over the tunnel, and fitted it with electronic charges connected to a switch box with two spark points: one in the command post, the other just inside the city walls.

At this point, Jason observed, the resurfacing machines outside were already at work laying the road over the top of the wooden boards. But even with all the machines working at once, it looked like it might take some time yet. Inside the city, the plan was that the trench would continue north of the command post all the way to the sea wall, albeit smaller. This two-metre wide and three-metre deep trench was only two-thirds dug, and a good 400 metres had not even been started. The volunteers inside the city were working flat out to dig it, along with all the excavation vehicles from outside the city walls now that their tasks there were complete. The only vehicles remaining outside were laying road as if their lives depended on it. Which they did.

The plan was that as soon as the trench in the city was completed, three huge pumps would begin pumping sea-water over the sea wall and into the narrow trench, from where it would flow through the trench inside the city and then begin to fill the space under the road outside the city. If it got completed in time, then a great surprise awaited the Notalians, who were bound to approach Ruwark by this highway, the only main road into the city.

Once the front part of the army was over the trench, the charges in the roof would be blown, the road would collapse into the water, and a good part of the invading force would fall into the trench. As a result, whilst they were preoccupied with trying not to drown, Anasiun archers would shoot from the city walls, hopefully bringing the Notalian Liberation Army to a standstill before it stepped foot in the city. Driving into the city would certainly be out of the question once the trench roof was blown. Since the unannounced Notalian invasion of Anasius a few hours earlier, hundreds of volunteers had been put to work on the trench in the city. On his arrival, Jason immediately contacted those in the subway and asked for more. Dozens of citizens came willingly to help with the excavations, almost all adding to the digging effort with machinery and even with garden forks, spades and shovels. Collectively, there was a massive effort made to get the trench dug and lined right up to the sea defences so that they could start the pumps and get the water flowing.

Jason calculated quickly – assuming the Notalians had commandeered goods vehicles in Port Diblaine or Maycross, and had departed as soon as Port Diblaine was overthrown, the journey to Ruwark would take them four or five hours at the most. Kia informed him that City Hall in Port Diblaine was overrun by 6:45 am, meaning that goods vehicles full of Notalian soldiers could arrive at Ruwark anytime after 10:45 am. And it was already 10:15.

Jason took out his Scroll and asked to contact the chief engineer at the sea wall.

"Where do we stand?" he inquired.

"The pumps and hoses are all in place, but the trench has not yet reached the sea wall. In fact, it is being dug in sections, and last time I checked, some of those in-between sections are also incomplete. The nearest section to us will require another couple of hours or so at least, at the rate we're working."

"We don't have that long," Jason responded. "Find out

how far the other sections are from being completed. And as soon as a section is complete, send the volunteers from that section to work on other sections not yet completed – that should speed up the process." He thought for a moment, then asked, "Do you have any more ducting you can fit to the city-side of the pumps? That way we wouldn't need to dig the trench all the way to the wall, only as far as the ducting reaches."

"Sir," the engineer responded. "We have already connected up everything we have."

Jason thought again, and then asked suddenly, "How long is the section nearest you, at the sea wall? How much still needs to be dug?"

"Sections are each eighty metres long. The section here has only the thirty metres furthest from the seawall dug so far."

"Okay," Jason said. "Get that thirty metres completed and lined and, for the rest, just dig a shallow trench, maybe half-a-metre deep – as much as you can get done in the next fifteen minutes. Meanwhile call up every spare tram driver from across the city to meet us by the sea wall in twenty minutes, bringing every vehicle they possibly can with them. And give me an update on the other sections within the next five minutes. Let's pray the Notalians are late."

"Yes sir." The engineer scratched his head wondering what Jason had in mind, but he made the necessary calls as instructed.

Twenty minutes later, Jason arrived at the sea wall in a

city tram. But he could not get very close, because there were goods vehicles and trams blocking his way. He jumped out and climbed on top of the tram he was riding in. A minute later, courtesy of Kia's communication skills back at XSHC, he was connected to every implant in the vicinity.

"Citizens of Ruwark and Overlord Academy officers," he began. "I know that you were expecting to be instructed by Outer Warrior One. I regret to inform you that he died around forty hours ago." Jason tried to keep the emotion out of his voice. "As a result, I have been drafted to fill his position here." He turned away from the loudhailer. "Chief engineer, what is the situation with the other trenches in the city?"

"All are completed except for the one nearest the wall. There are at least 120 workers there now with virtually every excavator in Ruwark and the surrounding farms either here or en-route, and the officer in charge thinks they can complete it within the hour."

"That's still too slow," Jason responded. He spoke again through the loudhailer. "Almost certainly, the NLA are sending a significant attacking force to Ruwark as we speak. They could arrive any time from now. As a result, I don't think we have time to finish this trench here, so listen carefully. I want every city tram lined up alongside where the trench would be, head to head, bumping up against each other. It looks like we should have enough trams to line both sides of the remaining fifty metres. Then the plastic sheeting needs to be laid over the trams and down to the ground on each side. Every other vehicle needs to be lined up bumper to bumper behind the trams on each side. We're attempting to make an above-ground channel for the water to flow into before it falls into the trench that's already been dug. We need to get it done in ten minutes flat. If your vehicle is not a tram, move it away from here to let the trams through until the sides of our improvised channel are in place. Xci3 here will direct you. As soon as they start getting in place, the chief engineer here will organise plastic sheeting to cover them, and every other vehicle needs to be backed up behind the trams to stop them toppling outwards under the pressure from the water."

An engineer shouted up at him excitedly, "When they're in place, burst the tyres!"

Jason looked at him quizzically for a moment, and then he understood. He repeated the words into the implants.

"Tram drivers. When your tram is in place, let down the tyres. Other vehicles too."

Then, for ten minutes, there was utterly feverish activity. At the end of it, the plastic sheeting was in place, each side lined with trams, and a clear channel through which the water could flow.

Jason called up to the chief engineer, "Get me the officer at the city wall." Within seconds, Jason heard a voice in his ear.

"Hello," Jason said. "Is this the Overlord Academy officer in charge of the trench just inside the city wall?"

"Yes, I'm Dez. And it's nearly finished, the plastic sheeting is going in one end, and we've just got to widen the channel at the wall end so that it empties clearly into the channel under the road."

"Great work. You have about three minutes to pull all your workers out of the trench, whether it is finished or not. The sea water pumps are being turned on here any moment."

"But sir..."

Jason interrupted him. "Sorry it will not be as great as you had hoped, but we are out of time. The NLA are probably only a few miles down the road, and if we don't get this water moving then all our hard work will have been for nothing."

"Yes sir."

Jason turned to the chief engineer. "Start the pumps now," he ordered.

Jason raced back to the guard post, instructing thirty Anasiun officers to join him there. By the time they arrived, water was already pouring into the trench under the road, but it would take hours to fill and he knew they didn't have hours. They prayed for more time.

He ordered all remaining officers trained in archery to be on the city wall, focusing on the newly resurfaced highway. Kia informed him that he had fifty troops in this capacity. The remainder were soldiers skilled in hand-to-hand combat, she told him, so they were to form the infantry. Jason groaned. A force of sixty men was pitiful against hundreds of Notalian warriors, but it was all they had.

At 11:20 am, the water came gushing past the city wall and began filling the trench under the road. At 11:50 am they heard the first cry from the volunteer look-outs at the city walls. Jason turned up the volume on his implant.

"Goods vehicles have just crested Gleeson's Hill, thirteen miles from Ruwark."

Immediately, Jason responded to all personnel. "All vehicles must return to the city now," he urged.

"Sir, we still have fifteen metres or so left to surface," a foreman protested. "Our machines are quick – it'll only take ten minutes or so." Jason thought for a moment.

"Okay. Any vehicle not in use must return here now. As you come down the new road, leave all the traffic cones. It will be obvious something has been going on, so the cones might simply suggest that new roadworks have been underway. That might help reduce suspicion. To those still surfacing the road, the NLA will be here in under fifteen minutes if they're travelling at full speed. So you are to return here ten minutes from now, whether the road is completed or not. And may Xcion the Sovereign be with you."

Miraculously, it was only eight minutes later the final resurfacing machine trundled into the city. Jason watched, deeply relieved, as they passed the guard post where he sat. The road was complete, steaming with its new tarmac. But before he could give the order for the gates to be closed, something else happened. Something that Jason was not prepared for and didn't understand. Twelve heavy-goods tankers, one after the other, trundled out of the gate, driven by volunteer citizens of Ruwark, and driving directly towards the coming Notalian Liberation Army.

He tried to contact them via the implants, but he simply could not get through. After trying repeatedly, he gave up and dialled Kia back at XSHC.

"Kia," he called her urgently. "Kia, there are tanker drivers heading out of Ruwark straight at the battle line. I can't get through to them on the implants to bring them back. I don't know how this happened."

"Jason, be calm," Kia responded. "That trench will take a long time to fill, so the longer we keep the NLA away, the better chance we have of success." Jason's head swam.

"What? Didn't you hear me?"

"Yes, Jason. Did you hear me?" Kia responded.

"You mean...You mean you knew about this?" he demanded.

"Yes. They called the XSHC privately, because they knew you wouldn't agree. Whilst the trench was being completed, they discussed how to defend Ruwark from such a large force. They knew more time was needed if the trench trap was going to be a success, and after some discussion they decided that if they all drove out of Ruwark together, they might be able to block the road. The terrain either side is not suitable for heavy goods vehicles, so the NLA would either have to move to let the tankers pass or they would need to stop them and drive them off the road. Either way, it will take some organising and provide you with a bit more time. The drivers have loaded their tankers with as much fuel as they could find. They're going to pretend they're unaware of the invasion and are taking supplies to Maycross. They probably won't be believed. In essence, though, they're just going to do everything they can to get in the way and hold everything up."

"But they'll be killed," Jason protested.

Kia sighed wearily. "Yes – I think they probably will. I said as much to them. But they said that saving the city was more important. And they told me that whether I agreed or not, they were going to do it anyway."

"So what did you say?" Jason demanded. "You didn't sanction it, did you?"

"This is war, Jason," Kia responded. "Their plan is a sound one, if somewhat suicidal. I cannot have them giving up their lives for the sake of their country whilst knowing that they were disobeying direct orders. So I sanctioned it, yes. On their request, I blocked your signal to them so you could not call them back – they were concerned you would find a way to persuade them of a different course of action. That's why you couldn't get through. I wished them Godspeed. And I prayed for success. I'm sorry, Jason."

Jason shut the call down in horror. How could agreeing to send twelve civilians into frontline battle possibly be the right decision? It made him sick to the stomach. He was glad it was Kia making such decisions and not him. He could never sanction such a mission. Somehow, though, he realised that Kia could see the best course of action, the bigger picture, and made the right strategic move even when it meant that more Anasiuns might die. Grudgingly, his respect for her deepened.

The last of the tankers was well outside the city wall, so Jason gave the order and the huge iron gates were closed. They locked into place above the roadway, so the approaching army would need to open them or remove them somehow. This left only the guard-post exposed, where Jason was watching proceedings unfold, but it was also bristling with Anasiun troops well-prepared for close combat. The guard-post was battle-ready, its reinforced steel defences raised. The city gates were sealed and the steel defences raised there too, with archers along the walls above the road. And under the roadway, the trench was slowly filling with water. The charges were set, and Jason had appointed an officer to push the lever and blow the charges on his command.

Via the implants, Jason instructed all citizens of Ruwark and all Overlord Academy officers to pray for the unarmed tanker convoy heading out to meet the Notalian army, like mice defying a pride of lions.

23

Forest Fires

Trey, Joe, Max and Marcia were hurtling back under the Tsarn / Crask border. Joe had changed, drank a gallon of water, eaten most of the available food and then gone to the back of the tram where he lay down and promptly fell asleep.

Kia's voice sounded over the implants. As Joe slept, she explained to the three friends what was on her mind. "Tsarn, the capital city of Anasius, has four major access points. This means that despite it being a walled city, defending it against attack is a complex operation. There are guard-posts at the gate for Tranton Road and the gate for the Tsarn / Crask turnpike. The guard-post beside Finiston Bridge protected it against access from Maycross over the river, and the final access-point was the Empress Ferry Terminal which received the ferry from Port Diblaine. Tsarn is bordered on the east by the River Dagon, but the city wall runs almost directly into the river, with only the narrowest of paths, now almost unnavigable, between the reinforced ramparts and the water."

Marcia was nodding along as Kia spoke – she had seen all these things for herself in her training.

Kia continued, "It is clear that the primary attack from the NLA is going to be two-pronged. Some troops will be arriving from Tranton, following their overthrow of Xanver. Hundreds, if not thousands, of others will come from Port Diblaine. Both sets of troops will be fatigued. They'll be tired from battle and tired from the lengthy journeys they have already endured. But they will also be full of adrenaline, knowing that if they take Tsarn, then Anasius will belong to Notalia once and for all.

"There are four Overlord Academy officers due to lead the last stand at Tsarn. Xci5 will lead a team to destroy Finiston Bridge, thus preventing an easy attack from the highway to Maycross. He's already in place in Tsarn and preparing his team. Outer Warrior Two will mount a defence at the guard post for the Tsarn / Crask turnpike. Derek is driving him and his team and they are almost in Tsarn already. They will be moving directly to the guard-post in a few minutes' time, and Xci5 is briefing the team on their defence strategy. We are not expecting many NLA soldiers on the turnpike. Outer Warrior Two should be able to defend that position successfully."

Kia paused for a second before she continued. "The Empress Ferry Terminal defence will be overseen by Xci2, supported by Joe."

"What?" Max almost shouted his disbelief. "Joe betrayed Anasius. It's foolishness to trust him to now defend us!"

Kia disagreed. "On the contrary. Joe knows what the NLA

are capable of, so he really understands the freedom we're fighting for. And yes, Joe did betray Anasius, but the most damaging result of his betrayal was on himself. He knows that now, and having been rescued from Crask by you, I reckon he is keen to cement his loyalty to Anasius."

"But Kia," Marcia said, clearly worried, "Joe's fast asleep now. And he's still recovering from being in Crask. He's eaten a bit and looks a good deal better than he did at first, but he's not in any fit state to go into battle."

Kia interrupted her. "I'm sorry, Marcia. I'm sorry to you all, but I don't have time to explain further. Please ensure Joe gets implants at our facility in Tsarn, and tell him I'll give him further instructions then. Your role, Marcia, is troop movement via the tram-tunnel system. There will be a lot of driving in the next few hours, most of it crucial to the success of the mission. Is that okay for you?"

"Kia, I'm very willing to play my part, but it would be nice to understand what's going on." Marcia was increasingly concerned.

"I know, Marcia, I know, and thank you. I will keep you all as informed as I possibly can. Max and Trey, your role is to oversee defence at the guard-post on the Tranton expressway at Tsarn city wall."

"No, Kia," Marcia pleaded. "The two most dangerous places to be are the Empress Ferry Terminal and that guard-post, and you're putting three of our friends in those very places? We have no idea what's happening with Jason, and we've already lost Zak." She swallowed the lump in her throat, but mentioning it brought recent and extremely painful memories to all four of them.

Kia responded, "Put those thoughts aside. Zak would have been here leading the fight, and he would want us to do the same. We are at war. There is not time now to consider our own pain. Instead, we must rise to do what Xcion the Sovereign calls us to do. There'll be time enough for pain and sorrow later on."

Max interjected, "But I'm not a warrior, Kia. I haven't been trained at Overlord Academy. What can I possibly do at the guard-post apart from get myself killed?"

"Let me explain. In Arelard Castle library, you have read the two-volume text on Anasiun warfare, yes?"

"Yes, but..."

"And you understand the electronics behind the auditory warfare project, yes?"

"Again, yes, but how will that help at the guard-post?"

"Max, you need to think really hard. If high-frequency soundwaves could be projected along the expressway, that would disable the oncoming troops somewhat, would it not?"

"Yes, but it would disable us, too!" Max objected.

"I'm wondering whether it would be possible, using the implants, to counteract any ultra-high-frequency noise?"

There was silence for a few moments, as a slow smile crept across Max's face. "That's a genius idea. Let me work on it. And I'll need some guys to help me." Max's mind was racing.

"Done," said Kia, pleased he thought it could work. "Trey, you will spearhead the repelling force at the guard-post. I can't think of anyone else to do the job. I'm supplying a total of over 500 troops. Judging by the speed of the NLA soldiers moving from Xanver, you'll have a few hours to prepare. Wait. Sorry, I have to go for a moment – we have a situation unfolding in Ruscorn Forest. I'll get back to you shortly." And Kia was gone.

The friends looked at each other. It was unbelievable. They were being instructed by one of their friends to fight in a real war. A war that looked unwinnable. A war in which many had already died.

Ten minutes later, Joe awoke and looked puzzled for a moment before he remembered where he was. He sat up, feeling much more human. He had another drink, and Max explained to him what Kia had said over the implants. Joe spent a few minutes taking it all in, already feeling much stronger, but unsure whether he had what it took to defend Tsarn.

A moment later, Kia was back online and speaking to them. She had managed to hack into the tram's intercom so that Joe could hear her, too. Her voice crackly through the speakers, she relayed some terrible news. News that left them shocked, white and even more sick to the heart.

"I instructed all citizens in Ruscorn to take shelter in the subway, because we had intelligence that NLA troops were approaching the forest from the north. Shortly after our warning went out, those troops invaded the forest and penetrated as far south as the clearing. From there, they set the Overlord Academy ablaze. Some Overlord Academy warriors, including Xci2, fought hard to defend it, but swords are no match for flamethrowers, and those warriors were killed. From the clearing to the northern edge of the forest, the NLA are burning the forest to the ground.

"Even worse, on the south edge of the forest the NLA found the secret entrance to the subway, opened it, poured gallons of petrol down it, and lit a fireball that caused the collapse of the shaft. It looks like a huge shockwave rippled down the tunnel, and the fire sucked the oxygen from most of the subway system. The vast majority of those taking shelter in the subway are dead." They heard a catch in Kia's voice. She was struggling to keep the emotion out of what she needed to say. "You are instructed to pick up the surviving warriors from the tunnel entrance in the Overlord Academy, and take them to Tsarn. The few citizens remaining, and the injured, will be cared for in the Overlord Academy hospital. We believe they will be safe there. The next few hours will be decisive in whether or not the Notalian invasion succeeds and Anasius falls. We need a miracle to repel this invasion now. Our troops have been decimated."

The four friends in the tram absorbed this news with horror. Joe was white-faced, and throwing up into a waste-bin he had grabbed. His shock was deeper and more guttural, and the others were worried about him. Trey was trying to bring some comfort to him.

"It's okay Joe," he said. "It's not your fault. We need to focus..."

But Joe interrupted him hoarsely. "You don't understand," he sobbed. "It is my fault...You should have left me in

Crask...I am the one who told them about the secret shaft into the subway system in that tree...It was me. If I hadn't done that, those Anasiuns would still be alive." His chest heaved and tears were falling fast as he tried to speak. "I didn't just betray you who are alive...I betrayed all of those Anasiuns who are dead. I betrayed Zak and he's gone, too. I can't..." But he couldn't go on, and he retched again.

The three friends didn't know what to do or say. Hundreds dead because of Joe? Who could live with that kind of guilt?

Max said suddenly, "But Joe, how did you know about the secret door? We didn't know about it, and we've done a shed-load of study."

Marcia spoke up from the driver's seat just in front of them. "I knew about it. In fact, I visited it as part of my Anasiun tour. It was a secret known by many of the Overlord Academy graduates, too."

Joe had stopped vomiting, but was still crying. He managed to say, "I saw Zak and Gloria use that elevator shaft on the day Zak first arrived in Anasius. And I told Zvarak exactly where it was, precisely which tree contained it. He'd never have known otherwise." Joe was sitting on a chair, clutching his stomach, and rocking back and forth as he tried to get the words out.

Max thought for a while and then said, "That is true. There is no getting around it. But the NLA knew about the Overlord Academy and always planned to destroy it and to burn the forest down. Their intention from the very beginning was to slaughter the citizens of Ruscorn

Forest. We never imagined they were plotting the kind of savagery we've seen over the last three or four hours. The commitment to mass slaughter; the refusal to take prisoners; the failure to provide any kind of warning or offer terms for a bloodless invasion – none of those things have anything to do with you. Those Notalian savages," Max spat the word out, "are displaying an evil we could never have imagined. Yes, Joe, you showed them the entrance to the subway. But no-one could have envisaged the way they would use that information and the catastrophic results. That is not your fault. And I don't believe you wanted to betray us either, whatever you might say. You might have behaved abysmally towards Trey, and you might sometimes make very bad decisions, but I do not believe you decided, of your own free will, to abandon us at Arelard and betray us to the NLA. Tell me I'm wrong." Max was demanding now and as he spoke Joe's sobbing subsided, and he looked up.

"No," Joe said shaking his head. "I betrayed you to protect myself." Briefly, he told them the story of the couple at the café on the Crask / Tsarn border, the knife pressed into his neck, the requirement for him to report to them each week. "I thought I could handle it. But in reality I was more interested in protecting myself than in protecting Anasius."

Trey spoke up, "Yes, Joe, you were. But if you had not been, you would be dead. And that is definitely not the master plan."

"How can you talk of a master plan when Ruscorn Forest is going up in flames and Anasius is being overthrown?" Joe said. "Seems to me like everything is out of control. I've made everything a whole lot worse. And I've no idea how we can even begin to put things right." Another few tears fell, but Joe sniffed and wiped them away.

Trey shook his head, "No, Joe. That is not right. There is a master plan. All of this has happened for a reason, a reason we don't yet understand. And whatever the case, Xci1 told us that you had a vital part to play in the defence of Anasius. Seems to me you've not played that role yet. You cannot redeem yourself. You cannot undo and put right your actions of the past. But you have been rescued from the death you deserved. And now you can live in the light of your rescue and fulfil the role set out for you. That is where your focus needs to be." He turned to look at Marcia and Max. "And that is where our focus needs to be also," he said. "We're heading to Ruscorn Forest to take aboard any we can, and to help any who need it. And then we're going to Tsarn. Kia has told us what we need to do when we get there. So, Joe, stop beating yourself up – it's time to be a warrior on the right side of the battle."

Joe's head moved slowly from side to side. "Trey, I have no idea how anyone could forgive what I have done. Especially you. And yet here you are, the one I humiliated and betrayed, asking me to get alongside you and fight with you? How are you doing this?"

Trey breathed deeply and smiled faintly. "Perhaps I have spent longer in the Scroll than you have," he suggested. "I know what humiliation and defeat look like, it is true. But Xcion the Sovereign knows better than the both of us. And he's rooting for you as well as Marcia, Max and me. It's not my place to question his judgment. Our role is to follow orders and to do so to the best of our ability. So, whether you like it or not, you're one of our friends. And as such, we're going to stick together and fight this war." Trey's steely determination was infectious.

They arrived at Ruscorn Forest a few minutes later. Joe had taken some time to compose himself and clean himself up, and he drank some more water and finished off the food. For Joe, recovering fully from his experiences in Crask, and from the knowledge of his betrayal of Anasius and the resulting death of so many people, was going to take a long time. And for all of them, underneath everything, although they tried not to think about it at the moment, they were still reeling from the death of Zak and the knowledge that Zika was in hospital and may not survive. But they tried to put all that out of their minds for now. They had jobs to do.

When they stopped at Ruscorn, they did not pick up everyone. Some were left behind to care for the injured at the Underlord Academy field hospital. The rest, though, were trained soldiers, determined to turn the tide of the war. So they jumped on-board, determined and battle-ready. Marcia released the brake, and they raced for Tsarn.

At 11:50 am they heard the news that the Notalian Liberation Army was advancing on Ruwark and would arrive within fifteen minutes. This was really worrying because they knew that Jason was leading a very small Overlord Academy resistance army against them. The friends prayed desperately for Jason's success.

Kia spoke up again, "Joe, I know you don't want to hear

this, but since Xci2 lost his life fighting in Ruscorn Forest, you are now the one who needs to spearhead the defence of the Empress Ferry Terminal."

"What?" Joe asked incredulously, "how can I possibly do that? Xci2 was a great warrior with defence experience. All I achieved as an Overlord Academy graduate was betrayal."

"Yes, Joe, you did betray us. But you are the most experienced Overlord Academy graduate amongst us and Xci2 intended for you to be his second-in-command. He believed deeply in your capabilities and therefore I do too. Also, you are an athlete with particular prowess in swimming, and that skill is central to the defence of Tsarn. Let me explain the plan to you."

Joe listened as she spoke, and admitted that it was a clever idea. After Kia had finished, he said, "The plan sounds like it might work, but can't you send someone else? I'm not a military leader. I'm pretty tired. And I've proved I can't be trusted. Why would any of them listen to me, knowing what I've done?"

"Because they trust Xcion the Sovereign. Here at XSHC we are all in agreement. You must spearhead this plan. And, if I may be so bold, these are orders from your commanding officer, not suggestions from your school-friend."

"Okay, okay," Joe said wearily. "I thought I'd be dead by now anyway, so I guess I've not got anything to lose."

The conversation came to a close, and an hour later they arrived at City Hall in Tsarn. As at Ruscorn Forest, the majority of the citizens of Tsarn were taking refuge in the subway system, but the tram-tunnel system was a separate entity entirely, still utterly unknown to most Anasiuns. Marcia brought the tram to a stop at a large intersection. The tram-tunnels radiated out from this point across all of Anasius, and so the paved area beside the crossings was really the hub of the whole system. When they arrived and moved up into City Hall, the place was swarming with Anasiun Overlord Academy graduates and officers, all waiting and preparing to fight the Notalians.

As soon as they arrived, they were swamped with questions about Ruscorn and Crask, which Max and Trey tried to answer as best they could. Within a few minutes though, the large crowd fell silent as all their implants came to life simultaneously and they heard the voice of Kia back at XSHC explaining the strategy for defeating the Notalians. She explained that Xci5 and his team were already at Finiston Bridge, and that the bridge was going to be destroyed to prevent access to Tsarn by that route. Xci5's team would then defend the guard-post on the city wall there, in case any of the Notalians tried to enter by crossing the river.

Kia continued, "Outer Warrior Two will lead eighty troops to defend the guard-post at the Tsarn / Crask expressway. Those eighty troops have already been assigned and they are en-route to the guard-post right now. For everyone here, 700 are assigned to the Empress Ferry Terminal, where they will be led by Joe, and just over 500 will mount a defence at the Tranton Highway guard-post on the city wall, led by Trey. The remaining troops have various assignments around the city, especially City Hall here, over at the administration buildings, and at the subway entrance points to protect the citizens sheltering below. Listen carefully to your orders," Kia instructed, "and beware that almost certainly the NLA offensive will begin within two hours from now.

"Finally," Kia said to all those gathered, "they may invade our land, they may take our possessions, but they will never possess our country. I wish all of you Godspeed and great success as together we seek to defend Anasius against the NLA for the honour of Xcion the Sovereign in whose name we fight."

24

A City Teeters

It seemed to take an age for the convoy of tankers to meet the advancing army. Jason was surprised those around him couldn't hear his heart as it tried to crash out of his chest. His muscles were taut and he discovered he was holding his breath, watching things unfold on a big screen in the guard-post, via some powerful electronic binoculars mounted on the roof. The roof held twenty-four archers who were all excellent marksmen, and there were more archers at the first floor windows. On the ground floor, troops highly trained in hand-to-hand combat waited, watching the screen on the back wall. In reality, the meeting of the vehicles took only a few minutes.

The tankers were travelling in a 5-4-3 formation, the front rank of five tankers filling the entire roadway. The Notalian Liberation Army were approaching in trucks they had stolen from Port Diblaine. This was good news, because the trucks from Port Diblaine had a top speed of 50 mph – that's why it had taken so long for the Notalians to arrive at Ruwark.

When the army and the tankers were still three or four minutes apart, a young man got down from the front truck and then climbed up onto its roof. He had shoulder-length black hair over which was clamped a bright silver peaked helmet and he carried a curving sickle at his side. Jason recognised him instantly from his reconnaissance mission in Ruscorn Forest a week previously. He was Qinoda, Captain in the Notalian Liberation Army. Qinoda barked some orders and then dozens and dozens of troops poured out of the first twenty vehicles in the column. Then the vehicles rolled forward again, with the infantry marching off to the side as the trucks moved out towards the tankers.

As the tankers approached, the trucks showed no sign of slowing or swerving. It seemed that a head-on collision was inevitable. This was an insane move on the part of the NLA – the tankers were massive vehicles, at least twice the size and weight of the trucks, so whilst the tankers would probably be damaged by a head-on collision, the trucks would come off far worse. And anyway, the result of a collision would be a blocked road that could take hours to sort out.

Now sitting on the roof, Captain Qinoda recognised the folly of their advance and again called a halt to his vehicles. He barked some orders to his infantry, and over a hundred archers armed with crossbows took up positions on the roadside. They drew back their bowstrings, aiming to kill the drivers and then try to bring the tankers to a halt and get them off the road.

The drivers from Ruwark were sitting as low as possible in their seats, only just able to squint over the dashboard at the advancing Notalians. They had seen the foot-soldiers and archers and had locked their doors and shielded themselves as much as they could. But they were very vulnerable, with only glass windshields protecting them from an advancing army.

In moments, the air in front of the trucks was filled with bolts from the crossbows. As the bolts began to hit, the fixed-blade broadheads had no problem penetrating the windscreens. Jason knew the drivers had only seconds to live. Then, almost in unison, all five drivers of the first row of tankers were lying on the cab floor in the tankers, jamming the accelerators to the floor creating the biggest problem they possibly could for the Notalian army. Jason discovered later that all the tanker drivers had disconnected the brake pedals before embarking on their suicidal mission. As a result, a minute later when all the drivers of the first five trucks had died, their bodies lay atop the accelerator pedals and the tankers ploughed mercilessly forwards into the advancing trucks.

Qinoda realised he had made two mistakes. First, he had misjudged the commitment and planning of the tanker-drivers. Secondly, he had failed to notice that there were more tankers behind the first five. The first row had filled so much of the road that their arrow formation had hidden the tankers from behind. He reacted quickly, sending orders to his drivers and his infantry within the vehicles. His troops swarmed out of the remaining vehicles as the tankers ploughed into the first trucks in the long stretch of Notalian troops and trucks on the highway.

It took Jason a moment to understand what the archers with the crossbows were shooting at, but then he saw the tanker at the very front jolt as two of its tyres burst almost simultaneously. It slewed across the front of one of the tankers beside it, and they collided. The two tankers screamed along the highway together, their engines wailing and the metal of one of the cabs scraping along the road. A second or two later, Jason and his troops heard the sickening noise of the crash and of tangled metal as the tankers collided head-on with the first of the Notalian trucks. Almost simultaneously, the fuel in the tankers ignited. The sound of the explosion made the guard-post's walls shudder, and they were nearly two miles away. The tanker on the far side of the road careered off the highway and ploughed into the soft verge, killing a few Notalian soldiers, and coming to rest fifty metres later with its back end still hanging across part of the highway. The nearest two tankers had flat front tyres too now, defenceless against the barrage of crossbow bolts. The one closest to the edge of the carriageway raced off the road and ploughed into the ditch. The two tankers that were well and truly ablaze and locked together came to rest a further hundred metres up the highway, having crashed their way through another five vehicles en-route. They took up half the highway and left a train of devastation behind them. The final tanker slammed right into them head on. It veered skywards, almost in slow-motion, and then fell back onto them both before its fuel-tanks ruptured and there was another almighty explosion.

The drivers of the following tankers had made a brave

decision as soon as they realised what was happening to the tankers ahead. They jammed the accelerator pedals to the floor and leapt from their cabs, taking their chances with the road, the other racing tankers, and the Notalian archers. Of those seven drivers, one was struck and killed by another tanker within moments of jumping from his cab. The remaining six made a desperate run for cover across the open country. The Notalian army was focused almost entirely on the unfolding spectacle of tankers crashing into one another and into their troops and vehicles, with the resulting explosions and fireballs. But Qinoda, who was now utterly livid, suddenly noticed their departure, and barked out a brief order. The fifty archers on their side of the highway began shooting bolts in their direction. At a distance of at least 120 metres, accuracy was out of the question, but accuracy was hardly required when dozens of bolts were coming simultaneously. The slowest running driver was killed within moments. The second was hit first in the shoulder, but he managed to stumble onwards nevertheless. Another bolt, though, hit his right thigh, bringing him crashing to the ground, and a third bolt hit him in the neck. He died about a minute later. Another driver was hit by a bolt in his left arm, and another driver was struck a glancing blow to the leg, but both they and the final two drivers were almost completely out of range by now, and they continued racing back towards Ruwark, despite their injuries.

As soon as he saw them running, Jason shouted orders. The steel defences were lowered and the gates of Ruwark opened enough for a truck to race out towards them. Within two minutes the four drivers reached the truck, it did the fastest three-point turn Jason had ever witnessed, and raced back to Ruwark at top speed. The gates clanged shut behind the truck and the steel barriers were raised again. Jason and his compatriots turned back to the screen to find out what was happening.

Amazingly, the whole episode had taken under fifteen minutes. But now the Notalians had a problem. Whilst five tankers were off the road, the other seven were blocking the highway, stuck and burning fiercely. In addition, quite a number of trucks had been hit by the tankers and were in varying states of disrepair. Some would never drive again. Others still moved but were severely damaged. And from the view they had, clearly dozens and dozens of Notalian troops had died or been injured in the carnage, especially those in the centre of the column, where troops had not managed to get out of their trucks before the tankers careered into them. It was going to take a long time to clear the road, and the Notalian army did not have suitable equipment for dousing the fires, let alone removing tankers from a roadway. It was obvious that the only way now for the Notalians to advance was on foot.

Even as Jason and the others inside Ruwark's walls realised this, Captain Qinoda had regrouped and gathered the troops into marching order. They were skirting the burning vehicles and would soon be back on the road. Jason calculated they were under two miles away. The bravery and sacrifice of the tanker drivers had won the Anasiuns nearly an hour. An hour of water pouring into the trench. An hour of preparation for defending the city. And they had also won the anger of Qinoda. As any Overlord Academy graduate knew, fighting an angry opponent made your task significantly easier. Anger inhibits clear-thinking and slows the formulation of strategy.

It was because of his anger that Qinoda did not think to divide his troops and attack the city at various places along the walls. Instead, his entire focus was on the highway, the gates and the guard-post. This increased Ruwark's chances of success, although it meant the danger to Jason was significantly greater. As they watched the marching troops, Jason tried to do a count. He realised that whilst perhaps 300 had died back on the road, there were still upwards of 700 men marching toward the city, armed to the teeth.

Twenty minutes later, Jason called for his troops' readiness. The Notalians were marching along the new stretch of road, and would soon be at the guard-post. They were still too far out for the archers on the walls to have a hope of hitting them, and Jason was keen to keep those archers hidden until the last possible moment. As the troops approached the guard-post, Jason's heart began pounding wildly in his chest and he felt he could hardly breathe. The tension in the air was electric. The only sound was the increasingly loud tramp, tramp, tramp of Notalian boots marching down the road, led by a red-faced Qinoda with his swinging sickle.

Jason reiterated to the archers to hold their fire, even though most of them could now find a target. He wanted as much of the column of soldiers as possible to be over the trench and as much water as possible to be in the trench before he launched their attack. Then, when Qinoda and those beside him were within spitting distance of the guard-post, Jason shouted the command to blow the road, and his officer pressed the lever.

For one silent, sickening moment, nothing happened at all. The troops continued marching, weapons out and slightly startled at the sound of Jason's shout. The archers still waited on the city walls and Jason and his men took a few final breaths before combat began. But then there was a long low rumble and the Notalians began to break rank. A second later, the middle of the road collapsed inwards and pandemonium broke loose.

Most of the Notalian army found themselves falling into a huge trench which was now more than half-full of water, with more water pouring in all the time. The archers from the city walls and from the guard-post were shooting frenziedly. Many Notalians close to the guard-post fell, and those who had escaped the collapsing trench were felled with arrows from the wall. Because the trench walls were almost vertical, climbing out of the trench alone was impossible. Many Notalians drowned within minutes.

Jason and the Overlord Academy officers rushed from the guard-post to find twenty-five Notalian army officers with swords drawn, and Captain Qinoda leading the charge. The archers focused their attention elsewhere to avoid hitting their own men. And then Jason met Qinoda face-to-face.

"You?" Qinoda shouted in rage.

Jason's sword flashed as he tried to defend himself against Qinoda's ferocious attack. He was a well-tanned young man with sharply defined muscles that flexed as he moved. He had the weight advantage, and he was highly experienced in killing people. Jason felt little hope that he could last long in this fight.

But Qinoda was also angry, and Jason was quick-footed. As a result, while Jason repeatedly failed to land any blows with his sword, he at least managed to dodge the repeated sickle sweeps. He wasn't getting anywhere, and he knew he would tire first, but Qinoda's rage was increasing every second Jason eluded him. Suddenly, Jason had a crazy idea and dived head-long between Qinoda's legs, sliced upwards with his sword as he did. His desperate intention was to disorientate Qinoda and use his sword to deflect the downward stroke of the sickle which he felt was sure to come. However, the adrenaline of the moment had made Jason faster than even he expected, and his upward sword-stroke struck Qinoda on the back of his right thigh. Blood streamed from the wound. Qinoda howled and fell heavily to one side. Jason was up in an instant, whirling around to protect himself. Qinoda was slightly slower in rising, and their weapons clashed again as they fought tooth and nail.

As Jason whirled around again to avoid another thrust from Qinoda's sickle, he was cracked on the side of the head with a rapid left-hook and then had the wind knocked out of him with a heavy blow to his midriff. He stumbled and fell, dazed, bruised and winded. Qinoda steadied himself and came at Jason again as he rolled to the side, sucked in as much oxygen as he could, and tried to get up. The world had gone blurry and there was blood dripping down his forehead and into his eyes. He knew he had only seconds to live. He prayed for help as he forced himself back on his feet and turned to meet his opponent for the last time. He could hardly see, he had no idea where Qinoda's sickle was coming from next, and he had milliseconds to react. A new idea came into his head, and instead of slicing with his sword, he simply hurled it at the blurry shape with all the force he could muster. He felt Qinoda's sickle cut into his left arm, then a heavy knock to his upper body, and then he fell and the world turned black.

25

A City Falls

Xci5 and his team set the charges on Finiston Bridge. Then they prepared to close the city gates on the Maycross Highway. They would wait until the Notalian forces were crossing the bridge before blowing it. As instructed by Kia, they inflated two large rubber dinghies, floated them in the river, and secured them with lines to the bridge trusses. Now the team were ready for action, with archers on the guard-post roof and fighters in the guard-post itself, ready to defend the city.

Outer Warrior Two prepared and readied the guard-post on the Tsarn / Crask expressway within the hour. The city gates were closed, the steel barriers raised and the guard-post was bristling with Anasiun fighters. The city walls held dozens of archers, and a makeshift secondary defence-post was set just inside the gates in case they were breached.

Joe's task was much more difficult, not least because the troops from Port Diblaine would be ready to begin an assault on Tsarn at about the same time he and his troops arrived at the Empress Ferry Terminal. But he knew what he had to do. He sent ten Anasiun special forces to the ferry-landing pad to provide up-to-date intelligence on any troop movements on the river.

Then he left 300 troops under the charge of an Overlord Academy veteran, to defend the entrance to the terminal. His instructions were simple: if the Notalian Liberation Army overwhelmed the inside of the terminal, make it impossible for them to leave it. The commander of that force got his troops to work setting up barrels of fuel just outside the entrance, primed for ignition at the flick of a switch. If the Notalians came out of the terminal, they would have to pierce through a wall of fire, a devastating volley of arrows from the archers, and then an Anasiun infantry of Overlord Academy graduates, all trained in hand-to-hand combat.

Inside the terminal, which ran right through the city wall, Joe appointed a second Overlord Academy veteran as commander over 350 troops inside the terminal, with detailed instructions on their defence mission. Then he took a carefully selected group of forty officers, all looking faintly ridiculous clad in wet-suits, and they moved swiftly through a clothes store, collecting what they needed as they went and storing it in the large dry-sacks they had brought with them. Then all forty moved out to the water's edge.

Joe received a direct report from the special forces unit – there was no activity on the river and very little activity in Port Diblaine docks either. The Notalian fleet was moored in those docks, and from what they could see through their field glasses, most boats were manned with only a skeleton crew. The Notalians were busy finishing their work in Port Diblaine and fortifying their positions there. But Joe knew it would not be long now before the fleet came steaming across the river to land troops at the terminal.

Joe had explained their plans to the troops with him, left the special forces to form a front line of defence, and moved around to the south side of the terminal furthest from Port Diblaine and out of the line of sight from any in Port Diblaine docks. Then he contacted Kia and said, "Defence forces are all in position. My unit will be in position within the next five minutes. Please release the boats."

Kia responded immediately, and shortly after, up at Finiston Bridge, Xci5 untied the dinghies and let them loose down the river. They bobbed unmanned and uncertain for a few seconds, before being caught by the current and pushed quickly downstream. They disappeared around a bend in the river, and Xci5 retreated to the guard-post, closed the gates and raised the steel barriers.

Downstream just north of the Empress Ferry Terminal in Tsarn, Joe and his men had located the narrow footpath between the city wall and the river itself. On occasion the path had fallen away into the river so that no-one could manage the path without getting the occasional wetting. They traversed it quickly enough, though, and managed to move 200 metres upstream where they found an iron mooring set in the city wall. Tying one end of a long nylon rope to the ring, the two best swimmers then struck out across the river, dragging the other end of a nylon rope with them. The river was about eighty metres across at this point, an easy swim in a swimming pool Joe had thought. But swimming in extremely cold water across the swift current of the River Dagon was exhausting, and the two men were being swept further and further downstream as they swam. They had expected this, of course, and tried to compensate for it by starting upriver from the terminal and swimming diagonally, but nevertheless the crossing was treacherous, and Joe began to wonder whether they were going to make it at all.

The men were well-trained, though, and excellent swimmers, and they were driven by the knowledge that they were swimming to save their country. After a ten-minute fight against the current, finally their feet found the riverbed. They climbed the bank on the far side and walked back upstream until they were level with Joe and his team. Here, they secured the other end of the rope and then, without wasting any time, Joe and the team plunged into the icy water, carrying the dry sacks with them and pulling themselves across by the rope. Even in a wetsuit, the cold took his breath away and made him gasp, numbed his senses and slowed his thinking. Worse, Joe had no idea how long he would be in the water. Slowly, the others spread out along the rope until there was an officer roughly every couple of metres. Then they waited for the dinghies to arrive.

Thankfully they didn't have to wait too long. The first little craft bobbed its way around the corner on the side nearest Tsarn within a few minutes, and three officers moved along the rope to grab it and harness it. One of them grabbed the painter from inside the dinghy and looped it over and under the rope so that it couldn't drift further downstream. Before they had finished, the second dinghy appeared more in the centre of the river, travelling backwards. Again, the men near the centre of the rope moved to intercept it and kept firm hold of the painter. Following this, Joe and all the troops with him pulled themselves across the river along the rope, dragging the dinghies and the dry-sacks with them. On the far bank, Joe gave the order and most of the men stripped off their wetsuits, dried off and put on dry clothes from the dry-sacks. Now there were thirty-four of their number dressed as Notalian Liberation Army infantry, a disguise they hoped would be enough for them to get into Port Diblaine.

Back in the Arelard Castle library, one of the texts Max had read included reference to a bunker under the dock-front at Port Diblaine. It had been used at the overthrow of the Handed Isles immediately prior to the Western Land Exchange over 250 years ago, but seemed not to have been used since. Assuming it had not been filled or sealed off at any point, these thirty-four troops planned to locate and set up a forward defence post in that same bunker. It was a risky business. If they were discovered, they were a few men against thousands of Notalian troops – no-one could survive those odds. But if they succeeded, then the Notalian plans to invade Tsarn from the west could fail before they even started.

Joe and the six remaining men remained in their wetsuits, carrying the dinghies between them, and following the disguised officers as they trudged northward up the little track on the western side of the river towards Port Diblaine. The distance was less than a mile, but all of them were nervous. If they were discovered now, they would be slaughtered without mercy – of that they were certain. They trudged forward as quietly as possible, praying for a clear passage to the edge of the port.

But then, as the group were about to round a bend, they heard voices on the track ahead. Joe motioned wildly to the six men with him. As silently as possible, they slid down the little bank and into the river and sank beneath the surface. Dragging the dinghies above them, and swimming briskly downstream underwater, they hoped to come up behind the men on the track. Then they could attack in a pincer movement and would have the advantage of surprise.

The thirty-four troops on the path ahead simply continued to walk, although much more slowly – they had no other option. As they rounded the bend they came within a few metres of a group of citizens of Port Diblaine, obviously trying to escape without being noticed. The citizens took one look at them and gasped in horror. One or two of them dived straight into the river to try and swim across. The water was icy and the current strong, and they would have drowned within minutes if two of Joe's men had not caught them and then dragged them to the bank further downstream. Two or three others threw themselves headlong over the fence and raced off across the open fields, expecting to be shot with arrows at any point. But the most difficult ones to deal with were the two men who decided to stand and fight. Their swords were out at the ready and the two Anasiun troops in the lead drew their swords also. Both the two men and the Anasiun troops stopped moving.

It was a terrible situation. If Joe's men killed the citizens, then they were murdering their own people. If they told the citizens who they were, then the danger of having their cover blown was significantly greater. Joe had surfaced again, now behind the two men, and took in the whole situation. He made a rapid decision, scrambled up the bank as quietly as he could, and then hailed the two men from behind in a low voice.

"Citizens of Port Diblaine, I salute you. I come in the name of Xcion the Sovereign whom we all serve." The two men jumped and whirled around as they heard his voice behind them. It seemed now that they were trapped between Joe and the three men in wetsuits who had climbed the bank behind him, and the group of Notalian troops in front of them. They turned back to back, and clearly were considering the river as an escape route.

"If you jump into the river, you will die quickly," Joe said matter-of-factly. "The two who tried that option are only alive now because my men rescued them – they're up the bank just ahead of us and in severe danger of hypothermia."

"Who are you?" one of the men asked suspiciously, expecting to be attacked any moment.

"I am Joe, trained at the Overlord Academy and now an officer of Xcion the Sovereign. In fact, all forty of the troops you see here are Overlord Academy officers."

"You look like Notalian troops to me," the shorter man said gruffly.

"I guess that's encouraging," Joe noted quietly.

"Are you really tellin' us that you're not Notalian officers?" the other man asked incredulously.

Joe was getting slightly frustrated. "Why would we have rescued your two friends from the river if we were Notalian? Why did we not shoot your other friends who ran across the fields if we were Notalian? We're all graduates of the Overlord Academy, I tell you. I trained under Xci2, who is now seated at the throne of Xcion the Sovereign himself, bless his soul."

"Well, would you believe it," the taller man said, shaking his head. "Just now, I thought we were certain to be dead pronto like. Nows I find we might live a bit. Praise be!"

"The light dawns," Joe said, still irritated. "Please – we need information. According to our sources, Port Diblaine has fallen to the Notalians, and it will not be long before they try to set out across the river to attack Tsarn. Our mission begins by getting these disguised officers into the port without detection. Are there any Notalian soldiers between here and there?"

One of the men responded uncertainly, "Well, there weren't any when we came this way, otherwise they'd 'ave caught us, wouldn't they? Back at the dock though, there's officers on every ship, there's a shed-load of 'em at the public 'ouse on the waterfront. There's heaps of others murdering their way through the streets. We're lucky to still be alive. Most of our mates is dead. If you's really Anasiun, then we'll 'elp you 'owever you like, but don't you go askin' us to show mercy to the Notalians – they're savages, like animals that need to be put down."

Joe thought for a moment and then asked, "You say there are lots of Notalian officers at the public house on the waterfront. Do they have a commanding officer? Are they organised well? How disciplined are they?"

"You gotta be jokin', sir," the short man replied. "There ain't much discipline with the Notalians. They do 'ave commanding officers, and those near to them are pretty good at staying in order and doing what they're told. But most of 'em is just chargin' through our city, killing anyone they find and lootin' the 'ouses. It's 'orrible – 'orrific. No honour. No chivalry. No moral decency. At the waterfront, mostly they be drinkin' and laughin' and waitin' for orders to get going to Tsarn."

Joe could hardly believe it was true. The Notalians still had the most important battle of all to fight and they were drinking? It was almost unimaginable. The senior officers he'd come across did not seem like people who would tolerate indiscipline.

Be that as it may, he thought, if they're drinking then clearly they think they're in control, so their guard will be down. "If what you say is true, then our mission is slightly easier than we thought," he said.

"I would hardly call it easy, sir," one of his officers commented. We have to locate the entrance to a bunker right out in the open, open the entrance, climb down into the bunker, seal it up and then set it up as a command post. And we have to complete that without being noticed by any of the soldiers spilling out of the bar or sitting outside or looking out of the windows or wandering past. We have our work cut out for us and we still require a miracle."

Joe turned to the two citizens. "I'm assuming you're still running away?" he questioned.

"What can we do? We're just a mechanic and a tram-driver. We're not soldiers. And we don't fancy being butchered by sword-'appy drunken Notalian officers. We're headin' up river."

One of the soldiers with Joe responded, "Well don't go too far. We're expecting the Notalians to approach Tsarn from Finiston Bridge, so we've closed the city gates there and the bridge is not navigable. Once they discover that, who knows what direction they'll take. The fields provide little cover, and some of the Notalian archers can shoot a good distance."

Joe interrupted him. "That's not the point. The fact is that Anasius has been invaded, from Ruscorn Forest right across to Ruwark. The forest and Xanver have already been taken with thousands of Anasiun casualties. Port Diblaine is overrun, as you know, and Ruwark is making a last stand right now. It looks like the final battle of the war will be at Tsarn. If Tsarn falls, this country will be Notalian by nightfall. So we're going to do everything we can to make sure that does not happen. We need to defeat the Notalians here once and for all. We need your help, and I have an idea how."

"Are you sayin' that the Notalians are all over our country? That we're not safe if we escape Port Diblaine?"

"Yes. And we're fast running out of time. Either be useful and come with us or find somewhere deep and dark to hide in for a very long time."

The two men looked at each other and then nodded. "We'll do our bit, sir."

"Good," Joe responded. "Then listen up." And Joe explained the plan as they began moving up the path once more towards the port.

Thrty-five troops dressed as Notalian Liberation Army officers managed to climb unnoticed from the path and up into a little lane leading to the docks. From there, they marched in formation towards the docks, hoping they would pass as a squad of Notalian troops returning from a mission. They noted one or two frightened citizens peering at them from house windows, looking utterly terrified, but they ignored them and kept marching. Within minutes, the lane reached the edge of the dock and, with hearts thumping like mad, the men marched out onto the dock front.

Meanwhile, Joe and his team were in the dinghies, rowing down the river and around into the docks, wearing full wetsuits and black caps and trying to stay as hidden as possible. It took longer than they'd hoped because the dinghies were hard to manoeuvre, but they made it into the dock mouth and then proceeded to split up. Five men took the two dinghies and worked their way slowly along the lines of merchant ships, fixing charges below the waterline to each one as they went. Joe and the mechanic were now in the water, swimming for the largest vessel in the dock. It was an offshore patrol vessel that had accompanied the fifteen merchant ships. The Notalian flagship was too large to come up the estuary, so it remained moored in the bay, a good half-mile above the river mouth.

The Notalian attack had come as a complete surprise to the dock workers in Port Diblaine, simply because merchant ships usually carry goods. It was only as the patrol vessel came into view that they realised they were under attack, and by then the merchant ships were docked, their cargo doors were opening, and Notalian troops were pouring out.

Some workers had tried to put up a fight, but with 8000 Notalian soldiers swarming on shore, none had survived longer than a few minutes. The Notalians were merciless, and every Anasiun worker or civilian remaining in the dock area was put to the sword. The dead were strewn across the waterfront. The Notalians then divided up and worked systematically through the streets of Port Diblaine, sometimes even going from house to house and killing everyone they found. In the first five hours of the attack on Port Diblaine, over 12,000 Anasiuns were killed, mostly civilians – nearly a quarter of its population. Anasiun troops stationed in the barracks near the docks were barely waking up when the first Notalian troops burst through the gates. They put up a good fight under the circumstances, and the Notalians lost upwards of a hundred men, but it only took an hour or so before the barracks fell to the Notalians. City Hall was overrun and ransacked three hours later. Perhaps 4000 citizens had managed to get into the subway system and avoid detection, whilst others were hiding in their homes, hoping the Notalian soldiers would not come to their doors. The city was on its knees.

Joe and his new mechanic friend arrived at the hull of the offshore patrol vessel and swam along the side facing away from the shore. The side of the vessel formed one long smooth reinforced steel bulkhead, virtually impenetrable. Joe had a whispered conversation with the mechanic.

"We need to find a way to cripple this boat. I have some charges, but if we attach them to the bulkhead, they're not going to do much."

"I agree. But I reckon this ship has an echo sounder."

"How does that help?"

"Well, it hangs beneath the bottom of the boat and relays signals into the vessel of the depth of the water. The point is, it hangs outside the boat and is controlled from inside. Put a couple of charges at the top of the echo sounder, and you have a chance of blowing a hole in the bottom of the boat."

"Sounds good. Can you do it?"

"No. I'm not a good enough swimmer. Maybe you could do it?"

Joe swallowed. "I'll give it a go, but I don't really know what I'm doing."

"If there is an echo sounder, it'll be the only thing sticking out of the bottom of the boat. Should be easy to find. And then you just need to lodge the charges at the top of it against the bottom of the boat. Then, prime the charges and you're done."

"Easy as pie," Joe said sarcastically, and then he took a huge breath of air and dived down into the water. A minute went by and the mechanic got uneasy. A few seconds later,

Joe's head broke the surface and he gasped in the air.

When his breathing had recovered a bit, he panted, "No echo sounder where I looked. But it's really hard to see because the water's opaque down there, and the only way to find anything is by touch. I'm going again a bit further along."

He dived down again and eventually resurfaced. "Found it," he said triumphantly. "Now comes the tricky part." He dived again.

For Joe, it was a very awkward job. It only took ten seconds to locate the echo sounder again, but getting charges fitted to the right spot in virtual darkness whilst fast running out of breath was a tall order. He tried for as long as he dared, and then surfaced again.

"You don't happen to have a torch or something, do you?" he asked. "I can't see a thing down there."

The mechanic rummaged through the drysack he was holding.

Nothing. "Sorry mate," he said. "Can't 'elp you."

"Yes you can," Joe said suddenly, and he pointed to the mechanic's wrist. He was wearing a basic Anasiun watch. Joe fashioned a bandana out of a T-shirt and tied the watch onto it with some thread he pulled out of the seams of the T-shirt. Then he turned the watch on its side, located the back-light button, and taped it firmly down to hold it in place. Now he had a head-torch. He grinned at the mechanic, and then dived back under the surface.

This time, when he was up close to the echo sounder, he could see a little of what he was doing. He located three screws, surveyed the area quickly, and then resurfaced.

"Screwdriver," he panted. "Cross-head."

The mechanic smiled. "That I can do." His hands were back in the drysack, hunting for his jacket. In the jacket pocket he had a multitool, one that was far better than anything Joe had come across before. He handed it to Joe, who admired it briefly and then dived back under the ship. This time he was down for an impossible length of time. The mechanic was virtually certain he was never coming back. When he did finally returned his eyes were popping from lack of oxygen and he was sucking in air like a vacuum-cleaner. He was looking very irritated. A couple of minutes later, he had recovered his breath a bit and explained.

"I've removed two of the screws, but the third is jammed. I've tried as hard as I can, but it's not going to budge. I'm going to have to try something else." He dived again. He was back within a minute, and now he was smiling. "I levered the panel out a bit and squeezed the charges into the gap. I just need to prime them, and we're done here."

"I'm just going to swim to the back whilst you do that," the mechanic said. "I have an idea."

"Okay." Joe dived again, and the mechanic swam slowly to the back of the ship.

When Joe resurfaced, the mechanic had disappeared. He looked about him, and then swam to the back of the ship. There was no sign of the mechanic. And then, suddenly, the mechanic surfaced a couple of metres away, heaving in air. But he refused to say what he had done. Five minutes later the whole dive team regrouped by the dockside and compared notes. All the charges were set and ready to go. Joe punctured the dinghies and sunk them quietly under a boardwalk. Then he contacted Kia.

"How did the Overlord Academy officers do, disguised as Notalian troops?" Joe asked.

"It has been horribly nerve-jangling, to say the least. After some discussion, they marched directly across the paved area less than twenty metres from the public house, with all those on the west side of their column staring firmly at the floor, trying to locate the access point. It was difficult because, while they marched as slowly as they dared, they had only a second or two to examine the slabs as they walked past. There must be upwards of 10,000 paving slabs on the waterfront, so it is hardly a surprise that they failed to find the one we need. They're now holed up in a bank out of sight of the waterfront, hoping they are not disturbed as we try to figure out what to do next. We're running out of time, though. I'm suspecting the bunker is reasonably central, but I'm not sure that helps too much. Do you have any ideas?"

Joe thought for a bit. Then he said, "What if we swim right up to the harbour front and see if we can locate the bunker from the water? We are unlikely to be spotted unless someone's looking for us, and we'll stay close in by the dock wall. At least if we can find the bunker, they'll know where to concentrate their efforts."

Kia gave him the go-ahead and Joe and his team moved into action. They were in the water at the harbour wall within five minutes, working their way slowly along it and looking for breaks in the brickwork. As it turned out, finding the front of the bunker was not difficult from where they were.

Its arrow slits were extremely thin and also cleverly disguised using the natural spaces where mortar would be between stones. Just like the paving-slab access points in the Crask dungeons, Joe found gaps instead of black mortar – completely invisible unless you were within a metre of them. Then Joe had a brainwave. He called Kia and they had a brief conversation.

Up above, the Anasiun officers got a call from Kia. After some heated conversation, eventually the call ended and they moved into action. Shortly after this, the Notalian troops in the public house noticed a tram coming along the harbour front. It was being driven, so they thought, by an Notalian army officer, and a few other officers were lounging in the back, laughing and joking. Suddenly, the officers got off the tram and wandered up to the street and around the corner towards City Hall. Then the tram came to a halt and the driver got out and meandered across to the public toilets beside a souvenir shop. He disappeared inside. The tram and its two carriages had stopped in such a way as to completely block the view of the dock-front from anyone sitting in or near the public house.

Simultaneously, a group of Notalian officers emerged from a side street and marched across the dock until they, too, were hidden by the tram. If any real Notalian troops had been watching from a rooftop and looking in the right directions, they would have noticed three things. First, the driver of the tram had gone in the front of the toilets and immediately climbed out of the window to the side and joined the officers from the back of the tram. Second, all of them had doubled back in a wide circle into the lane they had emerged from originally, and then marched across the harbour until they, too, were behind the tram and out of sight of those in the public house. Third, some faint smoke appeared from between the cracks of a flagstone.

This happened, because Joe had helpfully stuffed a small smoke-grenade through one of the arrow slots. The smoke had found its way to the roof and then seeped between the cracks of the flagstone. From the outside, an observer would have seen, almost comically, all the Notalian-dressed troops one by one dropped down a hole that had suddenly appeared, before the hole was then filled again by a flagstone and all thirty men had disappeared. A moment later the smoke stopped emerging from the flagstone holes (for the simple reason that two of the Anasiun troops now in the bunker had taped over the cracks), and the harbour front next to the tram was deserted again. The whole operation took less than fifteen minutes. And, luckily for them all, no-one noticed a thing.

Less than half-an-hour later, hundreds of Notalian troops began pouring down onto the harbour front and climbed back on-board the fifteen merchant boats and the offshore patrol-boat. By now, Joe and the six men with him had swum out of the harbour and climbed back onto the path they had left earlier. But they remained dangerously close to the harbour, because Joe wanted to get the timing just right. There must have been 4000 troops loaded onto the ships before the hatches were shut, the offshore patrol vessel took the lead and they set out across the river towards Tsarn. It was as the last three vessels in line moved slowly out of the harbour that Joe blew the charges. The result was spectacular.

The charges had been set over a metre below the water line, and each charge blew a massive hole in the boat. Seven of them listed over violently and sank almost immediately, with virtually no survivors. The patrol vessel up in front didn't list over at all, and seemed to press on for a while without any obvious signs of distress apart from the Notalian troops running frantically across its decks and shouting obscenities. However, after a short while Joe noticed that the boat began to get lower and lower in the water and veered round to the right. It seemed the rudders were jammed and it was at the mercy of the current. The mechanic next to Joe grinned to himself.

Seven of the other eight merchant vessels, some of them only just out of the docks, listed too, but less so. They also took on water, but they sank more sedately, giving many of the troops on board time to throw themselves into the river and swim for the shore. Many of those troops didn't make it to the shore because the water was icy and the river current strong, and they were swept downstream and out to sea, cold and lifeless in death. Dozens of others failed to get back to shore because they made the mistake of swimming back into the docks. As they approached, the Anasiun troops in the bunker on the harbour front went into action. The air filled with arrows, and many swimmers were hit as they hunted for a place to come ashore.

Within twenty minutes of blowing the charges, fourteen boats had sunk without trace. The patrol vessel had finally sunk to the bottom about half-a-mile north of the port, but her tall mast stuck a few metres out of the water, the Notalian flag waving forlornly in the breeze. But one merchant ship remained afloat, seemingly unaffected by the carnage around her. The charges on her had failed to blow.

Her engines were running, but she was not moving. In fact, her captain and his second-in-command were in a quandary about what to do. Returning to the dock at Port Diblaine was unattractive. Not only did they have no idea how many Anasiun troops had swarmed into the port as soon as they had disembarked, but also there were a number of their own merchant ships somewhere below the water line, and they were worried about hitting them. On the other hand, moving ahead with the planned attack on Tsarn would be almost suicidal with a squadron of only 300 men. The captain decided to contact his superiors on the flagship for advice.

There were still a number of Notalian soldiers trying to climb into the docks, and sixty or so succeeded without being hit with arrows. They arrived, dripping, on the harbour front and then staggered back towards the public house, presumably to dry off and then try and find reinforcements. Another hundred or so managed to climb onto the path beside the river. Those north of Port Diblaine continued north, hoping to be picked up by rescue launches sent from the flagship anchored out in the bay. Those south of the port made their way further south towards Finiston Bridge. It was agonising for Joe and those with him. They had jumped the fence and were lying in the ditch by the tow-path, hoping desperately that none of the Notalian soldiers would venture off the path and come their way. Fortunately, the Notalians who had survived the river were in no fit state to contemplate anything much apart from getting away from the docks, and they stumbled by on their way to Finiston Bridge. They thought they were walking away from danger.

Soon, the docks once again looked calm, but under the surface, the sunken vessels and hundreds of drowned NLA troops told their grim story. For Joe and the six men with him, the adrenaline and then euphoria of the spectacular success of their mission had kept them warm and energy-fuelled. Now, though, the adrenaline was gone and they were exhausted, wet and extremely cold. Hypothermia was a very real danger, and Joe instructed them to get up and onto the tow-path. Joe contacted Kia.

"Joe!" she squeaked joyfully as she heard his voice. "From what I see here, your mission went extremely well. It looks like you managed to take out upwards of 4000 NLA troops, leaving perhaps 3000 others scattered across Port Diblaine."

Joe was smiling as he responded. "Still far too many to make Diblaine a comfortable place to be, but it seems to have halted the invasion of Tsarn from the east, at least for the moment. What's the situation on the harbour-front?"

"From the cameras, it looks like there are quite a number

of Notalian troops at the public house, but apart from that, the front looks deserted."

"Is the tram still there?"

"Yes, I suspect they couldn't find a driver to move it."

"And how are our troops in the bunker?"

"I cannot possibly tell from the cameras. They did great work with their archery though. What are you thinking?"

"I'm thinking that if they stay much longer then they're going to be imprisoned forever."

"I'll contact them and get back to you," Kia said simply. She clicked off the line.

Twenty minutes later, thirty-five NLA-clad troops were scurrying furtively across the harbour-front and down onto the path by the river. They were spotted by some of the men at the public house, but no-one chased them down. And then they met Joe and the men with him, and the Anasiuns had a muted but happy reunion on the path. Joe knew what had to be done, but he didn't like it, and he knew the men wouldn't like it either.

"Friends," he said. "We need to return to Tsarn. Port Diblaine is not safe, and there are Notalian troops all over the place now, scattered from the carnage of the last hour or so. We need to use the rope across the river and return the way we came."

There was silence for a minute as the Overlord Academy officers absorbed what he was saying. The return journey to Tsarn was, in fact, easier than the original crossing. The rope across the river was still secured – none of the Notalian troops had spotted it, or if they had, they'd left it alone. So, one by one, the Anasiun troops dragged themselves back into the river and hand-over-hand along the rope and up onto the tiny path on the far side. They made their way slowly back to the Empress Ferry Terminal, where Joe hailed the troops from special forces. Kia had informed them of Joe's imminent return, so when they finally made it back into the terminal, towels, clothing and a hot meal were awaiting them at the restaurant on the main concourse.

26

The Final Fight

Back in Crask, Xci3 and the sixteen men with him had found the dungeons and the lower-ground floors of the building entirely devoid of Notalian troops. On the ground floor, they found various guards leaning lazily and bored against the wall or sitting at a desk here or there. The guards were dispatched swiftly, without noise and with surprising ease. Then the Anasiuns swept the building and found about twenty other Notalians, all of whom were taken by surprise and easily subdued.

Then they took stock. They could not hope to take the city of Crask with only seventeen men, so they contacted Kia. She informed them of the devastation at Ruscorn Forest and the preparations for the final battle at Tsarn. Xci3 made a decision.

"As soon as Marcia drops the others in Tsarn, she must return here and take us also," he said.

Kia agreed. "It will be done," she assured them, and relayed the information to Marcia.

The Notalian troops from Ruscorn Forest regrouped

on the southern edge of Ruscorn Forest and then began a march to Xanver to support General Qong's efforts there and provide some reinforcements.

Meanwhile, back in Ruwark Jason's eyes were beginning to open. He was back inside the guard-post which appeared deserted, and he had no idea how he had got there. There was blood all over his shirt, his head hurt horribly and everything looked a bit blurry. He shook his head to clear it and then wished he hadn't. He groaned.

Unbeknown to him, the remainder of Qinoda's group at the guard-post had been finished off by Jason's compatriots. Miraculously, it turned out that when Jason flung his sword desperately at Qinoda, somehow it had found its mark between two of Qinoda's left ribs, piercing his heart. Qinoda had died almost instantly and landed heavily on top of Jason. His friends thought Jason was finished and had hauled Qinoda off him only to discover that it was Qinoda who was dead, not Jason.

Qinoda's men were fast losing the will to fight, with two-thirds of them drowned or shot with arrows in the trench, hundreds more dead from the carnage of the tankers, and now Captain Qinoda was dead as well. They had not even managed to open the gates to the city and who knew what would lie in store for them there. Within a few minutes, they were surrendering, despite the knowledge that such actions might well result in their execution back in Notalia. As Jason was beginning to come around, his men had rounded up the ninety or so remaining Notalian troops, opened the gates to Ruwark and marched them to the City Hall, where they were now locking them in the cells, ten or twelve to a cell. It was not humane, but it was all they could think to do under the circumstances. In the whole process, the Anasiun side had lost around thirty troops, all from the guard-post, and eight of the tanker drivers. But Ruwark was saved – it was a victory without a doubt.

As soon as Trey arrived at the Tranton Highway guard-post in the city wall, he made a careful inspection of the whole area. The huge iron gates to the city hung on enormous hinges embedded in the castle wall. Once closed, at the flick of a switch the gates could run with a powerful electric current, proving fatal to any who touched them. There were large steel barriers which could rise impenetrably from the road at the touch of a button, fortifying the gates and providing a reassuring perimeter to the guard-post. Those steel barriers could also run with a pulsed electric current. Within the city wall, staircases and corridors ran on three levels, providing access to the ultra-thin slit windows through which archers could fire upon invading troops outside the city. The guard-post itself had a large open room at ground level, with a few arrow slits facing the road, but no windows. On the first floor, up the stairs running at each end of the open room, was a large screen displaying an enlarged view of the final few miles of road leading up to the city, obtained from the concealed video cameras on the roof. This room held larger windows, making it much lighter, and it also housed controls for the steel barriers around the guard-post, a direct video-link to City Hall in the centre of

Tsarn, and a direct intercom system to the corridors in the city walls to relay information to the troops there. The roof was ringed with battlements providing vantage points for archers armed with powerful crossbows.

Trey organised most of the troops with him under the command of three Overlord Academy officers. One oversaw the archers in the walls. One was in charge of the city access – the gates, the steel barriers and the electronic defences. And the third was in charge of the guard-post itself, ensuring the archers were all in position and setting a lookout for approaching Notalian troops. But he kept ten troops for Max.

Max instructed them to locate large speakers, some tools and as much cabling as possible. One of the city tram-drivers offered his services, and so his men disappeared on a shopping spree. Meanwhile, Max got to work preparing the loudhailer system in the way Kia had suggested.

In the hour that followed, there was a frenzied activity as the Anasiun forces at Tranton gate got themselves organised. Max's troops returned from their shopping expedition, with some huge speakers, nearly a mile of cabling and a plethora of tools. They ran the cabling to four specific locations on the city walls and also to the roof of the guard-house, and Max installed the huge speakers in each location. Max had calculated the frequency for a counter-signal and then informed XSHC of the details, instructing them to wait for a message from him before initiating this continuous counter-signal to all the implants within half-a-mile of Tranton gate. Finally, he connected the cables from all the speakers into the electronics board in the guard-room, ready to run with sounds generated from XSHC.

An hour later, the Anasiun forces at Tranton gate were as prepared as they could be for the onslaught that was coming. Trey kept in constant communication with the three Overlord Academy officers and also with Kia back at XSHC, trying to gather as much information as possible. At noon, he heard of Jason's highly successful defeat of the Notalians at Ruwark, and of the death of Qinoda. At 1:15 pm he heard about Joe's exploits in Port Diblaine. Both events were a great morale boost for his troops. But then the Notalian Liberation Army appeared from around the bend in the highway, not five miles distant.

Some were travelling in trucks from Tranton as expected, but the first third of the column comprised twenty-four armoured vehicles taken from Xanver Navy Base, each capable of carrying 100 troops. If all vehicles were full of men, Trey estimated that his little army of 500 were about to face an invading force of more than 5000. And if those trucks and armoured vehicles drove right up to the barriers, Max's audio weapon would be of little use. But he could think of no way to entice the troops from the trucks. He did not know what to do.

Then Kia's voice was in his ear again.

"Trey, you remember Xci3 and the troops who had helped with Joe's rescue in Crask? They have finished in Crask and I am sending Marcia to collect them and deliver them to you. They will be of significant use when they arrive."

"That's great, Kia, but we have thousands of NLA troops

approaching, outnumbering us ten-to-one. They are using Xanver armoured vehicles and may well be preparing to ram the barriers, so I don't see how an extra few on our side can make much difference. We have no hope of success."

"Yes you do, Trey. I know it seems futile. I know it feels like there is no hope. But Xcion the Sovereign has been right so far about posting Jason to Ruwark and Joe to undertake sabotage at Port Diblaine. Those missions were a spectacular success. Xcion does not get it wrong. Trey, our role is to trust and obey." Kia clicked off the line. A few minutes later, Marcia was on her way back to Ruscorn Forest to collect Gloria and then to Crask to collect Xci3 and company. She hoped they would return in time to be of use.

The sound of the approaching vehicles was growing steadily louder, and Trey's heart was already banging against his ribs and making his ears ring. He was watching the screen intently and then heard Max speaking in his implants.

"They're slowing down," he said matter-of-factly. Trey stared harder at the screen and then realised Max was right. Why in the world would they do that? What were they planning to do now? He could not imagine. Five minutes later, and a good half-mile away from the city, the vehicles came to a complete halt. Then, the troops from every vehicle came pouring out onto the road and took up positions both on and off the road. They proceeded to begin to march towards the city, but it was a slow march because half the troops were walking beside the road where the ground was soft, uneven and much more difficult to traverse.

Trey looked across at Max, who was smiling broadly.

"What is it?" he asked him, completely confused.

"They've heard about Ruwark," Max replied. "Look at the troops on the road, staring nervously at the ground and to the sides, wondering whether or not it's all going to collapse. And the reason they left their vehicles behind was in case some heroes from Tsarn decided to drive out in tankers and block the road." He repeated again, "They've heard about Ruwark!"

Trey understood and began to smile as well. Then, suddenly, he said, "Switch it on, quick."

Max grinned. "Already done," he said.

During his time at the library at Arelard Castle, Max had read a two-volume book on non-traditional warfare, a fascinating read by all accounts. It had provided the history of warfare across the known world, and the All-nations Arms Agreement, which banned the manufacture and use of all biological, chemical and nuclear weaponry. More fascinatingly, as a result of a global outcry regarding steeply rising instances of devastating gun-crime, the agreement also banned the manufacture, sale, purchase and use of firearms of any description in any situation. All nations had to retrain all their troops in hand-to-hand combat and direct-action warfare. Weaponry was destroyed in every nation under the watchful eye of the Cross-national Arms Enforcement Office, who was given jurisdiction to inspect any manufacturing or training facility in any country if there was any evidence of a failure to break the agreement.

Thirty years later, Pheglonia, a large country with a population of over 34 million, went to war against Nukait, an adjacent country much smaller and with a far smaller army. Pheglonia began using firearms in the fight, and in response, the CAEO cut all ties with Pheglonia from that point forward. No trade or travel was allowed in or out of the country. It underwent complete global alienation. Within five years, Pheglonia's government was overthrown from within, and the new government ordered an immediate withdrawal from Nukait. The international community refused to re-engage with them in any way until they surrendered all their firearms, paid for the rebuilding and restructuring of Nukait, built a strong and Nukait-operated border-wall between the two countries, and provided all funding necessary to get Nukait back on its feet. The international community matched their funding to Nukait. Ten years later, Nukait was a wealthy and thriving country, whilst Pheglonia struggled for another twenty years to recover from the crippling economic burdens placed upon it. After that, no country around the world had attempted to use firearms in warfare.

Since the inception of the All-nations Arms Agreement 150 years ago, whilst occasionally there appeared hand-made firearms by private individuals, instances of their use were few and far between. Nowadays, weaponry used in hand-to-hand combat was limited to bladed weapons, electronic weaponry and projectile weapons such as bows, crossbows and catapults. Many of these weapons had also become much more sophisticated with growing technological advances, but most wars involved traditional fighting with swords and archery. Anything greater risked the wrath of the international community, and no country wanted that.

As Max had read on, he found that one chapter included some comments about some experimental weaponry called auditory weapons. Four scientists at Arelard Castle had done some preliminary work on the effects of high-frequency sound-waves on human subjects. They had discovered that if the human ear is subject to certain frequencies of sound wave, over time those subjects developed increasingly strong head-aches. Typically, it was high-frequency waves emitted at high volume that had this effect. Older people were unaffected because their ears no longer detected the high-frequency sounds, but for younger people (a more typical age for soldiers on the battlefield) these high-volume-high-frequency waves (HVHF) could have a significantly debilitating effect.

The four scientists spent two years on the project, working hard to maximise the effect of the HVHF. Initially, it was hard to cause any problems to someone more than four metres away, but over time they developed a system which made the HVHF effective over a 200 metre arc, assuming at least three high-powered speakers were operative. The largest problem with the project was that any sound-waves so emitted would have the same effect on home troops as they did on the enemy, thus providing no tactical advantage. Finally, following a poorly-designed experiment in which two of the four scientists spearheading the project lost most of their hearing, the whole project was shelved.

In the eighty years since those experiments, the Anasiuns had developed the ring and the auditory implants. Kia knew about noise-cancelling speakers which use interference to cancel out a sound and, as a result, she suggested to Max that if he could figure out how to produce a sound-wave to cancel an HVHF, they could play it through the implants and so neutralise the effect of the HVHF on any Anasiun troops.

Since Kia suggested the idea, Max had thought and planned hard, and he knew what was required to get the system in place. So, whilst Trey had been organising troops at Tranton Gate, Max had been preparing the loudhailer system on the city walls by installing huge speakers directed towards Tranton Highway outside the gate. He had sent detailed instructions to the XSHC regarding soundwaves to be emitted on his call to every implant for the troops at Tranton Gate at the same moment as the HVHF was turned on. Everything was in place, and now he had sent his messages and flicked the switch. The HVHF was operational.

It was a moment of triumph. This had never been achieved before on a battlefield. As the minutes went by, though, the Notalian troops simply continued to march towards them, with no break in their formation and no slowing of their pace. It would not be long before the Notalians arrived at the guard-post, and defeat seemed inevitable. From where they stood, the auditory weapon seemed to be useless. For the Notalian troops on the road, though, the story was different.

All the younger troops noticed the extremely high squeal coming from the city as soon as Max turned it on. For the first minute or so, it was just an irritating, background noise, but within five minutes, all of them were developing headaches – headaches which slowly grew in intensity until the troops felt that their heads were pounding from the noise. They continued to march, but their eyes were half-closed, their thinking seriously impeded, and their reactions increasingly sluggish.

For the slightly older troops, it took a bit longer before the noise achieved anything, but slowly it began to take effect on them as well. Again, the effect was a slow but inexorable descent into a full-blown pounding headache. For the oldest troops, though, of whom there were few, the noise had no effect whatsoever. And one of those old troops was General Qong. The virtually totally white-haired man, with the forbidding Notalian military insignia tattooed on his forehead, was clearly unaffected and getting increasingly irritated with his ailing troops. He barked some orders, and those nearest to him straightened their shoulders and marched more smartly once again. But most troops struggled to keep going.

Trey and Max, however, were increasingly frightened. Within a few minutes, the huge column of soldiers would reach the guard-post, and while the archers would do their best beforehand, the 250 men in the guard-post would have the impossible task of fighting thousands of troops, hand-to-hand, unaided.

As soon as the first ranks of soldiers were fully in range,

Trey signalled to the archers and moments later, arrows filled the sky. Most in the front ranks died within moments, but as soon as the archers went into action, General Qong ordered shields up. Protected by their large, oval shields, a number of Notalian troops managed to progress reasonably well. While the archers shot furiously for a few minutes, only a couple of hundred Notalians fell – the rest marched relentlessly forwards, with General Qong now leading the charge. And as soon as it became apparent that the road was not going to collapse, General Qong ordered the return of the armoured vehicles. The troops divided into two columns, like the wake from a boat in the sea, and the three leading armoured trucks ploughed their way up the middle of the road. Two minutes later, the front troops arrived at the guard-post. Archers from within its walls shot as fast as they could, but they were about to be overrun and they knew it.

Trey shook Max's hand. "It's been an honour," he said. "Do not leave here until you have to." Then Trey was out of the main door, leading a group of thirty men into the first hand-to-hand combat of Tsarn. His sword was out and he was shouting orders as he went. He was fearless.

As Max watched in horror, Trey forged ahead, his sword flashing about as he ducked and weaved amongst the Notalian troops. In moments, Max realised that Trey was leading his men towards the armoured vehicles. Trey had covered half the distance before he was confronted with two older men, and it was then that he realised something. He had managed to get this far purely because of the effectiveness of the HVHF. The younger men he had cut down on his way were so debilitated by the auditory noise, that they could hardly function. But the few older men were not able to hear the HVHF and so were entirely unaffected. And here was Trey, a fifteen-year-old boy with only a few weeks' training with a sword, facing two fully-grown men who had been using swords in battle for longer than Trey had been alive.

As Trey lifted his sword and sought to find some space and develop an opportunity, the three men just behind him rose magnificently to the occasion. They thrust Trey to one side and attacked the two men with a ferocity and determination which was awe-inspiring. One of them fell with the first blow of his opponent's sword. The other two were fighting with everything they had. Trey circled and tried to help by attacking from behind, but a blow from the sword of one of the men sent his own sword spinning, and Trey grasped his bleeding wrist and cried out in pain. As he got up, he tried to locate his sword, but a voice interrupted his thoughts.

"You looking for this, vermin?" It was General Qong. He was standing to his full height, with a sneer on his face, and Trey's sword was dangling from his left hand. The fighting was continuing all around them, but those individual battles faded from his mind as Trey realised all hope was gone.

"Killed with your own sword! Hardly a warrior's way to die, is it?" General Qong lifted Trey's sword a little and drew back for the final blow. Trey closed his eyes and waited for the end. Then he opened his eyes again, annoyed with himself for being so cowardly. He would meet his death eye-to-eye. Then he saw the flash. And he heard the grunt. The battle was still raging around him, and his men were falling fast, but General Qong had hardly moved. Suddenly, on one side of his head, a black charred mark had appeared, and then General Qong fell headlong to the ground. Trey snatched his sword from the General's hand and leapt back, but the General never moved again.

Trey had no time to think, but ploughed on towards the armoured vehicle like a driven man. Only four men remained at his side, with the Notalian troops coming in waves, but there was a strange look on some of their faces, a look completely at odds with their situation. It was fear. Then he saw another flash, and this time he realised it had come from the roof of the guard-post. As he reached the armoured vehicle and turned to put his back to the metal, he looked up at the guard-post again. His knees went wobbly, he gasped and his jaw dropped. He was utterly floored.

There, up on the guard-post in-between two battlements was Gloria. And lying next to her on his front, was Zika. Zika who may not survive. Zika who was in a coma. Zika who had very serious injuries. And yet there he was. And strangely, he had his sword in his hand and was waving it about uselessly. Then, even as Trey watched, a sudden flash came from the tip of Zika's sword, and the Notalian soldier who was rushing towards Trey checked himself and then fell. Even as it happened, a flash came from Gloria's sword and another Notalian died.

Trey could hardly think straight. What was that flash? How were they doing it? He stared around him quickly, and noticed Notalian troops backing away fast. Now he understood the fear of the faces of the troops. Not only were they struggling to cope with the HVHF which continued to pound their eardrums, but now this second unknown weapon was being unleashed and they could not defend themselves against it. To top it all off, their general was dead.

Trey shouted to the command-post, but he need not have bothered. The Anasiun troops were piling out and launching a full attack on the Notalians as they began to retreat. Quickly, Trey affixed the charge he had brought for the purpose and rushed away from the armoured vehicle. In three seconds, there was a huge bang, and the armoured vehicle blew over onto its side. The Notalians needed no more encouragement. Ignoring the cries of the few older troops who were demanding that they press home their obvious advantage, the vast majority were racing back along the highway seeking escape from the battlefront and from the pounding headaches they were enduring.

Somehow, the tide had been turned. An army of 5000 had been defeated by 500. As they cleared the battleground later, they counted nearly 600 Notalian soldiers who had died, and fifty-four Anasiun troops had been killed in the process. In the midst of the carnage, though, Trey had only one thought. He wanted to see Zika. He ran for the guard-post and pounded up the steps. But when he reached the roof, Gloria was there but Zika was nowhere to be seen.

He looked quizzically at Gloria, and asked, "Zika...He was here...He..."

"Zika saved your life, Trey. He used an MPP to kill General Qong."

"Yes. But how did he get here? Where is he? And what is an MPP? I..."

Gloria interrupted him. "He was extracted to this point from his hospital bed. He was lying here in his hospital gown, looking somewhat confused, but as soon as he saw what was happening, he demanded a Scroll and a sword and went into action from his prone position. He dispatched General Qong first, saving your life, and then various others died at his hand before he was re-inserted. I expect he is back in hospital now."

Trey was sad not to see him, but overjoyed Zika was alive.

Xci3 arrived on the roof-top with an announcement. "We have just heard that the Emperor of Notalia has issued a press statement. He declares that the invasion occurred without his assent and was against his wishes. He has ordered a complete withdrawal of his troops with immediate effect."

"That's rubbish," said Gloria. "He planned and orchestrated the whole thing, I am sure."

"I agree." Xci3 nodded. "But this way he can save face whilst withdrawing his forces and we can return to peace. I'll take it."

They returned to the ground floor, where Max and Trey noticed a small golden circle, just off to the left. It grew and grew until, all of a sudden, they were re-inserted and they were right back at Max's gate where they had been chatting before Trey headed home. They looked at each other.

"Zika!" they said simultaneously.

They fired off messages to the others and then cycled off to the hospital. Twenty minutes later, Trey, Max, Marcia, Kia, Jason and Joe were crowding into Zika's room. He had just woken up, and they needed to tell him about Zak.

27

In Honour

Zika grinned when he saw them. "Battle over?" he asked, much to the nurse's confusion.

"Yes – and you saved my life, Zika," Trey blurted out.

Zika grinned again. "Not quite useless, even lying here with nothing to do! You must tell me all about it."

But his friends were not smiling and he realised something was very wrong.

"What is it?" he asked, worried.

"It's about Zak," Max said simply. And they told Zika the news. The friends spent two hours with him, talking about Zak, helping Zika to understand, sitting with him through their shared tears. Finally, though, the nurses told them it was time to go. Zika needed a wash, a rest, new bandages, and so on. Zika's mum was on hand, worried but delighted he was recovering. Reluctantly the six friends left him, but they promised to return straight after school the next day.

Because of his injuries Zika was in a single room. He had some privacy and slept really well. Had he been in the open paediatric ward, which was always noisy throughout the night with crying babies and children, Zika would have struggled to sleep at all. But sleeping in his own separate room was helping Zika's physical recovery enormously. His emotional recovery was going to take much longer.

After a difficult day trying to focus on maths and physics and history, the friends finished school and headed straight back to the hospital. They discovered that Zika was only just beginning to wake up as they arrived. The friends stayed with him too long, wearing him out with all their stories about Anasius and what had happened. But for Zika, it was a welcome and a sweet time that helped to distract him from the pain of Zak's death.

Just before they left, Zika commented, "I have so many questions about Zak. What happened? How is his mum doing? Is there a funeral? Where is Zak now? I don't know who to ask about it all."

The friends nodded their agreement.

"I don't even know whether he's still in the hospital or gone off to some funeral place somewhere or what?" Marcia said. "I think I'd quite like to see him."

"That's weird," Joe said bluntly.

"Is it? I don't know. I thought it might help somehow," Marcia responded.

"I think I'd rather remember Zak how he was before the accident, don't you think?" Joe asked.

"Well, yes, but also it might help me say goodbye, you know? I'm not sure," Trey said.

"We don't even know if we can see him," Joe said.

"Well, why don't we see if Tim can answer some of these questions?" Jason asked suddenly.

"I don't really know him," Kia protested.

"Neither do I," said Zika. "It would be a bit weird to talk to him, wouldn't it?"

"Well, he knows most of us," said Jason. "And Zak knew him really well – better than all of us. And he's really easy to talk to. I reckon he'd be happy to chat to all of us, even you guys who don't know him. And he might be able to answer some of our questions at least. I find it a bit hard to ask questions like these to my parents, to be honest."

"You're telling me," agreed Joe. "My dad's not around, and my mum's too stressed out. She worries way too much. I can't ask her."

"My mum's the same," said Kia. "Always stressing about something. I guess if we're all together, it would be okay. What d'you think Max?"

"It's okay by me," Max said. "As long as he doesn't give us some religious lecture – I couldn't stand that."

"He's cool," said Jason. "He has religious views, of course, but he's not going to force them on you. He'll just say what he knows and help where he can. And if he doesn't know, he'll know someone who does."

"I reckon Jason's right," Trey interjected. "I found him really easy to talk to."

Zika looked around. "So, then, Jason, can you ask him? Would he come here?"

Jason shrugged. "Don't know, but I can ask." He fired a message, the friends said their goodbyes and left.

Two days later, the friends met in Zika's room at the hospital again, and this time Tim was with them. Zika was just beginning to look a bit better. He was even sitting up in bed when they assembled.

His mum was not there because she'd had to return to work. This meant Zika had a lot of time lying awake, thinking about what his friends had told him about the war in Anasius, thinking about school and, of course, thinking about Zak. So when the friends arrived again, it was a really welcome distraction, and he was pleased to see them.

Tim introduced himself to Zika, and then said suddenly, "I was remembering Zak when he had long hair. Do you remember?" The friends nodded. "When Zak arrived at church one Sunday, we had an elderly visitor from downtown who obviously didn't know the family at all. She spoke to Zak's mum and said, 'Your daughter looks just like you!' Zak went bright red, but his mum didn't have the heart to tell the old dear that Zak was, in fact, a boy. Then, when Zak arrived at youth group later that week, he had short hair!" The friends were smiling at the story and remembering Zak's crazy hair before he had it cut.

There was a brief pause, and then Marcia asked, "Hey, Max, do you remember that school trip to Thorpe Park in Year 8? Zak insisted on doing the Nemesis Inferno right after lunch and nearly threw up all over you?" Max and Zika were both smiling.

"I missed that trip because I was throwing up," Jason commented. "The only school trip I have any interest in whatsoever, and I missed it."

"Oh yeah, was that when you had, like, three weeks off school for the flu or something?"

"It wasn't three weeks," Jason protested, "but yes, I missed the first day of exams and had to do them after school on the second day. It was awful."

The friends grinned, but their grins faded as they thought of Zak again.

"You remember when Calvin stuck a bug in Zak's sandwich and Zak didn't realise and ate half of it before we told him?" Joe asked.

"Ugh, that's disgusting," Kia almost shouted her horror. Her face was screwed up as she imagined the scene. "What did Zak do?"

"Not a lot he could do. He'd swallowed it by then," Joe laughed.

"Aaargh, that's so nasty," Max said.

"What's going to happen to Zak's dog?" Joe asked suddenly. They looked at each other.

"I don't know," Max said eventually. "I guess his mum'll have to give him up. She won't be able to work and look after a dog."

"Yeah, I reckon so. By the way," Jason said, "Did you know his dog got renamed 'Potato'?"

"What?" they were all laughing, wondering what he was talking about.

"It's true," he insisted, and then told them the story of their French class.

There was another pause in the conversation. The laughs and smiles faded and Jason began to feel guilty. He turned to Tim, "Tim – d'you think it's okay to laugh about Zak when he's not here anymore?"

Tim nodded. "I think it's helpful to remember the good times we've spent with someone we have lost. It helps us to celebrate their life. And I reckon Zak wouldn't want everyone sitting around crying all day for the rest of their lives."

"No, I know, but I kinda feel guilty if I laugh and forget for a minute that he's gone," Jason tried to explain. His bigger worry was that he couldn't cry, for some reason. He cried when his football team lost the cup final, but he couldn't cry when his friend had died. But he didn't say anything.

"I feel guilty, too," Marcia agreed. "It feels like a betrayal of him, somehow. To forget, I mean."

"I get it," Tim said. "But it's not a betrayal. That feeling is part of the whole grieving process. Zak's death is not the fault of anyone here. And, as I say, he wouldn't want us to be sad all the time. Somehow, eventually, we will figure out how life can go on even when there's a hole in it. But that's going to take some time."

The friends absorbed this for a minute or two. Tim broke the silence.

"It's always helpful to chat about someone you've lost – talking about Zak has been a help to me, somehow. Painful, but in a good way. So I'd encourage you all to be free to do that. It might be good to write a few of your memories down, too. Zak's parents might appreciate some memories to use at the funeral."

"When will it be?" Kia asked.

"It's not decided yet. Apparently after a fatal accident

there's usually an investigation, sometimes a post-mortem, and so on, and some of that has to happen before the funeral. I'm guessing it'll be in a couple of weeks' time," Tim said.

"What will it be like? I've never been to a funeral," Max said.

"Well, all funerals are different, and it depends what his parents want," Tim said. "I don't have loads of experience of funerals, although I have been to a few. There'll probably be some songs, someone will talk about his life – that bit's called the eulogy. There might be a talk from the pastor and there'll be some prayers."

"Will Zak be there?" Joe asked.

Tim smiled faintly. "Well, probably his body will be there in a coffin. Sometimes they carry it in at the beginning of the service, and then carry it out afterwards before it's taken to the grave where there might be a very short service called a committal. Unless they decide he's going to be cremated, in which case they won't take the coffin out of the service – it'll just disappear behind some curtains."

"I don't know that I'd like to be in a service looking at a dead body," Marcia looked a bit disgusted by the idea.

"You wouldn't see his body, Marcia. Just the coffin, probably with flowers on it."

Max, Trey and Marcia looked at each other. Then Trey asked, "Is it possible for us to see Zak?"

Tim thought about it. " Quite possibly. He's still at the hospital at the moment, but when they move him to the funeral home, it may be possible then. Shall I ask for you?"

"But isn't that really weird?" Joe asked. "I mean, that's

just his dead body. It's not really Zak anymore, is it." He said it as a statement, not a question.

Tim responded, "Some people find it helpful to see the body, Joe, especially in a death as sudden as Zak's. It kind of helps to accept that he is really gone. I was thinking of seeing Zak myself, to be honest."

"But what would it be like?" Max asked. "Will he be all bashed up from the accident, or will they fix him up a bit so he looks more normal?"

"Max," Marcia said, wincing at his words, "I'm not sure we should be asking about that..."

"Yes we should," Zika responded. "I want to know, too. Also, can you take pictures?"

"Zika," squealed Marcia. "Who would think of such a thing? How can you..."

But Zika interrupted. "Probably I won't be able to see him, because I'll still be here. But I'd like to see him somehow, so a photo or two would help."

"Okay, I understand," Tim said. "I've never been to a viewing, but apparently they usually try to make someone look as much as they used to look as possible. You would see his head and maybe hands and arms, but the rest will be under a sheet or something. Maybe it'll be a bit like visiting Zika when he was sedated, if you remember that?"

"How could we forget?" Jason said.

Twenty minutes later, they left Zika to get some more sleep, but Jason and Joe lagged behind the others, walking very slowly with Tim. They had some more questions, so Tim suggested they chat in a café just up the road from the hospital. When they were settled with drinks, Jason asked, "Tim, this might be a silly question..."

"Jason, one of your best mates has died. No question is silly. What is it?"

"Well, the thing is..." He was clearly embarrassed. "The thing is, what happens if I can't cry?"

Tim waited for Jason to say more.

"I mean, it's just that one of my best friends has died, and I haven't been able to cry. Last night I tried to make myself cry, but I couldn't do it. I just have this empty pit in my stomach that makes it hard to eat, hard to sleep, hard to concentrate on anything. But I can't cry. Maybe I didn't really care about Zak? Maybe I'm a bit weird?"

"I assure you that you are weird, Jason. No worries there." Tim grinned at him. "But on this thing, you're not weird. We all respond in different ways to death, especially sudden death. When my grandad died, I didn't cry either. I was surrounded by weeping relatives – even my dad cried, and he never cries – but I didn't. In fact, I don't know that I ever did cry about him. I missed him horribly, though. I missed so much about him. But when my dog died, then I cried."

"Maybe you're the one who's weird," Joe suggested.

Tim laughed. "Yes, you're probably right," he agreed.

Jason was comforted, though. It hurt horribly every time he thought of Zak and what they had done together. He missed his laugh, his football skills, his loyal friendship. But perhaps it was okay not to cry, even though he actually wanted to. He wanted some relief from the pain and tension, but it would not come.

As Joe listened to Jason and Tim talk he began to think about his own feelings. Joe's grief was mixed up with the realisation that the last thing Zak knew of him was that he had betrayed them all to the Notalians. Joe had never had the chance to ask for Zak's forgiveness or to try and put things right. There was unfinished business, and he couldn't finish it now. Joe's experiences in Anasius had taught him a huge life lesson about the things that really matter, about how important it is to do relationships well, about the need to stand on what is true and not give in regardless of the consequences. Put simply, Joe had grown up a huge amount in the last two weeks, but he had not been able to share any of it with Zak. Perhaps Zak still thought of him as a self-absorbed, fun-loving, happy-go-lucky guy who didn't really care about what other people thought, or how his actions or words might affect someone else. As far as Zak was concerned, Joe was often fun but also selfish and immature. Joe knew that this was how he had been. But things were changing, and he wanted Zak to know it, to know how much he was cared about, to know that Joe was going to look out for these friends now because he owed them so much. But now Zak would never know, and Joe hated it. He had cried for hours. He cried because his friend was gone. He cried because he had messed up so badly with Trey. He cried because he had thrown their friendship back in their faces and betrayed them. He cried because he was sick with himself. He cried because Trey had forgiven him –

something he didn't deserve in any way, and he felt it would almost have been easier if Trey had left him languishing in Crask as he deserved. And he cried every time he thought of Zak and all the things they had done together.

How could he explain all this to Tim without talking about Anasius? He didn't know, but he wanted to try.

"The last thing Zak knew about me was that I was self-absorbed, immature and betrayed his friendship. I'm changing slowly, but Zak will never see that. He will never know how sorry I am..." Joe choked down the lump in his throat. "Zak will never know, will he?"

Tim nodded and said nothing for a minute or two. Then he said, "Joe, over the course of the last two weeks, and then over the course of the rest of our lives here, there will be thousands of things that we do or say which Zak will never know. All of us, myself included, have grown up a bit because of what has happened, and Zak won't know that. Would you mind if I gave a bit of a religious answer to your question. I think it will help?"

"If you must," Joe said uncertainly. "My problem is that I'm guilty. I know it and I'm sorry, but Zak will never know."

"Yes, Joe. That's true. You are guilty. And so are all of us, including me. But the person we've really messed things up with is not Zak. It's God. The good news is that God offers forgiveness if we ask him for it. Real forgiveness. Even of the stuff between you and Zak. I've probably said too much, but it's worth thinking about, I reckon."

"Huh," said Joe. "You mean I can't be forgiven by Zak, because he's dead, but I can be forgiven by God because he's not?"

"Yeah – that's kinda it. One thing I do know, too. Zak's not at all concerned about the way you've treated him now. He's in heaven having an awesome time. I, for one, am looking forward to joining him there."

"You mean you want to die?" Joe asked incredulously.

"Not exactly," Tim tried to explain. "It's just that when it's time for me to die, I'm happy to. Because I know where I'm going. That's what I mean."

Joe looked sceptical and thought that Jason's comment about Tim being the weird one was not so far wrong.

Then Jason's phone went off and he looked at it. "Sorry," he said. "Gotta go. Mum's wondering where I am."

Joe sighed. "Yeah, me too, I guess."

"Thanks Tim," Jason said.

"Thanks," Joe repeated.

"See you later," Tim said as he returned to his coffee. Jason and Joe left.

The funeral was set for a Tuesday morning at the church, with a private family-only committal service over at the cemetery shortly afterwards. Zak's parents had asked for some memories of Zak from the group of friends, and Marcia had also seen them on her own to talk to them about music for the funeral. In fact, for the past week Marcia had been really busy with something musically, but she wouldn't tell them what. They would not find out until the funeral.

They arrived early for the service, unsure of themselves and nervous. Tim had told them that whilst many of the

344

family might wear black, Zak's parents had asked for a bit of colour if possible – they wanted the funeral to be a celebration of Zak's life, not just a mourning of his passing. As a result, while both Jason and Joe were in black suits with white shirts, Jason had chosen a red tie, and Joe's blue tie matched his eyes. Trey arrived on foot with his parents, and he wasn't wearing a tie at all. Instead, he wore a dark blue blazer and chinos with an open-neck blue shirt. Kia looked stunning in a knee-length black dress and black heels which made her almost as tall as Max. Max, in a grey suit, arrived with his mum, both of them looking nervous. Marcia, who had arrived first along with her parents, looked most nervous of all. She was wearing a velvet brown dress with a striking green sash, and her hair was wound up in a tight knot on the back of her head. She went straight into the church even though everyone else was standing outside.

Various other kids from school arrived, some carrying musical instruments. Many were accompanied by a parent, and all of them milled about uncertainly in front of the church. Tim and Pastor John were both there, greeting people and making low-voiced conversation. Marcia came out of the church again a few minutes later and signalled to various students from Raynesborough County to follow her. All those with instruments traipsed into the church after her.

"They're obviously going to play something in the service," Kia said quietly. "That must be what Marcia's been up to over the last week or so."

A few moments later, a shiny black hearse and a second

black car arrived, and seven grim-faced men in black suits and black ties got out. Pastor John invited everyone to move into the church, the family first followed by friends. It appeared that Zak had a large extended family, and they filled the first three rows in the church. As they took their seats, Trey realised that the church was going to be quite full, and Tim told him later that there had been well over 300 people at the service. He noticed Marcia sitting at the front along with a sizeable band, far larger than they had on a Sunday morning. Many of them were music students from school, although the usual church drummer, bass-guitarist, pianist and vocalists were there as well.

There was an order of service on each chair, so Trey picked it up to read it as the church was filling up. There was an excellent fairly recent picture of Zak's face on the front, smiling broadly on a sunny summer day. He looked so carefree and happy. The front page announced, "Zak Harper, October 3rd 2004 – June 14th 2019." It seemed so definite, so final. The familiar lump arrived in Trey's throat.

The background music that had been coming from the piano came to an end, and there was quiet in the room. A new number began on the piano and everyone stood up. The doors were opened and the seven grim-faced men walked solemnly into the church, six carrying Zak's coffin on their shoulders, and the seventh following them. At the front, they lowered the coffin onto the table that had been prepared for it and then withdrew to the side. The music stopped and Pastor John walked to the podium.

"It is with great sadness and a heavy heart that we meet

to remember and celebrate the life of Zak Harper. I extend a warm welcome to you all, and I trust that together we may give thanks for Zak's life, commit him into the hands of our heavenly Father, and rejoice that even as we meet, Zak is standing near the throne of Jesus with joy in his heart and that cheeky grin on his face. We will remember Zak in a number of different ways today, and we will all hold our own memories of him, too. In many ways, life will never be the same for us. There will always be a hole, a space that Zak used to fill but now, suddenly, is empty. But for those of us here who are Christians, we know that somehow God has not lost control. Somehow, even this pain is woven into his great and eternal tapestry. And so we give him praise. Let's stand and sing together."

They all stood, and the hymn followed. There was a confusing reading from 1 Corinthians 15 which contained something about being raised "imperishable". Trey didn't know what it meant, and he was fairly sure that Zak's aunt, who did the reading, didn't really understand it either. Then there was a eulogy from Zak's dad, a eulogy that reminded all of them about the Zak they knew and loved, a eulogy that included two or three of the stories they had shared about Zak. It was a eulogy that resulted in tears from many in the congregation. Somehow, though, Zak's dad managed to hold it together and make it to the end. His wife was crying softly when he finished.

Then they sang another hymn, and Pastor John preached a short sermon in which he talked about Zak's faith and the promises in the Bible about where Zak was now. Trey lost track a bit and began to daydream.

Suddenly, Pastor John finished preaching and said, "This music is new to us all. But apparently it means a huge amount to Zak and to some of his school friends, so Marcia Hawksworth has arranged the music and now the little orchestra are going to play it."

There was a pause. And then the music began. One long note played by a single trumpet – a deep, sonorous note. Somehow, Marcia had transcribed from memory the music from the Overlord Academy graduation ceremony. Now, in Zak's funeral, the orchestra were playing the majestic and emotive music of the "Eagle's Egress" stirring the whole congregation with its achingly beautiful melody. And Trey, through his own tears, noticed something he had not seen before. Jason was crying.

About the Author

Rich Castro has taught in boarding schools for twenty years. He has an MDiv from Reformed Theological Seminary. He is passionate about preaching, discipleship and youthwork, with a particular focus on finding ways to irradicate Biblical illiteracy in the church and to point young people and adults alike to the wonder of Jesus.